HOLLAND

D1387508

Holland

Its History, Paintings and People

ADAM HOPKINS

ff

faber and faber

LONDON · BOSTON

First published in 1988
by Faber and Faber Limited
3 Queen Square London WC1N 3AU

Phototypeset by Wilmaset Birkenhead Wirral
Printed in Great Britain by
Redwood Burn Ltd Trowbridge Wiltshire
All rights reserved

British Library Cataloguing in Publication Data

Hopkins, Adam
Holland.
1. Netherlands—History
I. Title   II. Stephens, Tim
949.2   DJ109

ISBN 0-571-14681-3

Contents

Illustrations

by Tim Stephens

Maps

by Paul Margiotta

Erratum

A reference to Queen Beatrix on page 189
says she has four sons. The correct
number is three.

Note on names

The main difficulty in writing about Holland is what to call the country. Officially it is the Netherlands and this is what the Dutch call it – Nederland or the Low Country. For most English speakers, however, Holland is the customary name. Unfortunately, this produces an inaccuracy which grates on the ears of the Dutch. For them, Holland is the name of a single province, the province which has dominated throughout history. (Today it is divided into North and South Holland.) Using 'Holland' for the whole country is rather like using 'England' when also meaning Wales and Scotland. The dilemma has no real solution. In the text, I have generally preferred Holland because it is the English vernacular. I have used the Netherlands when the context – often geographical – required it. When referring to the province of Holland, I have always labelled it as such.

Two other small points: when IJ occurs at the start of a name, as in IJsselmeer, it is treated as a single letter and both constituent parts are capitalized (IJ is in practice the Dutch Y); names of individuals ending in the very common 'zoon' – son of – are always abbreviated, e.g. Pieter Claesz., the still-life painter, and of course Rembrandt Harmensz. van Rijn.

Introduction

The reasons why a writer undertakes one book rather than another are often enough obscure. Looking back, it seems to me that this book began somewhere in my childhood before I had ever crossed the channel from England to continental Europe. In the years immediately after the Second World War my family lived in East Anglia. As children, my elder brother and I frequented the banks of the Rivers Stour and Orwell. Sailing barges still plied the estuary, their sails red and fading brown. But of all craft that went on water it seemed to us from an early age that it was Dutch barges, with their leeboards to let down on either side and their swelling, sensuous lines, that were most beautiful. I must also have learned during childhood about the sky in flat country – how it arches over all, continually visible, occupying most of one's vision whichever way one looks. Certainly, I recognized the phenomenon with a familiar shock twenty years later when I visited the Fen country as a journalist to report on an agricultural reversal – the farmers had planted their carrot and onion seed and thanks to the flatness and the lack of hedges, the wind had blown both seed and top soil clean out of the neighbourhood and out to sea for all that anyone knew. And all around the enormous sky was full of clouds like giants' pillows.

By now, I knew from the experience of several visits that this flat farming country had its parallel just across the sea in Holland, with the added bonus of curious and compelling architecture and a school of painting that echoed the huge skies.

So my introduction was first through landscape, then through landscape painting. Like most visitors, I knew little about the people whose art and countryside I was eager to enjoy.

Then, just a few years ago, on a visit to Amsterdam, and wishing, finally, to learn more about the country, I looked for a book that would carry me deeper not just into art and architecture but into the lives of the Dutch – historically, politically and socially. By then it was clear to most people who read a newspaper or watched television that remarkable re-adjustments to the twentieth century had been taking place in Holland. It was not just the Provo's of Amsterdam with their white bicycles or the city's reputation for drugs and liberty, but a sense that serious issues were being tackled in many other fields – though a deeply entrenched conservatism still existed alongside radical *joie de vivre*. Small though Holland is, there might be lessons here for others. But there was nothing I could find to read that seemed entirely suitable and so I sat down to try to fill the gap. There is much that I have not had space to mention – holidays among the sea-birds of the Wadden islands up on the north-west corner of the country, or a bicycle ride I once made to Staphorst, most conservative of all Dutch towns, where the inhabitants, the women at least, wear traditional dress, where television is frowned upon and vaccination sometimes still refused. All writers wish they had been able to write longer books; but I hope that in what follows I have been able to tackle at least some of the subjects of importance to readers.

Many people have helped me, in Holland and in Britain, some through virtue of the posts they hold, others precisely because they are private citizens. The spirit of democracy and independence is so strong in Holland that in some universities it is a condition of appointment that the customary thank yous should be omitted when learned works are published. For this book, that would never do, but a suitable compromise might be to cite the names of those who have helped me most in a single list and without further explanation. I am particularly grateful to:

Raymond van Asperen Vervenne, Charles Batchelor, Epke Beens, Marianne and Martin Bierman, Pieter Brusse, Henk van den Burg, Mieke Davies, Radnum and Miranda Dros, Carol van Driel Murray, Erik Holm, Jeremy Hooker, Jan-Derk Jansen, Christina Janssen, Luc de Jong, Akkie van der Kerkhof Kikkert, Ronald de Leeuw, Wiepke Loos, Jan Michael, Angela Needham, Sue Roach, and Meina Westerouen van Meeteren-de Bel. The names of many of those who helped me in the town of Wolvega in Friesland are mentioned in the text but I should like to include them here as well: Robert Blauw, Berend Brummelman, Jan and Allie de Haan, Fennie, André, Anja and Sieni Koning, the Kramer family and Hanneke Zonderland.

The book could not have achieved its final shape without the generosity of Michael Hoyle, Monique Kroese, Barrie Needham, Hein van Meeteren and Laura Raun. While not being responsible for its faults and errors, they will know how much they have given.

At home, the heat of the battle has been borne by Gabrielle Macphedran, who first urged me to turn the idea of a book on Holland into reality.

General Map of Holland

Heavily Populated Area
M Museum/Gallery

NORTH SEA

Vliel
Texel
Hoorn
Den_Held

○ Alkmaa

Zaand
M **M**
M **Am**
Haarlem
○ Aalsmeer
○ Leiden
Scheveningen

M
The Hague
○ Delft
○ Gouda
('s-Gravenhage) **M**
Rotterdam

○ Dordrecht

Bergsche Maa

○ Zierikžee

○ Breda Ti

○ Middelburg
Vlissingen

BRUGES

ANTWERPEN

ℰ GHENT

MECHELEN

○ YPRES ℰ ○ LEUVEN

BRUSSELS

ONE

Land and water

Most people, it would seem, have two contrasting images of Holland in their minds. There is the original, old-fashioned version from picture books, made up of open landscape with black and white cattle and canals, a windmill in the background and possibly a milkmaid in bonnet and clogs. The town nearby is built of brick, with gables and canals. The scene is quaint and timeless. The other image is of Amsterdam, nightmare or dream, with near-naked prostitutes on view in windows, heroin for sale on every corner, magnificent mansions along fine canals and in the Rijksmuseum the most extraordinary home-made art in northern Europe. Rembrandt's tumultuous vision is open to all and not far down the road the intensity of poor one-eared van Gogh. The message, unmistakably, is one of extremism, a radical Holland where all is permissible.

The trouble is, there is a little truth in both these versions. But neither is the place to start in the search for Holland beneath the commonplaces.

Water is the first essential. Surprisingly, you cannot see the sea from anywhere inland in Holland. At all points it is held in check by dikes or dunes or huge sea walls or sluice gates, some so enormous you can scarcely comprehend them. To look beyond, you have to stand on top of them or go upstairs in a house behind the dike or, best of all, climb a church tower. Then on one side you will have the North Sea full in view and on the other a receding landscape, flat as the kitchen floor, with villages or towns or bright green meadows and more church spires and

I

very often the proverbial windmill. In many places, the whole of the landscape will have been won from the sea in long campaigns during which the dikes were little by little advanced and the ground so gained was gradually made fit for agriculture. Whether old or new, the landscape visible from the church tower will be tidy. All seems the essence of tranquillity. But if every dike and dune, sea wall and sluice gate were obliterated, the waters would rush across the land to overwhelm a third of the country. In 1953 the dikes were breached along the southern coast. Huge tracts of country disappeared in a tidal immolation. One commentator wrote: 'As children we had been told in the schools that we had a dragon living next door, and of course we knew it was there, but we had never ourselves felt the quick, sudden, tiger-like stroke of that dragon.'

Now, after another generation of large-scale works, the barriers against the sea are reckoned, rightly or wrongly, impregnable. Inside the barriers, the fragile landscape is again composed in considerable part of water. Sun gleams or cloud reflects on brimming lakes and a network of canals for ships and drainage, often higher than the surrounding land. Vessels on these canals appear to be travelling across the fields. In two places that I know, one just east of Leiden, the other south of Gouda, open aqueducts cross motorways with ships riding high in them, right there in front of you, so that, as you drive, you suddenly plunge down to pass beneath their keels. Grown-ups as well as children burst out laughing. And through this man-made land-and-water-scape flow the greatest rivers of northern Europe. The Maas (or Meuse) comes up from France and Belgium, the Rhine from Germany, dividing and sub-dividing as they near the delta mouth, bringing their long barges from the French and German cities and millions and millions of gallons of water every minute of every day and night.

Like the sea, the inland waters must be held in check. The rivers are diked and excess water from the lands below sea-level is continuously pumped upwards till it is high enough to drain off into the sea. If the pumping ceased, much of the land behind the sea-defences would drown as thoroughly as if the dikes were breached.

Nowadays this work is carried out by vast machinery invisible inside pumping stations. But it was the windmill, introduced to the task of drainage in the seventeenth century, which first gave the inhabitants of Holland the capacity to convert inland lakes and marshes to dry land. These towering machines brought unimagined power. Those who built them best were fêted and their names are still remembered. The mills, too, were given individual names and often stood in rows, each one lifting the water a few feet and the next one raising it a few feet again till it arrived at the proper level. Windmills working together were called a gang – one of many Dutch words so thoroughly embedded in the English language we scarcely recognize them as borrowings.

All land won from the water goes under the generic name of 'polder' and it is the polder landscape, its summer pastures copiously dotted with black and white cattle, which provides the first of the familiar images of Holland. A better version of that image will be linked to a landscape where control of water is sometimes tenuous and the necessity for it never to be forgotten, a landscape made of working parts.

But even when the position of water is properly acknowledged, there is still much in Holland that seems cosy, over-safe, perhaps with a hint of toy-town – too long a succession of neat little villages and towns, 'Dutch' gables and trim brickwork. Around the IJsselmeer, the enclosed waters behind Amsterdam once open and called the Zuider Zee, many of the inhabitants of the old fishing villages still don traditional costumes. Sometimes this is done for tourists but it happens, too, well off the tourist trail. And tulips do flourish, just as the preconception has it.

There is great pleasure to be taken from all this. But it can begin to cloy, to bring out a touch of impatience in the traveller. It is then that it is necessary to persevere. For just as the quiet landscape has been won from a wilderness of waters, so the trimness of town and village has been achieved against a background of tumult.

3

Whatever its people's wishes in the matter, Holland has in practice been one of the great cockpits of history. Almost every large idea which European societies have lived by has met a fundamental challenge here and this tiny nation has at different times dominated intellectually, artistically, commercially, even imperially.

When the Romans occupied the land they were unable to hold all of it against the local tribes. After the Romans the territories that now comprise Holland and its neighbour Belgium, the Low Countries or Pays Bas of history, were absorbed into the empire of Charlemagne, re-emerging in the Middle Ages as the richest fief in the possessions of the Dukes of Burgundy. These dukes were kings in all but name and their court far outshone that of France. Van Eyck was court painter during the heyday of the Duchy and he and the other so-called Flemish primitives gave the Low Countries a name for artistic excellence.

After the Dukes of Burgundy the Low Countries passed under Spanish rule. Rich before, they were now indisputably the wealthiest part of a far larger empire. While Bosch painted and Bruegel after him, the wool and cloth trade flourished and the Catholic church grew wealthier than ever. But now the Reformation was posing the first systematic challenge to the combined authority of pope and emperor. Throughout the Low Countries opposition grew around the figure of William the Silent. Reluctantly and for many years professing loyalty to his Spanish sovereign, he launched himself on what proved to be an Eighty Years War with Spain. By the end of it, the Dutch provinces were established as the first substantial European republic of modern times.

Now literally hundreds of painters were at work. They included not just Rembrandt, Frans Hals and Vermeer, but scores of others acknowledged today as major artists. It was a period of intellectual activity and erudition, of new sea voyages and brilliant map-making. The Dutch emerged as the main sea-carriers of Europe, and as they travelled and traded they founded an early empire in north and south America, in what was known as the East Indies (Dutch-ruled for many centuries) and, with ominous consequences, moved into South Africa.

A comfortable retreat from greatness began with the eighteenth century. Napoleon came at the end of it and, through his brother, briefly reorganized the country. Next, Holland became a constitutional monarchy. The tradition of painting lived on through the nineteenth century and into the twentieth, yielding the Hague School, van Gogh and Mondrian. Life at home was stable but the empire became increasingly uneasy. Then, with the Second World War, calamity occurred. Holland was overwhelmed so thoroughly it was as if the dikes were down in every aspect of life. The many Jews who had found protection over the centuries together with recent refugees from Hitler were singled out by the invaders and sent off further east to their death. Fifteen thousand Dutch people starved to death in the last winter of the war. After the war, the empire fell to pieces.

It is against this background – tribes against the Romans, Protestant republic versus Catholic empire, Dutch mastery in painting, seamanship and commerce, Dutch empire and modern disaster – that Holland has achieved its poise and the atmosphere of stability it conveys. These are matters the visitor may ponder as he tries to look beneath the vision of Frisian cattle and canals and pretty towns.

Amsterdam, the other half of the image of the country, makes its disclosures openly. Elegant and scruffy, distinguished and whorish, sophisticated and gauche, international in outlook but its historic centre tiny by comparison with Rome or Paris, Amsterdam is the embodiment of the seventeenth-century Dutch Republic which rose on a mixture of pride and modesty and practised the art of tolerance more thoroughly than any other state in Europe. Amsterdam has retained its ability to accommodate, to provide what people want; and it is this which has given it its name for open sex, the ready availability of drugs and its capacity to put up with any kind of do-as-you-please behaviour. But the truth is that the image has outlasted the reality. It was the 1960s and 1970s which saw the furthest reaches of tolerance, as if the city was an escape hatch for all the pressures in Dutch society and a playground for the young of many nations. Today there is a realization that tolerance, as recently practised, had allowed some people's freedoms to limit the freedoms of others. The city remains accommodating and easy-going. It continues to put up with its very *outré* red light district but hard drugs are now reckoned a menace and dealing in hard drugs a criminal activity. You can still see plenty that is surprising, sometimes shocking, sometimes funny; you can still get your car broken into in a flash on the apparently safest of canal sides. But some kind of corner has been turned. From the visitor's viewpoint the mixture of canals and canal houses, of intellectual and artistic liveliness, the flower market along the Singel canal, the old 'brown' pubs with quiet talk and sometimes carpets on the tables, the unexpected as well as what one may have planned for – all this makes Amsterdam a place to wander endlessly. It is an admirable city, but not quite the city of popular folklore.

As capital of the Netherlands – though the seat of government is paradoxically in The Hague – Amsterdam stands at the centre of one of the most densely populated areas of Europe. Within what seems a stone's throw, certainly within an hour or so on the train, one may reach a large number of substantial cities. There is The Hague itself, gracious and expansive; Leiden and Delft, both of them astonishingly beautiful, representing the Dutch water town on a more intimate scale than Amsterdam; Haarlem, stuffed with curiosities; Utrecht, with its canals sunk to a lower level so that they run, as it were, two storeys below the street; and Rotterdam, busy and workmanlike at the mouth of the Rhine, with the largest port in the world and, out towards the sea, a petrochemical industry whose tanks and gantries and bright white lights gleam in the dusk like a sinister Cape Kennedy. On the inland side of the city there is a busy working waterfront where barges moor in abundance after their long journey from the interior. During the daytime it is an active, even a splendid place. At night, the city sleeps as if it had no dreams.

All of these towns together have acquired a common name – the Randstad, sometimes translated as Rim-City Holland. In discussions of contemporary life, the Randstad as a whole must be an even greater presence than Amsterdam considered singly. Most people who visit Holland, arriving at Schiphol airport in the centre of it, seldom see anything else. Even their meadows with canals and cows are likely to be encountered in the green spaces inside the Randstad.

And this, of course, provides a distorted view, for there is another Holland, too, far less familiar, far more diverse than one might imagine, full of interest, often extremely beautiful. For my own part, having seen the country in bits and pieces on expeditions beginning and ending in the Randstad, the experience became so frustrating and my view of Holland evidently so Randstad-centred that I decided on a cure. Arriving from England on a car ferry at Vlissingen in the south – sometimes still called Flushing by the English – I spent the whole of a fortnight making a slow circle of the country, anti-clockwise, passing through the Randstad on the way back but, with one exception, refusing to enter its multitudinous cities. The experience enabled me to construct a different geography in my mind, one which has left me with a richer sense of the whole.

Take, for example, my first port of call, Middelburg in Zeeland, a few kilometres from Vlissingen. It is a medieval city, heavily damaged in the Second World War and lovingly restored, with a town hall crammed with pinnacles and gables, and a massive abbey, also lovingly restored. Here ancient civic splendour mingles quietly with the remnants of religious authority. In its heyday all English wool was disembarked in Middelburg before being sent off down the River Scheldt to Antwerp but now the sea has moved away. The old harbour forms a cul-de-sac of canal almost in the centre of the town. Boats are tethered to wooden piles right under bedroom windows, the branches of trees extending over them.

Though the public is only trusted to go half way up, you see Middelburg to best advantage from the abbey tower. (It is, by

The Author's Route Round Holland

〰〰 Hoge Veluwe

〰〰 Betuwe

〰〰 Author's Route

RTH SEA

Dokkum

Appingda

Fruncker Leeuwarden

Groningen

Bolsward

Sneek

Almelo

Deventer Hengelo

Ensch

Zutphen

Arnhem

Nijmegen

Dordrecht

Breda Den Bosch

Tilburg

Middleburg

Eindhoven

Vlissingen

Maastricht

Valkenburg

the way, entirely necessary to climb every available tower in Holland. The Dutch, who have long since adjusted to the flatness of their landscape, are not so assiduous in this as they should be.) Once you are high enough you see what you may have begun to suspect on the ground – all the main streets run concentrically around the middle of town. First, there was a fortified mound at the centre, a *burcht* surrounded by moats. As the moats were filled in, their place was taken by roads. The combined effect in Middelburg of town hall and abbey, relic of harbour and circular street pattern is, so it seemed to me, entirely charming; and a world away from anything I had seen in the Randstad.

But now I was off across the south, making my way through a series of cities whose names will be familiar – Breda, Tilburg and Den Bosch, officially 's-Hertogenbosch. The painter Bruegel was born in or near Breda; Hieronymus Bosch took his name from 's-Hertogenbosch and lived there all his life. In the early days many of these towns were important places, religious and commercial centres. Then, under the Protestant Dutch Republic, they remained largely Catholic. Their religion was tolerated but they were cut off from power. The Catholic south became relatively poor, the butt of jokes, inhabited, so grander northerners thought, by uncouth yokels. There was no equality of wealth or educational opportunity. By the end of the nineteenth century, matters were evening up and the Catholic south began to produce surprises. First, there was the rise of Eindhoven, where the Philips light bulb factory, founded in 1870, has grown during the present century into a mighty multinational. Counting in Shell and Unilever, both half British, Holland now has three of the world's biggest companies, an extraordinary phenomenon. More recently the Catholic south has become a hi-tech zone, a kind of silicon flatland along the border with Belgium. This makes the area, once so despised, among the richest in the country.

Next stop was Maastricht in the very south-east corner of the country. Here, through a mixture of historical accident and dynastic bargaining, the province of Limburg stretches down a narrow hand between Belgium and Germany to greet the River

Maas. In this tract of country, until the 1960s, there was a working coal-field. The river itself, ample and gracious, flows past the welcoming town, likewise gracious and ample and a world away from any conception of canals and folksiness. Maastricht has been there for a long time and the area is rich in Roman remains. It has hills, too. As you turn your back on the French and Belgian south and face downstream towards the centre of Holland, there is on your right, to the east, a positively hilly district based on the little once-walled town of Valkenburg and known, with affectionate humour, as the Dutch Alps. Foreign visitors gather here for its wooded vantage points and valleys and its good location as a centre for visiting the German Rhine and Luxembourg. Dutch walkers hike here and school trips go riding and inspect the Roman ruins. In August the maize grows quite as high as the eye of an elephant.

Now, as it emerges at the wrist of the downstretched hand and enters Holland proper, the Maas is still flowing north. Away to the left, on the west bank and beyond, in the deeply rural fringes of the silicon country, asparagus grows richly on flat ground, its feathery foliage contrasting with the solidity of tightly bulging cabbages, so green they glint with iridescent blue. The farms here often have a patch of woodland. Fallow deer are kept in paddocks between the houses and the road and though the houses are quite small there may well be a discreetly expensive car outside the door.

The river flows due north for only a short way. No distance in the Netherlands is half so big as it seems on the map. On the trains which criss-cross the country with frequency and punc-tuality, you open your book and have to pack it away again before you have finished half a page. Map-reading in a car, you hardly seem to have found the motorway exit before you have passed it and swept on towards the next town, all of ten kilometres away.

So it is no surprise when the Maas soon turns westwards to aim straight for the coast. What is a surprise is the way it practically runs into the Rhine before it turns. The great Rhine, arriving from the southerly vineyards of Germany and the industrial Ruhr, bearer of barges and effluent, enters Holland as a single stream and then divides in two, so that now, all of a sudden, we have three great rivers – the Maas and the two branches of the Rhine, known at this point as the Waal and the Lower Rhine – running parallel across the body of central-southern Holland. A further branch of the Rhine, the IJssel, soon flows off in a northerly direction to give its waters and its name to the modern IJsselmeer. There are endless complications of sub-division and nomenclature and a network of canals linking these and other navigable waters – but essentially, once the Maas has turned west for the sea and the Rhine has come to join it, the map Dutch people understand has come into being. It consists of the country south of the Great Rivers and the country to the north. Though the religions overlap, the essential point is that the Netherlands south of the Great Rivers is mainly Catholic, while to the north the country is predominantly Protestant. This division has dominated history.

In due course I reached Nijmegen on the Waal and to my own surprise I fell in love with the city and the area. Nijmegen lies on the southern side of the river and on a high bluff of land here the emperor Charlemagne had a palace called the Valkhof or Falcons' Court (his main court was at Aachen, further south). This eminence, now mostly greensward with one or two ecclesiastical remains, looks out northward, across the stretch of land between the Waal and the Lower Rhine. On the far side of the Lower Rhine, on an opposing bluff, stands Arnhem.

Because of the hilly ground to north and south of the double river bed, the river scenery, the wide reaches of open sandy ground, both Nijmegen and Arnhem were places of delight and retirement right up to the Second World War, with a sprinkling of former civil servants, bankers, colonial officials, living in large houses. Families came to hotels and boarding houses here for their summer holidays. All around there stand enormous trees. And to the north of Arnhem there is a large tract of sand and forest, the Hoge Veluwe, containing a national park and a quite outstanding museum of painting and sculpture – the Kröller-Müller, of which more in another context. This, like the better-known galleries of Amsterdam and the Randstad, is a world-class museum. (One of the realizations a visitor makes on a grand circle of the country is the extraordinarily high quality of art collections outside the centre.)

I left Nijmegen with regret, swung north through Zutphen and Deventer, both on the River IJssel, both fine medieval cities. The English poet Sir Philip Sidney fell in defence of Zutphen in 1586, fighting against Spain. The view of Deventer across the water is peaceful and delightful, even though it was the bridge at Deventer which stood in for Arnhem's in the film *A Bridge Too Far*, based on the battle in September 1944. Next I backtracked east to inspect the fairly dull textile towns of Enschede, Hengelo and Almelo on the German border, then up and off again for Groningen, the major city of the Dutch north-east. To get to Groningen, you cross the few remaining stretches of heath in an area once almost entirely heathland, site of some of the earliest human settlements in the Netherlands.

Groningen is a substantial city. After Utrecht, it has the highest church tower in the country, very good for climbing. There is a big university, a mixture of canal-town elegance and serious business. Any account of the Dutch has to reckon with Groningen. Again I broke my journey for days, again regretted my departure. Next, though, to the delicious water-town of Appingedam in the far north-east, then westwards back across the top of the country in the direction of England to visit a hoop of other water-towns – Dokkum, Franeker and Bolsward, all in a ring round Leeuwarden, the biggest but the loveliest, a feast of canals and elegant red-brick houses. The two northern provinces – Groningen, centred on the city, and Friesland, round Leeuwarden – make up the territory of the one-time independent Frisia or Friesland. Like Wales or Catalonia, it has a language of its own, though this is now in serious decline. Leeuwarden is full of the memorials of Frisian independence and has a seductive statue of one of its native daughters – Mata Hari, that *femme fatale* of the First World War.

Inevitably, discussion will return to Friesland. For the moment all that is necessary is to register it as the polar opposite of the country south of the Great Rivers. Leeuwarden and Groningen are the centres of quintessential Protestant country, with huge farmhouses and, at one time, a rural gentry to live in them. Historically the people of this area have had plenty of faith but have in the last analysis preferred hard work to faith, regarding their Catholic compatriots in the south as little better than helter-skelter pleasure seekers. This is the other side of the great Dutch divide and precious little of it can be understood from merely visiting the Randstad.

In terms of general inquiry, this was the end of my journey. But I had reserved one final pleasure for myself – a visit to Dordrecht on the way south again to Vlissingen; and though Dordrecht is in reality a part of the Randstad I chose for the moment to forget this. I set off through the lively Frisian port of Harlingen and across the Alfsluitdijk which closes the mouth of the IJsselmeer. This, I am afraid, is a fairly dull experience. You cannot see the North Sea from the road and so you miss the scale of the undertaking unless you stop to visit the memorial in the centre.

Soon I had slipped between Amsterdam and The Hague on the southbound motorway and after another surprisingly short distance found myself entering Dordrecht, past the slightly leaning tower of a cathedral flanked by barge-basins and elegant old warehouses and surmounted by one of the most odd-shaped clocks that has ever stood on top of a cathedral tower. Dordrecht was a favourite town of painters and the silhouette of the cathedral clock appears, distant but unmistakable, in many canvases. The point of my visit that day was to meet the Great Rivers again now they had traversed the country east to west, like a straight line drawn across the lower portion of my own full circle. At Dordrecht there is a meeting place of two wide streams. You can stand here on a hoop-shaped terrace at the point of confluence, on a little headland called the Groothoofd. Glass-balconied hotel and cafés and a gateway of armorial splendour behind, you look out across the water to see the long barges swinging in the current to take the waterway of their choice. It is not exactly an original thought, but this, as much as Amsterdam, could stand as a shorthand for Holland.

TWO

From swamp to Flemish primitive

First, before the ice age, there were the Neanderthal people. Cold beat them back and it was not till 14,000 years ago – in this long time-scale almost the modern era – that the next arrivals came, hunters living off reindeer on what had now become a vast tundra pasture. Little by little the weather grew warmer. Pine forests appeared and then gave way to alder in the swamps. In due course a wide waterway came into being, separating Britain in the west from the rest of continental Europe. The Dutch coast was now fringed with a long streamer of sand-dune partially separating the sea from a miserable terrain of swamps and lakes in the interior. In some places the ground was solid and the next arrivals, farmers and stock-rearers, settling this firmer land, made clearings in the forest and then moved on when they had spoiled the ground.

None left much behind except for pottery. But next there came a group whose bold constructions – megalithic dolmens known in Dutch as *hunebedden* – have outstared time almost 5,000 years. They came in top right on the map, along the sandy ridges and through the heathland of the north east, following geographical features easily recognizable today. One of their routes was along the Hondsrug or Dog's Back, a low ridge angling in a few kilometres south of Groningen. Today it is a favourite route for Sunday cyclists and outings in the family car. It isn't much of a ridge, though it offers a view of further undulations in the land, but it has a deeply comfortable feeling of long use, with large farmhouses, their vast barns built on to the house as part of the main structure, traditional in form but solidly wealthy, generally modern in appearance. The farm-houses stand among the smaller dwellings of almost continuous villages along the ridge. Surprisingly, the villages, too, are modern, built mostly in the nineteenth and twentieth centuries. There are woods and riding stables, a general impression of outdoor sporting life. To anyone who has read of the brooding presence of *hunebedden*, forbidding in a forbidding landscape, this approach along the agreeable Hondsrug will come as a surprise.

You know you are getting close to the Funnel Beaker folk – the name given them because of the pottery they made – when you start to see the occasional large boulder marking a farm front door or lesser boulders spaced along the road in place of garden fences. These are ice-age erratics carried down from the Baltic and known in Dutch as *zwerfkeien*, wandering stones. They were the raw material for the *hunebedden*, rings of standing stones topped by great lids or capstones. Fifty-four *hunebedden* still survive, mostly near the Hondsrug though there are a few further south. Some are tiny, the largest 60 yards or more in length. In most, the stones have been laid bare. The first I ever saw, though, was still a mound. A little hole had been excavated in the upper part, revealing a very domestic-looking capstone. There were young oaks all around, with swelling green acorns, harebells in bloom and a goat tethered just five or ten yards away. Other *hunebedden*, like those of Bronegger, for instance, are at the edge of corn fields or almost buried in thicket. The classic *hunebedden*, those of Brouwer or Borger, say, all close to the Hondsrug, look like battleships or prehistoric monsters, long and low, with lumpy backs.

The Funnel Beaker people and their descendants and the various new migrants who arrived in succeeding centuries cannot have been rich or particularly comfortable. Their methods of agriculture continued to be destructive and away from the ridges it was still necessary to move mostly by water in canoes and coracles – except where local people had made causeways laying logs and branches side by side on sleepers, a system that was to endure for many centuries in northern districts.

The geography and the times were difficult but immigrants continued to arrive. There were several waves of them, mostly Germanic people, and they now spread out over most of the watery terrain of modern Holland. Once again they left little behind that can be seen today – that is, until about 300 BC. The new arrivals at this stage were cattle farmers, the ancestors of the independent-minded modern Frisians. They came down from the north east into the north of Holland and because their territory was subject to flood, swept either by the tide or inland water, they turned, very sensibly, to the construction of artificial mounds or *terpen* (*terp* in the singular). The Roman author Pliny wrote in his *Natural History* of AD 47 that the terp-dwellers of these coasts looked like sailors out at sea on the flood-tide, like castaways at the ebb. He seems to have been describing fishing, not farming settlements and the people of his description were poor. They attempted, Pliny said, 'to warm their frozen bowels by burning mud, dug with their hands out of the earth and dried to some extent in the wind, more than the sun which one hardly ever sees.' The reference to peat is clear enough. So is Pliny's assumption that their lives were miserable.

Many of the *terpen* still exist and if once they were the symbol of a desperate way of life, today they are delightful, the embodiment of two thousand years of continuous habitation. First there would have been just one or two farmhouses on a single mound, then at the next rebuilding a higher mound with more houses on it and so on in successive layers until the time of Christianization when the central position was generally taken by a church. One of the most thorough excavations of a *terp* took place at Ezinge, a village a few kilometres north of Groningen. It is possible to follow the stages from the exhibits in the provincial museum of Groningen and then make a pilgrimage to the village, a place with a sober little main street, all red brick, flanked by brick pavements of a still deeper red, running

17

up to a red-brick church with tower standing separate from the main building. The only ornament in the village on my last visit was a single ice-cream sign. The object of the visit, of course, was not just the village but also the *terp* that lay beneath it. This can be seen to best advantage from a little way away. Then it becomes apparent that the church itself, standing at one end of the settlement, is built on a substantial mound, one that must represent centuries of digging and earth-moving. In its quietness and its witness to the labour of generations it is genuinely moving.

There were, it has been calculated by those who like this kind of mathematics, 1260 *terpen* in the provinces of Groningen and Friesland, in total volume thirty times greater than the largest single pyramid. Nowadays they lie under some substantial towns – Leeuwarden, the Frisian capital, is built on two adjoining *terpen* and nearby Dokkum rises up quite steeply from its inner-ring canal on to a central mound. *Terpen* lie under some small villages and even isolated farms and churches. Is it really a *terp*, you ask yourself as you pause by a farmhouse, ringed with its own canal or moat, ducks on the water, classical façade, and underneath the farm a distinctly swelling artificial mound. The province of Friesland is the richest hunting ground. Groningen has fewer though those that exist are often more remote.

My own most memorable *terp*-hunting expedition was undertaken in the very top righthand corner of Holland in the company of the English poet Jeremy Hooker, then living at Groningen. We set out early on a bright and windy day just at the end of summer, striking the coast at Eemshaven near Delfzijl, a modern container port in the middle of nowhere. A ship had been moored or beached on the far side of the sea-dike, green hull beyond a green dike the far side of a green, green field, each green in the composition a little different from the others.

Beyond Eemshaven we stop to climb the sea-dike, with its tight cropped turf, tangy with sheep's dung. The tide is out, revealing mud flats marked out in squares with stakes, a bent figure in the distance digging for bait. The sky reflects in pools of sea water in the mud flats. Oyster catchers with their long black beaks walk delicately on the surface of the mud. In the distance we see Borkum, one of the Wadden islands, a German one, not Dutch. This little patch of sea, with mud beneath the water and narrow channels through the mud, right on the German border, is *Riddle of the Sands* country, celebrated in the Erskine Childers' novel and given wider currency by a film made in 1978.

Now, as we turn to look inland, the landscape is wide and spacious with no high buildings to be seen, nothing more obtrusive than the odd windmill and a few church towers, brick-built and capped by the little pitched roof characteristic of this part of the Netherlands. One of the attractions of the district is that it is entirely blank on the general road map I've picked up at a garage. Not even a minor road is shown. But the large-scale map reveals a network of lanes and dikes and even gives the names of windmills. 'Goliath' is in view here, with 'The Four Winds' and 'de Jonge Hendrik' a little way along. (When you approach a windmill you will see that its name is painted on the head, just below the point where the sails are attached.) Meanwhile high clouds wheel above us, propelled by the brisk wind. 'Clouds are our only mountains here,' says Jeremy Hooker. 'It's a paradox but I sometimes think you have to come to a flat place like the Netherlands to find out about mountains.'

We are in fact on new land here, captured by the dike builders well after the times of *terp* construction, so we abandon the sea and set off inland, crossing successive lines of dike, each in its day the foremost in the battle against the sea. The land here seems almost to smell of salt. We feel, a shade irresponsibly, a sense of proxy satisfaction that so much has been done on our behalf. We pass a little gas field fenced off behind tall lines of fast-growing trees. Much of Holland's considerable wealth of gas lies under the northern provinces, with still more out in the North Sea, but it is evident from the trees that here at least we are not entirely welcome.

19

Soon we are back in far more ancient land and the *terp* hunt is on. I have no exact recollection of how many we saw or thought we saw, how many of the mounds were truly ancient, how many made by modern earth-moving machinery. Plenty of the former, certainly, but the pleasure, we supposed, lay in the whole assembly of the day – bright sky and clouds, the villages, the little brick-built churches, windmills with proper names, the sea-dike and mud flats, bait-digger and oyster catchers as well as in the *terpen* we happened to encounter.

The Romans arrived two and a half centuries after the *terp* builders. Julius Caesar led them in in 57 BC. During the course of his various campaigns in the area he savagely set about the Eburones, south of modern Nijmegen, and he seems to have annihilated the Nervii, another local tribe. The name is familiar from Shakespeare. In *Julius Caesar*, Mark Antony picks up the fallen leader's bloodstained mantle, remembering

> the first time ever Caesar put it on;
> 'twas on a summer's evening, in his tent,
> that day he overcame the Nervii.

In 12 BC, forty-five years after their arrival, the Romans crossed the Rhine and moved into the delta area they called the Insula Batavorum. The Dutch themselves later used the name Batavia for Jakarta in the East Indies, and Napoleon dubbed Holland the Batavian Republic before he turned it into a kingdom under his brother Louis. The fertile fruit-growing countryside running west from Arnhem and Nijmegen is still called the Betuwe, a name associated with the Latin Batavia and probably meaning, originally, Good Land. Fittingly, Betuwe is also the name of a popular brand of jam, visible on every supermarket shelf.

When the Romans moved north of the Rhine they encount-ered difficulties. In AD 28 the Frisians rebelled so effectively that from that point the Romans ruled the land only in name, formally abandoning it in AD 47. Thus they held their territories north of the Great Rivers for only fifty-nine years. But they continued to hold the south for another three centuries, a difference which seems likely to have helped create the later north–south divide.

The Frisian revolt of AD 28, however, was not the whole story. Though the Batavians became relatively free of Rome, they nevertheless supplied mercenary soldiers for the empire. One Batavian soldier went by the name of Claudius Civilis – his original name is lost. He had already served in the Roman armies for twenty-five years when he and his brother were accused of conspiracy and taken to Rome in chains. The brother was executed and Claudius Civilis next appears back in his native country as a hostile chieftain. He rallied the German tribes against Rome and for a while, in AD 69/70, was triumphant against his former masters. But his support leached away and finally he was forced to negotiate, parleying with the Roman commander, each man on opposite sides of a bridge that had been broken in the middle.

Tacitus has given us an account of the rebellion. Unfortunately, this is where it ends. But the revolt of the Batavians against foreign despotism was an inspiration for the Dutch in their struggle against Spain in the sixteenth century; and the oath which Claudius Civilis swore with his fellow tribesmen in their 'conspiracy' was celebrated in the seventeenth century in a forceful painting by Rembrandt – though one which failed to give universal pleasure in its own day.

The trouble lay in Tacitus, who said quite clearly Claudius Civilis only had one eye. Most versions accordingly showed him in profile, only his good eye in evidence. There was also a problem with the oath-taking. Tacitus told how Claudius Civilis summoned the nobles of his tribe to a sacred grove and spoke to them vehemently on the evils of slavery. His speech was 'received with great approval, and he at once bound them all to union, using the barbarous ceremonies and strange oath of his country'.

Rembrandt's contemporaries represented this scene as a clasping of hands but for Rembrandt himself this was not barbarous enough. He chose to show Claudius full-face and one-eyed, a ruffian among ruffians, and in the vivid flare of torchlight Claudius and his fellow-conspirators cross swords. Rembrandt's work was commissioned for the new town hall in Amsterdam but hung there only briefly. It seems then to have been cut down drastically in size, perhaps to make it easier to sell. Today it is in the National Museum in Stockholm, at last an acknowledged masterpiece.

Whatever Rembrandt's initial lack of success, however, *hunebedden*, *terpen* and the revolt of Claudius Civilis all strike themes that are to be developed over time. The *hunebedden* may stand for religion and concern for the after-life. The *terpen* usher in the unceasing fight against water; and the struggles of Claudius Civilis introduce the major theme of resistance to foreign domination.

The Romans departed, suddenly, between AD 260 and AD 270. One contributory reason may have been a sharp rise in the level of the sea and so the loss of profitable land to water.

Over the following centuries, the water rose several times, always with massive consequences. It was during these centuries, too, that the pattern of habitation we recognize in modern Holland began to take shape. Villages were established on sites that have endured down to the present and then came the slow growth of the medieval trading towns, one of the country's greatest glories, still often visible beneath later additions.

First, there were more immigrants. Place-names give a strong indication of what the land was like when they settled it. *Holt* means 'wood', as in English. *Lok* or *lo* at the end of a name indicates woodland with openings, as in Almelo and Hengelo, the smaller textile towns near Enschede. *Woud* and *wold* suggest a forest with *broek* for marshy thicket, *vledder* and *vlier* for marshy meadow. In general, the map gives a strong impression of near-ubiquitous swamp and woodland with scattered clear-ings. In the provinces of Drenthe and Overijssel, farms were sometimes grouped around a central clearing, a kind of common called a *brink*. (The central square of the town of Deventer, among others, still goes by this name.) On the sandy ridges, villages were longer and more straggly, just as they are today. Some soon began to develop into towns.

The Frisians of the north retained their independence. They were great traders, selling their own produce north and south and dealing in an impressive range of goods from Rhineland wine to Scandinavian amber and including English wool, tin and lead. First efforts to Christianize them were largely wasted. According to the nineteenth-century American historian John Lothrop Motley – whose *Rise of the Dutch Republic* remained a classic work for several generations – one Bishop Wolfran was despatched north to do his sacred duty by King Radbod of the Frisians. As Radbod stood with one of his legs immersed in the baptismal font – the account here is Motley's – a thought struck him:

> 'Where are my dead forefathers at present?' he said, suddenly turning upon Bishop Wolfran. 'In hell, with all other unbeliev-ers,' was the imprudent answer. 'Mighty well,' replied Radbod, removing his leg, 'then I will rather feast with my ancestors in the halls of Woden than dwell with your little starveling band of Christians in heaven.'

As late as 1088 Adam of Bremen refers to the Frisians as 'able-bodied heathens', adding the observation that they 'jump-ed over the creeks and ditches of their marshes with the aid of long poles, so that nobody could get at them'. There is still an annual pole-vaulting competition in Friesland.

In fact, Christianization seems to have proceeded at a brisker pace than Adam of Bremen suggests. In 692 one Willibrord, from Northumbria in England, was sent on a mission of conversion and later rewarded with the newly established bishopric of Utrecht. There is an equestrian statue of him there, looking rather tired and bowed but with the model of a church held firmly in his hand. This bishopric grew to be one of the great powers of the land. The Counts of Holland, in The Hague, were a countervailing force.

Christianization was linked to the Carolingian dynasty. They controlled a powerful empire in northern Europe in the early Middle Ages. Charles Martell managed to subdue the Frisians somewhat and then came Charlemagne, the most powerful Carolingian. He ruled, of course, from Aachen, now in West Germany, but seems to have enjoyed his subsidiary palace at Nijmegen. This was mostly built of wood. Destroyed by Vikings in the tenth century, it was rebuilt in the twelfth, in stone, by the emperor Frederick Barbarossa. It stood as one of Holland's greatest memorials till Napoleon's troops delivered the *coup de grâce* in 1796.

The Vikings were highly disruptive for some 200 years but by the tenth century their fling was nearly finished. The water level was steadying as well, making it more practicable to attempt to control the sea. It is from about this period that we get the first real evidence of systematic diking. The first simple sluices also appear to have originated at this time, opening to allow the ebb tide to escape and closing under the force of the returning flood. Apart from buckets, the sluice was to be for some centuries the only available means of draining the land.

The departure of the Vikings meant that trade could flow again. Flanders, in the southern half of the Lowlands, soon became the centre of a major cloth-producing industry. Bruges, Ypres and Ghent, now all in modern Belgium, became rich and powerful. Between the tenth and sixteenth centuries Antwerp rose to become one of the great cities of the known world. In a Flemish play of 1561, a character observes: 'When I name Antwerp, you think you hear the names of Venice, Florence, Genoa, Naples, Augsburg, Cologne, Lyons and Paris, for all these come together in Antwerp for the pursuit of trade.'

Further north, in what has since emerged as the Netherlands, development was slower. There was some spread of wealth northwards from Flanders. Middelburg, where wool from England was trans-shipped for Antwerp, is the most obvious example. Other towns grew rich by trading northwards, again with the Baltic. One of these is Kampen, about an hour and a half's drive north east from Amsterdam and in the same league of excellence as Middelburg. It is a quiet place today, with ancient streets and that irresistible Dutch harmony of canals and handsome houses, at once both comfortable and stylish. The town hall here is extremely venerable with brick buttresses to hold it up and a tower leaning at a crazy angle. There is a sombrely medieval open space around the principal church and on two sides of the town the original gatehouses survive, brick-built and turreted.

The main joy of the town, however, is the river on which it stands. This is the IJssel, that northernmost branch of the Rhine. In medieval times it debouched into open sea and Kampen became a formidable port, distributing the goods that travelled up the Rhine and, of course, receiving in return the corn and pitch and pine that came down from the north. Kampen was at times a member of the Hanseatic League, that powerful association of Germanic trading towns, and at times in deadly enmity with the League. It was at all times a major trading city – until the silting of the river and the rise of Amsterdam.

Nowadays the IJssel rolls fatly through, with barges moored along the Kampen waterfront. For some reason, the bollards are on the far side of the pavement from the water. The passer-by is obliged continually to step over outstretched hawsers. A kind of Bailey bridge crosses the river here and just beside it, on the town side, a little boat sells eel and herring in bread rolls (*broodjes*, for rolls, is an essential word). There is no better way to experience the passage of time than to eat your *broodje* here, surveying today's pleasure boats and yachts on moorings away towards the west and watching the students of the local colleges of art, religion and journalism potter across the unimposing modern bridge on bicycles. Is this what a mighty Hanseatic town has come to, you may think, and then reflect that it is at all events extremely agreeable to be here. The view back from the further bank reveals one of the most deeply pleasing of all Dutch waterfronts.

Among the main features of the medieval period were the rise of Flanders and economically dependent Dutch towns like Middelburg, the rise of the towns along the IJssel – Zutphen, Deventer and particularly Kampen – and, equally important, huge changes to the shape of the land caused by another so-called 'marine transgression' or rise in the sea-level. This took place between 1130 and about 1500, accompanied, as the other 'transgressions' had been, by severe storms and devastating high tides. An estimated 50,000 people were drowned on the north coast in a flood in 1287. During this period the coast actually broke open. The sea flowed into the large lake behind, so forming an open stretch of water which acquired the name of Zuider Zee or Southern Sea. The new arrangement of the waters meant that many former lakeside settlements like Hoorn and Amsterdam now found themselves with the possibility of becoming seaports.

In the interior, a large area south east of Dordrecht had been diked, too daringly perhaps, in the early thirteenth century. It was open to long-distance flooding from the sea and, more pressingly, from the Great Rivers. Peat-cutting had allowed water to seep in under the dikes. There were many lesser floods and alarms. Then on the night of 18–19 November 1421, St Elizabeth's Day, under a storm tide and a westerly gale, the dikes gave way on both sides of the polder. The terror of the flood, right in the middle of the country, has entered popular legend. Seventy-two villages were drowned and it was thought at the time, though the figure is now believed exaggerated, that 100,000 lives were lost. Dordrecht, once the centre of a prosperous rural community, now became an island and remained one for a long time; behind it a district called the Biesbos, or Forest of Reeds, still occupies land once under cultivation. It is today a place for summer boating.

The ever-present threat posed by the water brought an interesting reaction. From a very early date, there were fierce laws intended to keep slack dikers up to the mark for the communal good. But this was not enough. Grants of land were made at low rental to people willing to work on the dikes and free status was conferred on many for the same purpose. In this way, feudalism was undermined at an early date. The Counts of Holland and the Bishops of Utrecht led the way in diking and land reclamation but their activities were accompanied by the rise of dike, drainage and polder boards. These local organizations derived legal authority, ultimately, from the fact that they were working for the general benefit. Many believe the Dutch have achieved a sense of common purpose from their struggle against water. It is certainly reasonable to see some kind of democratic structure emerging in the Middle Ages with the polder boards.

But the larger power structures were thoroughly non-democratic. From 1384, first Flanders and then more and more pieces of the Low Countries' jigsaw were assembled, effectively as a single state, under the Dukes of Burgundy. These were among the greatest potentates of Europe and anxious to centralize their dominions. The Duchy's main centres were Dijon in France and Brussels in the Low Countries; the most notable of the dukes were Philip the Good who ruled from 1419 to 1467 and his son Charles the Bold who reigned for just ten turbulent years. Philip was the most important. After a bitter struggle he succeeded in forcing his cousin Jacoba van Beieren, one of the heroines of the Middle Ages, into surrendering her territories to him; and by a mixture of force and purchase he laid his hands on most of what now constitutes the Netherlands, Luxembourg and Belgium. So far as the Dutch provinces were concerned, the dukes were forced to tolerate a number of local rights and privileges. When they wanted money for campaigning they often called together the representatives of the provinces in a central States General.

Historians used to see a sort of democracy in the way each town had its own government and each province sent its own representatives to the States General. The contemporary view is rather different. It has been shown that the colleges which elected local officials were restricted to the richest and most influential of the burghers who were in practice a closed and self-perpetuating oligarchy.

At the same time, the ambience remained medieval. Out of a welter of narrow beliefs and proliferating symbolism, the court of the Dukes of Burgundy rose like a fantastic pinnacle of wealth and ostentation. According to Johan Huizinga, the great Dutch historian of the first half of the present century, Philip the Good lived on bread and water four days a week, gave alms on a huge scale and fathered a goodly number of illegitimate children. The lavishness of the display for his wedding in Bruges in 1430 entered popular folklore. When Charles the Bold met the Emperor Frederick III at Trier in 1473 he wore a mantle entirely encrusted in diamonds. The feasts of the Burgundian quasi-monarchs were an orgy of excess, not just in the elaboration of the food but in the decor too. At Bruges again, in 1482, an orchestra of twenty-eight persons played in a pie. One of the table decorations was a 46-foot high representation of the tower of Gorcum, a town near Dordrecht. 'Boars' played trumpets and 'goats' sang a motet.

Not everybody was pleased. In the northern part of the Low Countries a religious lifestyle of considerable austerity evolved. This was the Devotio Moderna, based first in Groningen and then in Deventer. Its tone can be surmised from the fact that members deplored the great cathedral tower of Utrecht as a symbol of worldliness. Thomas à Kempis wrote *The Imitation of Christ*, a devotional work still widely read today, within the circle of the brotherhood.

This was one of the great achievements of the age. Another was the religious art produced for a court where splendour was matched by an extravagant piety. In their attempts to reconstruct a Middle Kingdom between France and Germany the Dukes of Burgundy were able to draw on both northern and southern artistic strength and it was against this background that the outburst of painting known as Flemish primitive occurred.

The Flemish primitives are the direct precursors of Dutch painting and their story is inseparable from the story of Dutch art. Though there was probably some difference of temper and tradition to the north and south of the Great Rivers, the Flemish masters painted at a time when there was at least uniformity of belief. Ghent, Bruges, Antwerp and Brussels were the first to achieve prominence and the work done in these towns flowed in an unbroken stream of cumulative tradition into the later work of Utrecht, Haarlem, Leiden, Delft and Amsterdam. The greatest lessons were concerned with realism and realistic detail.

Much Flemish painting is now abroad, above all in London and New York. But the greatest concentration still remains in the towns where it was originally produced. This means that the serious visitor to Holland must at this point in his inquiries go to Belgium.

Ghent, with its rather gritty urban feel, is possibly the place to start because there, in the Cathedral of St Bavo, the most famous of all early Flemish paintings, van Eyck's *Adoration of the Lamb*, remains triumphantly on display. The chapel it is in is tiny; the number of visitors is immense; and the experience of joining them is unforgettable.

The *Adoration of the Lamb* is an enormously full and complicated work, an altarpiece made up of many panels, each extremely arresting. It is true that the work in general shows no great mastery of perspective and that the faces in it seem mostly to represent types rather than individuals ('good' perspective and individual characterization sometimes being taken as proof that a painting belongs to the Renaissance rather than the Middle Ages). But there is in this work a crystalline clarity, a delight in the observation of detail and surfaces, of skin, hair, horses' manes, hands, eyes, that establishes, within a very medieval arrangement of parts, an inextinguishable sense of vividness and realism. Here is painting, one might say, poised on the mountain-top of the medieval at such an altitude that all who come after must now follow the example and use the new techniques employed in the ascent.

One of the great conundrums of art history is who was actually responsible for this work. A Latin inscription suggests the honour should go to 'Hubert van Eyck who was surpassed by none'. But the inscription also says the painting was completed by 'Johannes, second in the art'. Hubert remains a shadowy figure; there are many extant paintings by Jan van Eyck. We know that he first worked for the counts of Holland, then as court painter and 'varlet de chambre' for Philip the Good of Burgundy. He lived in Bruges for the twelve years up to his death in 1441.

Bartolomeo Fazio in his *Book of Famous Men* of 1455–6 calls Jan van Eyck 'the leading painter of our time'. Carel van Mander, writing about Dutch painting in an important work in 1604, treats him quite simply as the founding father, a view which seems to have been unanimous among Dutch painters. All credit him with the invention of oil painting though this is no longer regarded as a tenable view.

There are many other fine pictures in Ghent but perhaps the next port of call after St Bavo's should be the Groeningemuseum in Bruges, just down the motorway. Bruges, though slightly pickled in its own past, is a pretty town of canals and unexpected corners, brick buildings full of crannies, and geraniums on window ledges. The Groeningemuseum is entered by a cobbled forecourt. Then, suddenly, there one is, face to face with other works by Jan van Eyck and in far more intimate relationship with them. The van der Paele *Madonna* is the same marvellous mixture of brilliantly observed detail and archaic perspective. The figures in the foreground are nearly as large as the church they are seen in; the treatment of textures and textiles creates an astonishing illusion of reality. There is unfortunately in the Christ-child one of those typical Flemish babies with the features of a forty-year-old. But one can see from the painting as a whole what the art historian Max Friedländer was thinking of when he praised van Eyck for offering a soft colour harmony which 'encompasses and unites the steely sharpness of the formal design'.

In the Groeningemuseum there is a van Eyck portrait of his own rather sharp-nosed wife, bearing the inscription 'My husband Johannes finished me in the year 1439 on June 17/my age was thirty-three.' This seems unusually personal for the times. And nobody should end the encounter with van Eyck without a quick trip, at least in the mind, to the National Gallery in London to see the Arnolfini portrait – a couple shown full-length and frontally with the greatest clarity and apparent tenderness, a pair of wooden sandals higgledy-piggledy on the floor in front of them and the painter dimly visible in the small mirror on the wall behind. There is no other work like it from the fifteenth century.

After van Eyck in fame comes the anonymous Master of Flémalle, now thought to have been Robert Campin of Tournai, and after him Rogier van der Weyden, the 'Brussels master', as influential on his immediate contemporaries as Jan van Eyck. His work is more sculptural in tone and less declamatory than van Eyck's, more sombre and spiritual, retaining many Gothic attitudes but developing, within backgrounds often devoid of space and depth, enormous emotional power. Van der Weyden's accepted masterpiece is *Descent from the Cross* in the Prado in Madrid but there are magnificent works in the (magnificent) Musée des Beaux Arts in Brussels and also in the Antwerp Beaux Arts (where van Eyck's fantastical and lovely drawing of St Barbara is displayed).

Rogier van der Weyden, though in some ways the most old-fashioned, remains for me at least the most moving of the Flemish painters. Van Eyck was the most revolutionary; and in this respect his successor was undoubtedly Hugo van der Goes. Van der Goes worked on a larger scale than many of his contemporaries, avoiding the schematic and presenting character and emotion very directly. He introduced everyday figures into his biblical scenes, sometimes seeming in this to prefigure the paintings of a later period. One of his finest works, *Death of the Virgin*, is in the Groeningemuseum in Bruges and it appears to be infused with huge emotional pressure.

Whether there is anything that may be called specifically Dutch at this period is a far harder question. During the Reformation, almost all early works of art in the Dutch churches were destroyed by zealous Protestants anxious to suppress idolatry. The only really useful source of knowledge, or perhaps source of tradition, is Carel van Mander who wrote a hundred years and more after the event and with the evident intention of making as much as possible of the Dutch tradition. Van Mander was at pains to claim as Dutch three painters now acknowledged as considerable masters: Dieric Bouts, Albert Ouwater and Geertgen tot Sint Jans.

It is generally believed that Dieric Bouts, whose work is fairly plentiful, came south from Haarlem as a mature painter in about 1440, perhaps with some specifically Dutch artistic traits. His figures are short and have massive heads (except for the *Judgement of Count Otto* in Brussels which appears to have been finished by somebody else after Bouts's death). Ouwater probably worked as pupil to a Flemish master and then came north again having mastered his technique. Little is known of his work though there is a remarkable *Raising of Lazarus* in Berlin.

As for Geertgen, far more of his paintings survive, even though van Mander claims he died at the age of twenty-eight. This would have been, perhaps, between 1490 and 1495. He was a native of Haarlem and seems never to have left Holland. In him we see a most delightful painter, full of quirky observation and with an eye for the burlesque. A good deal of emotional and religious concentration is in evidence and there is nothing sentimental. Experts consider him important to the development of landscape painting because, unlike many Flemish masters, he achieved an easy and natural-looking movement from foreground to background. His *Nativity at Night* in the National Gallery in London is an extraordinarily beautiful work;

some of the finest of his paintings are in the Kunsthistorisches Museum in Vienna; but there is enough to get started on in the Rijksmuseum in Amsterdam.

The surviving fragments of the earliest Dutch painting certainly show possibilities, though perhaps it is only hindsight which allows us to make out in them the first stirrings of anything distinct from the general Flemish style. Most of the most important work must surely have been done in Brussels, Antwerp, Bruges and Ghent.

As for the Dukes of Burgundy, the end was both sad and ignominious. Philip the Good, van Eyck's master, was broadly successful in centralizing rule and extending the territory of the Duchy. But Charles the Bold, his much-loved son, waged wilder and wilder wars against all about him, entirely at the expense of his unwilling subjects. He perished at the battle of Nancy in January 1477, killed by an unknown hand. The body, once so magnificently attired, was discovered, stripped naked, in a frozen pond. Charles had been so dominant a figure during his lifetime that simple people could not accept that he had really died. Up to ten years after the battle of Nancy, money was still being lent out for repayment on the day of his return.

Charles left a nineteen-year-old daughter named Mary who was to outlive him by just five years. Her brief, traumatic reign over the Low Countries was to prove critical in several respects.

Mary's decisive deeds were done in the year her father died. Hard pressed by the French and in trouble from the moment she succeeded, she could only raise the money to fight back by granting her burgher-paymasters a comprehensive set of liberties. These were enshrined in the Great Privilege, a document as important to Dutch history as the Magna Carta to English. Though repudiated by Mary's successors, it became a touchstone for the future. The Great Privilege provided, above all, that the States General could meet whenever it wanted to and without being summoned by the ruler.

In that same year, at the instigation of her nobles, Mary married the Archduke Maximilian of Austria. This meant that when she died the two tiny children whom she left behind were Habsburgs.

Before the enormous consequences of the Habsburg connection are even hinted at, it is necessary, sadly, to record the loss of Friesland's independence. The Archduke Maximilian, left in charge of the Low Countries as a result of Mary's death, was having a terrible time with, among other turbulent folk, two rival factions named the Hooks and the Cods. The complications and ramifications of the strife between these groups are as dreary for the student as the struggles of the Guelphs and Ghibellines in Italy. To subdue his Hooks and Cods, however, Maximilian had to bring in a foreign general, Duke Albert of Saxe-Meissen, and finally, because he had no money, he found himself obliged to settle his debt to the duke by awarding him the hereditary governorship of Friesland. This arrangement came unstuck at a later date but for the Frisians it was a definitive farewell to their primordial freedom.

And now that greater matter – the Habsburg supremacy in the Low Countries. The story begins, of course, with the marriage of Mary of Burgundy and Maximilian of Austria. Their two children were named Philip and Margaret. Philip, known to history as Philip the Handsome, in due course married the Spanish Infanta Juana. Juana, daughter of Ferdinand and Isabella, stood fourth in line to the crowns of Aragon and Castile. By chance, all those who came before her in the list now perished one by one. In 1504, she became Queen of Castile and her husband Philip became king. Juana herself went mad and spent the rest of her life in confinement; Philip died of fever in 1506. Six years before, however, at the turn of the century, a child had been born to them.

This child's name was Charles and he was brought up as a Flemish-speaking prince. By 1516, he had become king of both Aragon and Castile. In 1520, his twentieth year, he was crowned emperor in Aachen. This meant that he was now, by process of addition, ruler of the Low Countries, of what remained of the Holy Roman Empire, of Spain and all her vast possessions. The political shape of Europe had been changed beyond recognition and with it the prospects for the future of the Low Countries.

THREE

The Struggle against Spain

In 1504, two years before his death in Burgos, Philip the Handsome, the father of the future emperor, commissioned a painting of the Last Judgement. The painter, who signed himself Jheronimus Bosch in neat Gothic lettering on the altarpieces he produced, was then about fifty-five years old and appears to have lived his whole life in 's-Hertogenbosch, the town from which he took his name. Today a prosperous city in the Catholic south of Holland, Den Bosch was well away from the artistic mainstream of Antwerp, Ghent and Bruges. Much has been made of the supposed provincialism of the town's most famous citizen. In fact Den Bosch stood on the junction of three main roads, all used as trading routes – this is why the main square forms a triangle; and when its cathedral burnt down in 1442, it was rich enough and cared enough to erect in its place one of the more impressive Gothic churches of northern Europe. As you look up from the car park just beside the cathedral into a thicket of stonework above swirling tracery, the grandeur of the conception is evident. Though distant from the centre of Flemish art, Den Bosch was evidently on some kind of map.

Hieronymus Bosch himself, of course, is one of those universally acclaimed great masters of the Low Countries, ranking with van Eyck, Bruegel, Rembrandt, Vermeer and van Gogh. His work must have seemed quite extraordinary to his contemporaries. Some still believe him the most extraordinary painter who has ever lived.

A number of his paintings are relatively simple. In *The Cure of*

Folly, for example, perhaps an early work, a quack doctor has opened the skull of a trusting idiot in an operation of evident lunacy. The action in this picture, which is probably an illustration of a proverb, concentrates on just four figures with a flat countryside stretching away behind. The great altarpieces form another distinct category. These are crowded with fantastical demons and burning cities, profuse eroticism, gluttony, anal fantasy, dismembered limbs, gallows and gibbets, scenes of grotesque torture, luxurious sin and utterly hideous punishment. Another of Bosch's themes was the suffering of Christ, generally depicted in tightly framed works showing little but degradation in the minutely observed faces of his assailants. Then there is a series of individual saints, solitary figures still many times pursued by demons, set against landscapes of great depth and beauty, with distant mountains and pinnacled towns.

In style the work is partly Gothic, particularly in the treatment of the human figure, and partly based, it seems, on the new realism. The grasp of landscape alone would establish Bosch as a considerable master if he had painted nothing else. At times he offers burlesque, low-life scenes, striking yet another theme which was to be developed in Dutch painting of later years. In content his work seems to anticipate not just his great follower Pieter Bruegel, but also, centuries later, surrealism and even contemporary science-fiction film-making.

Here are paintings done late in the fifteenth century and early in the sixteenth, showing humans with torsos made of houses and buildings with heads emerging from them, hybrid creatures made up of extraordinary mixtures, human, animal and inanimate, vast knives protruding between pairs of ears, weird plastic-looking bubbles, buildings like space-age architecture and casing made of glittering metal covered with knobs and buttons.

This work, at first so individual, was soon profusely copied, imitated, even forged – all signs of admiration. Charles V's son, Philip II of Spain, grandson of Philip the Handsome who commissioned *The Last Judgement*, bought up works by Bosch

37

when he was a young prince in the Low Countries. He carried them off to Spain where many still remain, mostly in the Prado, and continued to collect throughout his reign. Philip's lifelong enemy, William of Orange, also bought Bosch works and so, at a later date, did the painter Rubens.

But questions soon began to emerge. As early as 1605 we find Fra. José Sigüenza, in his *History of the Order of St Jerome* (which owned a number of the paintings) defending Bosch against the charge of heresy, an indication, perhaps, that the key to understanding his profuse symbolism was already lost. Sigüenza offers the penetrating insight that while other painters dealt with man from the outside, Bosch alone 'had the audacity to paint him as he is on the inside'. Earlier in our own century, the great art historian Panofsky conceded sadly that the interpretative key was indeed lost. Since then scholars have offered great numbers of ingenious explanations of Bosch's symbolism. These have been worked up from modern research into astrology, and from consideration of puns and riddles, alchemy, hallucinatory drugs and heretical rituals. All have been presented quite seriously and in detail as keys to the understanding of Bosch's work.

It would defy the laws of probability if not a single symbol had been read correctly. The trouble is, we do not know which ones. Fundamentally, there is agreement only that Bosch's work is medieval in many aspects, troubled, even tormented, with hell and torture as the final outcome rather than salvation. He remains a central figure in the contemporary imagination.

Bosch died in 1516. Some ascribe the sense of trouble in his work to the troubles in the world around him and a growing sense of insecurity as Catholicism itself came under attack. There is no certainty about this. What is clear is that during the latter years of Bosch's life a chain of political, intellectual and religious changes had begun against a background of unprecedented social development. There was to be no slackening in the pace of events till the Low Countries were split in two with the northern half – effectively the modern Netherlands – an independent Protestant republic more densely populated and more industrialized than anywhere else in Europe. It is tempting to say, if only for the sake of neatness, that the movement from Flemish medieval to the modernity of the Dutch golden age, began in 1500 with the birth of the future Charles V and was fully accomplished by 1609 with the grudging Spanish admission of Dutch independence. During this period the Low Countries first became part of the Spanish empire and then, in a slow-moving contest, the northern provinces fought off the might of Spain to achieve a political solution of their own. Somehow, as they did so, economic and intellectual energies were released on a scale to rival Elizabethan England.

The story starts with the challenge to the Catholic church; and this, as experienced in the Low Countries, was closely related to the intellectual activities of Erasmus of Rotterdam.

Erasmus was born in 1469, making him about twenty years younger than Bosch. He was educated in the agreeable town of Deventer, on the River IJssel, by the Brethren of the Common Life. The ideals of the Brethren were essentially to live out the teachings of Catholicism in a pure and simple spirit. It was quite common at this time for fierce onslaughts to be launched against the excesses of church and clergy and the Brethren contributed to a tide that was already flowing. Up to this point, though, the church had seemed quite capable of absorbing the criticisms.

In the hands of Erasmus the criticisms seemed to take on a new gravity. Moving freely at first between London, Paris and Louvain in the Low Countries – later he moved to Basle – he wrote and talked and made a great personal impression. Technically he was an Augustinian canon but he finally put off clerical habits to wear the clothes of a cultivated gentleman. His intimates were people such as Sir Thomas More and John Colet and, to most of us today, he will be familiar from the Holbein portrait in the Louvre – long nose with slightly flaring nostrils, the tiniest double chin, wisps of greying hair curling out from under a floppy hat as his quill moves lightly across the page. His

39

pen linked him to his many friends in a voluminous and influential Latin correspondence and he was among the first writers whose works became generally available through the printing presses.

Essentially, he took the inquiring methods of contemporary Italy, with its excited rediscovery of the writings of ancient Greece and Rome, and applied them to the interpretation of the Scriptures. With no apparent sense that he was undermining Catholicism, he offered the suggestion that each person individually should study the Bible and so assimilate the spirit and teachings of Christ. This was central to the way of thinking soon labelled Protestantism. But Erasmus wrote in a style which often appeared ambiguous and elusive, indicating a possible lack of commitment and, in the eyes of his critics, a lack of courage.

Many believed Erasmus was a key figure in the spread of Protestantism. But soon he was swept aside by that far fiercer spirit, Martin Luther, who attacked him for having stopped half way along the road and failing to declare his position openly. The name of Erasmus lives on as a synonym for humanistic inquiry and tolerance of individual belief. As Protestantism developed, however, it was Luther who dominated, and then, with greater consequences for the Low Countries, John Calvin of Geneva.

Meanwhile, as all these currents of thought were beginning to swirl in a quickening river, the young prince Charles was growing up in Mechelen under the care of his aunt, Mary of Hungary, a near neighbour of both Bosch and Erasmus. Charles, of course, spoke Flemish as his first language; to his subjects in the Low Countries he appeared throughout his life to be one of them. They felt pride when he became king of Spain and pride again when he was elected emperor.

During the remaining thirty-five years of his reign, Charles fought incessant wars and the rich Low Countries were taxed to pay for them – so much so that in some areas farmers moved off the land and wolves moved in instead. But Charles was a Lowlander, after all, and, groaning, his countrymen, put up with it. Charles also unified the Low Countries to a greater extent than had previously been achieved, taking over nearly the whole of their Seventeen Provinces for himself and ensuring, under the Pragmatic Sanction of 1549, that his son Philip would succeed to the territory as a single unit. The other strand in Charles's rule was the unceasing battle against the new religious ideas, defined quite simply as heresy.

Charles actually met Luther at the Diet of Worms in 1521 and lived to regret his failure to deal with him then as decisively as he might have done later in his career. Though Lutheranism was banned in the empire and Luther's books were burned in Erasmus's Louvain, the tide of Protestantism swept on, with a proliferation of sects, a joyously disrespectful refusal of the authority of priests and insistence on individual pursuit of salvation through the Bible. Dutchmen were prominent in the wildly anarchic Anabaptist 'Kingdom of Munster' – a seizure of power which led to ferocious repression, the perpetual fate of the Anabaptists. In the Low Countries a special state-run inquisition was set up alongside the church's own disciplinary system. This enraged the individual cities who feared, correctly, that their rights to judge their own were being taken away from them. Some 2000 inhabitants of the Low Countries were executed during Charles's reign. It seemed that 'heresy' might be entirely crushed. Many fled to England and Germany. In fact, the forces which were to tear the Habsburg inheritance apart and, paradoxically, to usher in the golden age of Holland, were already in place.

On the one hand stood Charles's son, the young Prince Philip, reared as a Spaniard, proud, obsessive over detail, immensely concerned to act correctly, above all in the eyes of God. He represented a vast orthodoxy and an equally vast imperial bureaucracy and military machine. On the other stood the man who was to become his principal adversary, Prince William of Orange – aristocratic, ambiguous, accessible, slow to act, as concerned as Philip to act correctly yet finally pushed by conscience and political circumstances into actions which led to the birth of a new state. These men were not the only actors; at many crucial moments their views were of no importance at all to the development of events; yet in a curious way both served directly as a channel for the forces which they also symbolized.

William, originally William of Nassau and later known as William of Orange or William the Silent, was born in the turreted German castle of Dillenburg in 1533. At the age of eleven, quite unexpectedly, he inherited the Princedom of Orange under the will of a cousin who had died on a military campaign. This made him one of the richest nobles of Europe with major possessions in the Low Countries. Immediately he moved to Brussels and there, though born a Lutheran, he grew up in the Catholic court of Charles V. He became a particular favourite of the emperor.

In 1549, when the succession to the throne of the Low Countries was made safe for Philip under the Pragmatic Sanction, William was one of the party who accompanied the prospective ruler on an elaborate and well-documented tour of his future possessions. This involved gargantuan feasting, meetings with the nobility and even a boat trip to the Biesbos behind Dordrecht to see the spires of the churches inundated in the St Elizabeth's Day flood more than a hundred years before. Charles abdicated in 1555, worn out with the cares of office and crippled by rheumatism. It was on William's shoulder that he leaned during the ceremony in Brussels. There, according to the English envoy John Masson, 'the Emperor begged the forgiveness of his subjects if he had ever unwittingly omitted the performance of any of his duties towards them. And here he broke into a weeping, whereunto, besides the dolefulness of the matter, I think he was moche provoked by seeing the whole company do the lyke before . . .' His weeping would have been more doleful still if he had known that within nine years his son would be engaged in open war with the much-trusted William.

In trying to disentangle the events which now ensued, the question of perspective is all-important. For a powerful myth was erected during the nineteenth century and it has been the task of twentieth-century historians to sort out which parts of it are reasonable and which must be discarded.

The author of the myth was the American historian, John Lothrop Motley, a well-connected and wealthy Bostonian, Harvard-educated, author of two early romantic novels, dabbler in politics and a passionate libertarian within the understanding of the day. He felt himself, as he confessed in a letter to a friend, drawn on irresistibly by the subject. In his eyes, the rise of the Dutch Republic was the story of democracy – Protestant democracy, of course – emerging through the black night of Catholic tyranny. The final success of the Dutch was the precursor of similarly successful quests for liberty in Britain and then America, forerunner of nineteenth-century liberal demo-cracy, the British empire and a global equilibrium.

Armed with these notions Motley spun an enormous web of narrative in which all true Dutchmen were noble Protestants, and all Spaniards and all they represented utterly evil – and told his tale so well and in such impassioned prose that his version was entirely dominant for eighty years and more. As a result, all who received a liberal education in Britain or America during the early part of the present century took some part of their own political identity from the valiant struggles of the infant Dutch Republic. Even today, though now perhaps at several removes, we derive from Motley a folk-history of the cruel Duke of Alva, heroic Dutch resistance in the sieges of Haarlem, Alkmaar and Leiden, the long and crafty struggle of William the Silent, and finally his cruel murder in Delft for a bounty offered by his enemy, King Philip II of Spain. 'As long as he lived,' wrote Motley, 'he was the guiding-star of a whole brave nation, and when he died the little children cried in the streets.'

The Dutch historian Pieter Geyl, writing in 1931, and then the British scholar Geoffrey Parker, in 1977, have shown that it was not so simple. Geyl stressed the common elements between the north and south and the part the Catholics had played in the rebellion. Parker, drawing on contemporary small-scale studies and an intimate knowledge of Spanish history as well, has

43

brought the story up to date again in a subtle narrative. It is now clear that there was not one monolithic upheaval whose only possible consequence was the formation of a Protestant Dutch Republic. Far from it. There were three separate revolts, or at the least three distinct phases, all based on different grievances among seventeen provinces more interested in their own particularist causes than in any 'national' unity. The Dutch succeeded in the end largely because of the financial difficulties of Spain. The Calvinists who carried the day for Protestantism in the north were always a minority, though highly organized and highly successful. Nor was the outcome even a particularly democratic one, for the States General and the Provincial States were still dominated by the oligarchies which had developed under the Dukes of Burgundy. There were new elements in the system, it is true, but not many and they joined with the rest in keeping power from the people.

Even so, the events themselves, the personalities, the issues and the outcome remain fascinating both in their own right and because they opened the way for the extraordinary developments in art and civilization achieved by the Dutch at the end of the sixteenth century and persisting through the seventeenth.

The troubles, in a real sense, began in 1549 when Philip II left Brussels for Spain, never to return. The Low Countries, accustomed for half a generation at least to being the centre of empire, now became a dependency of Spain. There were Spanish garrisons in the towns and Philip's aunt, Margaret of Parma, the governor, was clearly there to rule in the Spanish interest. She herself was under the immediate guidance of her minister Antoine Perrenot, soon to become Cardinal Granvelle, and ultimately under the guidance of Philip. Philip himself was like a puppet-master trying to run the theatre from so great a distance that he initially achieved no more than to keep the strings agitated and the puppets confused.

The indignant provinces refused to pay their taxes till Spanish troops were removed. They succeeded in this campaign in 1561. Meanwhile Perrenot pushed ahead with a reform of the bishoprics which maddened every interest in the Low Countries but made him Archbishop of Mechelen and a cardinal, the dominant figure, under Philip, in both church and state. But soon he so greatly overstepped even his own great power that the most powerful nobles of the Low Countries – William of Orange and the Counts Egmont and Hoorn – formed an anti-Granvelle league, sardonically dressing their servants in livery intended to parody a cardinal's dress. Hostility to Granvelle was a challenge to Philip's authority that he could not deal with at so great a distance. By 1564 the king was obliged to sacrifice his minister and Granvelle now left the Low Countries under pretence of visiting his sick mother.

Events in the Low Countries still continued to outrun Margaret of Parma and Philip. The winter of 1564–5 was a terrible one. The countryside was gripped by ice. There were bread riots in the cities. At the same time, Calvinism was openly on the march, reaching all social classes despite the inquisition. Orange, Egmont and Hoorn petitioned Philip to soften his policy but he would not. As a result, the challenge to Spain passed out of the control of the grandees and into the hands of the lesser nobles. These now drew up their own petition, a document called the Compromise of the Nobility. They stormed into Margaret's palace in Brussels and threw it, in effect, into her anguished face. She wept. The Count of Berlaymont beside her, trying to rally her, observed: 'Quoi, Madame, affreuse de ces gueux?' – frightened of such beggars?

At once the movement had a name – The Beggars. Their badge of office was a begging bowl worn round the neck; and soon they too lost control. For now the Calvinists who had fled during the earlier persecution (Norwich in England was almost forty per cent Dutch at this time) came streaming back in defiance of the authorities. There was a wild ouburst of open-air assemblies, huge crowds flocking to hear vehement preaching in the safety of the countryside. Next, all in a rush, events occurred that still affect the look of Dutch religious interiors, accounting for the bare splendour of the great Protestant churches.

The 'iconoclastic fury' in which paintings and images were destroyed in the north began when the former hatmaker Sebastian Matte preached so effectively that twenty or so of his audience leapt up to smash the images in a monastery. According to Geoffrey Parker, the bulk of the subsequent damage was done by 'an organized itinerant body of image breakers who came over from England'. They were paid by the Calvinists of Antwerp and were not anywhere resisted.

In Antwerp itself it was William of Orange who finally succeeded in quelling general disorder. He had been sent there by Margaret of Parma and in March 1567 he refused to put himself at the head of a 'Beggars' army' led by John Marnix, one of the lesser nobles. Marnix died in the disturbance and throughout the rest of William's career, whenever his loyalty to the revolution was in doubt, the sinister question would go up on the walls of Antwerp: 'Who killed John Marnix?'

It was a reasonable question. For William's position was extremely cloudy. While protesting loyalty to Philip he urged moderation on Margaret in a way that seemed to her disloyal. Though he had colluded against Granvelle with Counts Hoorn and Egmont and had consorted openly with the Beggars, he nevertheless appeared to be on the king's side when matters came to a crunch in Antwerp. Many believed he was playing a double game.

William of Orange puzzled his contemporaries. Those hostile to him called him William the 'sluwe' or 'sly'. In inflated Latin this became 'Taciturnus' and finally, in English, William the Silent. It was an inappropriate name. He kept his own counsel but he was in fact extremely sociable. As a young man he enjoyed the wealth and splendour of his great palace in Brussels and was an outgoing host at his favourite residence, the Castle of Breda. As circumstances darkened and his character deepened, he became more self-contained – as adept as Erasmus at concealing his own motivation. He worked prodigiously and once he had set his hand to a task he carried on with stubborn obduracy. 'It is not necessary to have any success when trying,

nor to have hope when you want to make a start,' he is reputed to have said. People often doubted him, partly because of his seemingly expedient changes of religion from Lutheran to Catholic and finally to Calvinist. His slowness to act was also held against him. But he evoked great love and his almost unbelievable sticking power over and over again made him a rallying point when all appeared lost. He was a romantic figure, too, four times married, twice made a widower, once calamitously betrayed.

Philip finally decided William in favour of open rebellion by sending the Duke of Alva to the Low Countries on what was clearly to be a punitive expedition. As Alva made ready to bring up troops from northern Italy, the unrest in the Low Countries petered out. William withdrew to his estates in Germany. On 24 June 1567, sixty years old, gouty, ferocious and inflexible, Alva crossed the Mont Cenis pass in snow at the head of an army of 10,000 Spanish veterans. Within five days of his arrival in Brussels Alva had pushed aside Margaret of Parma and established a Council of Troubles – known more appropriately, even without benefit of Motley, as the Council of Blood.

At first the pace of executions was slow. Time was needed for sequestration of property, questioning and torture. Counts Egmont and Hoorn were arrested, both still believing they had acted in accordance with their duties to King Philip and his subjects. William was stripped of his possessions – meaning that his only way back was through force of arms. Next January, 84 leading citizens were publicly executed. In March a further 1,500 were arrested. 'Now', wrote an Englishman from Antwerp, 'the very papists do perceive that the Duke of Alva doth go about to make them all slaves.' Later in the year, still uncomprehending, Egmont and Hoorn were publicly beheaded. William of Orange, who would plainly have been with them if he had not withdrawn to Germany, emerged now as the single focus for revolt. During 1568 he succeeded in putting together four armies to attack from four different directions. But he was unable to synchronize the separate campaigns and in the end all four were totally defeated. Bankrupt and disgraced, William retreated once more to Germany. 'We may regard the Prince of Orange as a dead man,' the Duke of Alva wrote. The first revolt was over.

The Spanish repression raged through 1569. This year also marked the death of a person better known to the twentieth century than either William the Silent or Philip of Spain. The painter Pieter Bruegel was a Dutchman working mainly in the Flemish tradition, born about 1525, in or close to Breda. Its great Gothic church was already standing when Bruegel was a child. Today there is a market every Tuesday morning – and a lively one, its stalls hard up against the cathedral apse, with fish sellers from Scheveningen and bulb sellers from Haarlem and Indonesian and Surinamese traders. In Bruegel's day there were thirteen sycamore trees where storks nested each year and a market that was cosmopolitan for its own time. Just round the corner was the castle, soon to be occupied by William. Today it has been rebuilt and is a military training academy, off limits to the public.

Much of the medieval is still discernible in Breda though the modern world is also bursting through. The same may be said of Pieter Bruegel.

Although his paintings make him seem a familiar friend, Bruegel's life is documented about as sketchily as that of Shakespeare. Carel van Mander, writing in 1604, says he was apprenticed to the figure-painter Pieter Coecke van Aelst whose daughter he married at a later date. In 1551 he joined the guild of St Luke in Antwerp as a master-painter. Shortly afterwards he set off for Italy.

During the latter years of Hieronymus Bosch and in the decades following his death, Italian art had become extremely influential in the Low Countries. The Dutch painter Lucas van Leyden – who took his name from his native city – acquired a positively Italianate brilliance; a trip to the Lakenhal Museum in

Leiden to see his altarpiece of the *Last Judgement* makes the point. Van Leyden's contemporary Jan van Scorel was canon of the St Mary Minster in Utrecht. He travelled to Rome in 1521. When a fellow citizen of Utrecht became pope for a brief, unhappy reign – this was Adrian VI – van Scorel was appointed curator of the papal collections. He returned to Utrecht a master of the art that was to lead to northern Mannerism, his canvases full of narrative invention and Italianate human figures. Van Mander, keen to a fault on the Italians, called van Scorel 'the lantern-bearer and road-paver of the Arts in the Low Countries'. Van Scorel's own pupil, the increasingly well-regarded Maarten van Heemskerk, also went to Rome and came back a changed artist, treating classical themes in a style that proved another step along the road to Mannerism.

With Bruegel, by far the greater master, the extent of Italian influence is more doubtful. He was away four years and the effects of his trip remain controversial among scholars. This, however, is secondary to an appreciation of the vast scope of his work. Bruegel ranged over a number of distinct genres and achieved masterpieces in each.

According to the Italian writer Guicciardini in his *Description of all the Lowlands*, published in Antwerp in 1567, there were now 300 painters working there. It was virtually a factory town with elaborately organized art workshops. Bruegel, returning from Italy in 1555, went to work for a leading print publisher named Hieronymus Cock. He had clearly fallen in love with the Alps and produced a number of mountain landscapes in which the high vantage point and colossal vistas customary in Flemish painting were entirely naturalistic. Some of this work is almost topographical, second cousin to map-making.

Bosch had been dead for forty years but his work was all the rage and Bruegel turned out drawings in the old master's style. Some, when published as engravings, were even signed with Bosch's name – as in the famous *Big Fish Eat Little Fish*.

In addition to prints, Bruegel produced paintings based on Bosch's style. Most of these are well known from reproduction.

There was *Dulle Griet* – Mad Margaret plundering at the gates of hell, her huge frame striding through a demonic landscape – and the spectacular *Fall of the Rebel Angels*. This was a little softer-edged than an original Bosch, the hybrid demons now more comical than terrifying. Erasmus, after all, had in the meantime referred to demons as 'mere spooks and bogeymen'. The greatest painting in this series and the least like Bosch, despite the lurid skies and teeming landscape, was *The Triumph of Death*. In this masterwork of the sixteenth century the massed armies of the dead, skeletal and horrifying, fall upon the living against a charnel-house background of executions, fiery horizons and sinking ships. It speaks to the human condition with unbearable urgency.

Even this was only part of Bruegel's achievement. Erasmus had published a huge collection of Latin and Greek adages, with an extensive commentary. During the middle part of the century, the busy Antwerp presses produced many collections of contemporary proverbs. Bruegel now painted an encyclopedic illustration of the proverbs and another one of children's games. It seemed as if the intention was to hold the whole of human life to view, perhaps as part of a great theatre of folly.

At about the age of forty, Bruegel married his former master's daughter and moved to Brussels. Here, in the last six years of his life, he produced masterpiece upon masterpiece. These include complex scenes of rustic revelry, *The Peasant Wedding*, *The Peasant Dance*, *The Peasant Fair* (or '*Kemis*'), all world-famous, likely to be found on table mats in motel restaurants. Bruegel's paintings of the seasons – among them *The Hunters in the Snow*, *The Return of the Herd* and *The Corn Harvest* – are among the most brilliant landscapes in the history of art. And then there were two extraordinary paintings, sinister and beautiful in the same breath, with biblical scenes set in snow and ice in Flemish villages. One was a rendering of the census at Bethlehem, the other a massacre of the Innocents.

In this an alien soldiery assaults the village people, butchering the children. Mothers tug at the soldiers or turn away to weep.

In the background a troop of cavalry is drawn up in the snow. Their commander, dressed in black, hunches on his horse, awesome and white-bearded. The painting is thought to date from one of the hard winters immediately before Alva's arrival, and many would like to see it as a work of prophesy. This may be so. Other Bruegel paintings have also been claimed as political commentary. His *Sermon of St John the Baptist*, for example, shows the saint preaching to a large open-air crowd just as the Calvinists were doing at the time. But this was a well-established scene, painted in similar form in the Low Countries before the rise of Calvinism.

It would have been surprising if Bruegel had been politically combative or mounted an open religious challenge through his work. One of his principal patrons was the banker Niclaes Jonghelinck, known personally to Philip II. Philip's Habsburg cousins bought Bruegel's pictures avidly (with the result that the best collection is now in Vienna). Cardinal Granvelle himself owned several Bruegel works, among them *The Flight into Egypt* (though he had to leave some behind at the time of his own hasty departure). With this kind of custom it would have been rash for Bruegel to have stepped out of line. The only real hint of unorthodoxy is his deathbed request to his wife, reported forty years later by van Mander, to destroy certain 'biting and sharp drawings'. Van Mander speculates that Bruegel might have ordered their destruction to prevent them getting his wife into trouble.

Bruegel was enjoyed in his own day mainly as a follower of Bosch and admired as a peasant-loving humorist. This may have been how his successors in the Dutch golden age also thought of him. There was a tradition, probably mistaken, that he was himself a peasant by origin. Certainly he lacked the high Italian finish, but with hindsight it can be seen just how much more there was. In landscape, for example, he maintained the intense, indwelling observation of the early Flemish masters, adding contemporary Italian flourishes and some of his own as well. He loved to represent deep foliage and twisted trees. He portrayed human beings either in burlesque terms as part of the theatre of folly or as closely observed individuals, often enough with compassion. Almost incidentally, he set a vogue for snow scenes worked round silhouette and outline. From a modern perspective he seems one of the most generous of artists, whole-hearted and all-embracing. It is no accident that in this century he has attracted the attention of such poets as W. H. Auden and William Carlos Williams.

1569, the year of Bruegel's death, was William of Orange's nadir. Dispossessed, distrusted, a failed military leader, he waited in Germany, attempting without success to put together opposition to Alva. But Alva himself now made a decisive error. With heretics already burning by the thousand, he decided to impose a series of heavy taxes to defray the costs of his own large standing army. One of these – in effect, a ten per cent value added tax – led more directly than the repression to the next round of hostilities.

For several years a rather doubtful band of high-seas pirates and marauders, known as the Sea Beggars, had been in operation under William's nominal command. On 1 April 1572, flying banners protesting at the new tax, they captured the Dutch port of Brill not far from Middelburg. Numerous towns at once declared for William. With huge energy he gathered an army and by the summer had it in the field. Meanwhile at Dordrecht, in one of the principal rooms of a monastery there, the deputies of William's towns met to give their revolution some kind of legal form. Dutch children learn today that this meeting was one of the great turning points. It was addressed on William's behalf by Philip Marnix, brother of John who died at Antwerp and now, after years of bitter estrangement, once more a staunch ally of William's. The room where the meeting was held is called the Statenzaal or Chamber of State and is open to the public. Despite some fairly heavy restoration, the atmosphere of desperate alliance seems easy to imagine.

A desperate alliance and within a short time desperately unsuccessful. William once again attempted a multiple invasion and once again had difficulty coordinating his forces. At first the rebels were successful in the north and the north east. In the south they depended for help on the French Huguenots. But the St Bartholomew's Day Massacre in Paris in August had temporarily destroyed Protestant power there. Philip II, hearing the news in Spain and immediately realizing its significance, for once in his life was unable to restrain himself. The historian Geoffrey Parker says, 'he laughed out loud and danced about his chamber'. William was soon in trouble, his camp assaulted in the night, two of his secretaries and an equerry killed by a special raiding party. He himself, so the story goes, was woken by the scrabbling of his pug-dog Kunze and ran out into the dark to save his life.

William had been defeated once again. Alva, triumphant, now broke the recognized rules of war by allowing his troops to sack the towns of Naarden, Mechelen and Zutphen as they surrendered. The carnage was enormous. Four years later one witness to the sack of Mechelen declared: 'One could say a lot more about it if the horror of it did not make one's hair stand on end – not at recounting it, but just at remembering it.' William now showed his capacity to endure, moving north to the province of Holland with a remnant of barely eighty men, and pledging himself to 'make that province my tomb'. This time it was to be a fight to the death.

Almost at once Haarlem was besieged by forces under Alva's son, Don Fadrique. During a bitter winter the inhabitants of the city suffered grievously from deprivations of all kinds. Some wanted to give in – despite the memory of Naarden, Mechelen and Zutphen. But hard-liners gained control and maintained the defence. Skaters and pigeons carried William's messages of encouragement. The defenders continued to hold out. Next summer William gathered together the best force he could find to relieve the city – but this was cut to pieces by the Spaniards. Haarlem finally fell on 9 July 1573, and Don Fadrique, under orders from his father to show clemency, executed just under 2,000 people – the garrison and a selection of citizens. William was at Leiden and angry crowds threw stones against his windows. Alva himself was amazed at the unfavourable reception for what he genuinely thought an act of clemency.

First, Haarlem. Next, Alkmaar. This pretty provincial town is half an hour north of Amsterdam by train or car and site of a market much loved by tourists. Porters in white boaters carry glossy rounds of cheese on wooden stretchers. In 1573 the town came under siege from Don Fadrique. But the Dutch cut the dikes and sea-water rolled in over five miles of fertile ground won by infinite effort over centuries. Don Fadrique's men waded out, cold, disconsolate and wet.

The rebels now won an important sea victory over the Spaniards. Realizing that it was Alva's policies rather than the religious question which had provoked so determined an opposition, Philip decided to withdraw him. It was just nine years since Cardinal Granvelle's failure.

Next spring, two of William's brothers were killed in battle. And now Leiden, in the heart of the province of Holland, came under siege. Could this town, too, though further inland than Alkmaar, also be relieved by cutting the dikes? What consequences would flow from breaching the complicated tangle of sea and river defences in that part of the country? Even though it would mean great loss of land and homes, William was certain the attempt had to be made. The States of the province of Holland were meeting in Rotterdam. William put the case to them and put it over and over again to the point of personal exhaustion, scrupulously observing the niceties of democratic decision-making. Finally the States hardened in favour of the plan.

The water had to flow twenty-two miles to Leiden and it flowed extremely slowly. A fleet of barges had been prepared in Rotterdam and on 10 September it set out for the city. In Leiden, plague and famine had made existence almost intolerable. Adriaen van der Werff was burgomaster and the story has it that he shamed an angry mob by offering them his own flesh to eat rather than surrender. He had, he said, only one death to die – there is an heroic picture over the main stairway in the city's Lakenhal Museum, showing him making his declaration.

The barges finally neared Leiden. They encountered a protective earthwork, breached it, then came to a raised road defended by cannon. Now the citizens of Leiden could hear the sound of gunfire. But the Dutch were held at the road and the water, which had been three feet deep, dropped to a mere six inches. The barges foundered. As the next days passed the expeditionary force grew terrified that Leiden would finally surrender, not knowing how close rescue lay. There was general prayer in the churches in nearby Delft – William now had his headquarters here in the former Convent of St Agatha. As if in answer, on the night of 1 October a high tide combined with a north-west wind to raise the water level. The barges floated off. Two days later, with the Spaniards in confusion, the water-borne rescuers reached Leiden. White bread and herring were distributed to the people; white bread and herring are still distributed each year on the anniversary. The city was rewarded for its valour by the foundation there of the first Dutch university.

The war dragged on. Peace talks at Breda settled nothing. In 1576, the Spaniards took Zierikzee in Zeeland in a victory of such strategic significance that it looked as if William and the Dutch might finally be beaten after all – but within hours the victorious Spanish troops had mutinied for pay arrears. The rebel provinces were saved. Now multiple Spanish mutinies, anarchic and dangerous, provoked resistance from all of the Low Countries, not just the north. This was the start of the third phase of the revolt. Philip II's brother, Don John of Austria, arrived to take control on behalf of Spain and promptly sacked Antwerp in the most signal act of brutality of the century. The Spanish Fury lasted several days. Eight thousand citizens were killed, a third of the city burned.

It might now have seemed that all the Seventeen Provinces

would unite against Spain and the whole of the Low Countries emerge as a single nation. But the Protestants of the north, attempting to take religious control, replaced Catholic magistrates by Calvinist 'committees' in a series of coups in individual towns, replacing Catholic worship by Calvinism. This so dismayed the Catholics that the opportunity for unity, if it really was an opportunity, was lost. In 1579 six of the provinces of the Catholic south were reconciled with Spain – effectively the birth of Belgium – while the Protestant-dominated provinces of the north formally banded themselves together under the Treaty of Utrecht. Two years later, by the Act of Abjuration, they threw off the sovereignty of Spain – not that Spain accepted the legitimacy of the Act.

Philip II put a large reward on William's life. William, moving between Delft, Antwerp and Brussels in the frantic politicking of the hour, was open and accessible, always ready to receive petitions. He refused to change his ways. The first would-be assassin put a bullet through his mouth in Antwerp in 1582. He recovered, haemorrhaged, reached the point of death – and then recovered again. Two years later a cabinet-maker's assistant named Balthasar Gérard struck at him at the foot of the stairway in the Convent of St Agatha in Delft as he and his family came out from lunch. The pistol bullets entered his lung and stomach and within moments he was dead.

St Agatha's Convent has been re-named the Prinsenhof or Prince's Court. Most of its wide and airy chambers, now a museum, are comfortably domestic rather than baronial. There are some improbably large gashes in the wall at the foot of the stairway, supposedly the holes made by the fatal bullets. A statue of William lies nearby in the fourteenth-century Nieuwe Kerk, replete with allegorical figures and with the faithful pug-dog Kunze lying at his feet.

Politically all was now in doubt. William had died at a moment of confusion. The United Provinces were hard pressed militarily. Once again it seemed that all which had been won with patience and suffering might suddenly be lost. But then, after many years of dallying, Queen Elizabeth of England intervened. She helped the infant state directly by sending a military expedition and at the same time gave Francis Drake permission to harass the Spaniards in the Caribbean. By 1588, with the defeat of Philip II's great, ill-judged armada against England, Spain's imperial power was on the wane. Philip died at last in 1598, frustrated in all his efforts to subdue the Dutch.

During a further ten years of warfare the Dutch provinces held their own. By then, both sides had dug to the very bottom of their public purses. Under the Truce of Antwerp in 1609, an exhausted Spain conceded temporary independence to the Dutch. The struggle, already a long one, was in fact to last another forty years.

FOUR

Amsterdam and
Rembrandt Harmensz. van Rijn

Something extraordinary had been happening even while the war with Spain was at its most confusing and destructive, something which amazed contemporaries and has remained a source of wonder. This was the rise of Amsterdam. In 1546 it was a town of 14,000. A century later it had a population of 200,000 and had become a grandiloquently beautiful canal city to compare with Venice, headquarters of an empire, world capital of commerce and focus of a school of art which has given more delight and insight than almost any other. Amsterdam's astonishing development had already begun in 1578 when William of Orange, at a moment of political satisfaction, predicted that it would surpass all other cities. By 1615 the French writer Antoyne de Monchrétien was pointing out that the Dutch ascent had been swifter by far than that of Ancient Rome. Nor was it Amsterdam alone. All the other cities that make up the modern Randstad – Utrecht, The Hague, Delft and Rotterdam, even siege-torn Haarlem and Leiden – were also developing at a furious pace, with fine buildings proliferating as if there were nothing to it. Utrecht and Haarlem, Delft and Leiden seem on a smaller scale to have been as fecund in art as Amsterdam.

It is possible none of this would have taken place without the herring. During the late Middle Ages the massive shoals of the Baltic moved down to the North Sea. A Dutchman, William Beukelsz. of Biervliet, is credited with discovering a method of curing the fish when freshly caught. Herrings could now be

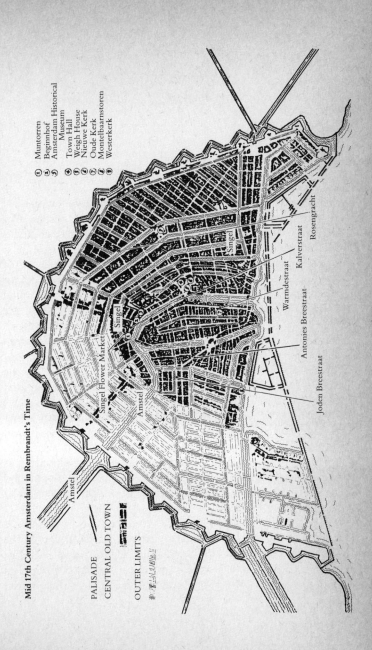

Mid 17th Century Amsterdam in Rembrandt's Time

1. Muntorren
2. Beginhof
3. Amsterdam Historical Museum
4. Town Hall
5. Weigh House
6. Nieuwe Kerk
7. Oude Kerk
8. Montelbaarnstoren
9. Westerkerk

PALISADE

CENTRAL OLD TOWN

OUTER LIMITS

Amstel

Amstel

Singel Flower Market

Singel

Singel

Warmdestraat

Kalverstraat

Rosengracht

Antonies Breestraat

Joden Breestraat

transported inland and sold at a later date. They quickly became a staple protein food in northern Europe and as they did so the little towns round modern Rotterdam and the small fishing harbours on the Zuider Zee – Hoorn and Enkhuizen, Monnick-endam and Amsterdam – began to engage in the profitable new trade. You can still see in Hoorn, to take just one example, the solid, stolid prosperity brought by herring and amplified by commerce. The seamen's trim and tiny cottages along the front, the quirkily formal warehouses behind, the official buildings with their small-scale dignity, are a major attraction for contemporary tourism and it is delightful, though not exactly surprising, to find that this little sea-port sent out its own adventurers and even gave its name to Cape Horn. Such, ultimately, was the power of the herring.

But effective diking and drainage were a precondition if Amsterdam and the province of Holland were to achieve more than isolated pockets of growth. The Spaniards, as it happened, were well-organized administrators and they were responsible for an efficient diking programme in the early part of the sixteenth century. William of Orange carried on where he and his fellow-revolutionaries obliged the Spaniards to leave off. He employed his own dike-master, one Andries Verlingh, whose writings express the gradualism and sense of community which the Dutch have brought to their fight against the sea. 'The foe outside must be withstood with one common resource and one common right,' wrote Verlingh, 'for if you yield only slightly the sea will take all.' He advocated patience and prudent use of time, with something attempted each year to make the work grow steadily. It was essential to direct the streams away from the shore 'without vehemence', he said. 'With subtlety and sweetness you may do much at low cost.'

The system of earthworks and sluices grew. The windmill, too, made great advances. Early windmills had been small and awkward, built round a single post. When the wind changed direction, the whole mill had to be rotated around the central pole. Now a new kind of mill evolved. The sails were attached to a round cap at the top which could be rotated on its own to catch the wind. At once the size and strength of the mills increased enormously. Just to the north of Amsterdam, in the Zaanstreek area around Zaandam, the land burst out in windmills. There were soon hundred upon hundred of them – windmills to grind grain and hull barley and rice, to crush flax and extract dyes from wood, to grind snuff, pepper and mustard. Later Zaandam also went into the noxious business of boiling down whale blubber for train oil. Everything that smelled or caused pollution seemed to be gathered together in one spot. In 1596 Cornelis Cornelisz. of Uitgeest arrived in Zaandam with his new invention, a mill which converted rotary motion to vertical thrust. The sawmill, handling timber for houses and ship–building, had finally arrived. Now, too, the windmill, originally used for grinding, began to be widely used for draining water.

Herring, dikes and windmills. During the thirteenth century a dam of sorts was built across the River Amstel, a couple of hundred metres back from the shoreline of the Zuider Zee. This became the focus of a small riverside settlement. The earliest known use of the name of Amsterdam occurs in a document of 1275 in which one of the Counts of Holland offers its citizens freedom from tolls throughout his territory. The settlement slowly became a transit point for Baltic grain and a place where tolls were paid on beer from Germany. The Oude Kerk or Old Church, still standing in the modern city, is mentioned first in 1334, the Nieuwe Kerk soon after 1400. But even though beer and grain had laid a useful foundation for trade, growth was not particularly rapid.

This changed dramatically in the sixteenth century. The Hanseatic League was weakening and with it Kampen, the medieval trading centre on the far side of the Zuider Zee. In 1527, in a symbolic readjustment, the right to set buoys in the Zuider Zee passed from Kampen to Amsterdam. Before another half century had passed, the changed trading conditions had turned the small town on the Amstel into the grain emporium of the north.

The open space around the dam, Dam Square, remained the centre. The Nieuwe Kerk stands on one side and next to it was a medieval town hall with stubby tower. Next to that stood an arcaded weigh-house with tiny pinnacles at each end of its pitched roof. The old town-hall and weigh-house, though absent now for centuries, feature in great numbers of surviving paintings and become familiar and friendly as one's knowledge of the city deepens.

Trading took place on Dam Square. Goods arrived by sea but the river mouth was blocked off by a large palisade of stakes stretching right across the shallow hoop of bay (the Central Railway Station, on artificial land, now lies along the original line of the palisade). Ships reaching Amsterdam dropped anchor just outside and their cargo was off-loaded into lighters which came ashore near the dam. By the time of Amsterdam's ascendancy, all goods weighing more than 50 lb had to be recorded at the weigh-house and were tested for quality. Contemporary pictures show scenes of great activity, with goods being trundled along in wheelbarrows or pulled across the cobbles on sleighs. Merchants and their wives, attended by servants, mingle with Middle Eastern traders wearing turbans. Quacks tempt the crowds with patent medicines and all kinds of unlikely objects are on sale.

The town hall on Dam Square was the focus of civic power. In February 1535, in the early days of Protestantism, a group of Anabaptists, men and women, enraptured by a doctrine proclaiming absolute simplicity and absolute equality, rushed naked into the streets to call the people to repentance. They also, briefly, took possession of the town hall. The civic guard retook it and the Anabaptists who survived were put to death on a platform just outside. Their chests, the sentence said, must be opened while they were still alive, 'the heart removed and thrust into their faces, whereupon they are to be beheaded and quartered. Their heads are to be mounted on stakes on the town gates, and their parts to be hung outside the gates.'

The city evolved a system in which power lay in the hands of four burgomasters, in practice always drawn from a group of wealthy merchants. They devolved the administration downwards, appointing various other bodies to carry out the practical tasks involved in running the city. The civic guard were initially a set of military organizations intended for defence and to keep order in the city. There was an archers' company, an arquebusiers' company and a company of crossbowmen. In the fullness of time they became more social than military, engaging in elaborate processions and cheerful dining parties. According to one account written by a member, the colonel needed 'only to see beer foaming in the glasses to report for duty' while the lieutenant could drink his 'brimful glasses even while kissing and cuddling'. The companies often commissioned group portraits of themselves and these have become an evocative part of late sixteenth- and seventeenth-century Dutch painting. Best known of all, of course, is Rembrandt's *Night Watch*.

In the early days the merchants' homes and warehouses were mostly on a street parallel to the river and running into a corner of Dam Square. This, the Warmoesstraat, somewhat battered and bruised by modern building, still exists. All along it, though today only at the northern end, the tall warehouses leaned forwards towards one another like chickens ready to peck. Signboards swung from the inclining frontages. The names and occupations of all the householders in the Warmoesstraat are listed in tax returns for the mid-sixteenth century. A fair number were women, in business in their own right, and there were shopkeepers and sailmakers as well as merchants. Hendrik de Brederode, leader of the Beggars at the start of the conflict with Spain, lodged here in 1567. Later the Duke of Alva stayed in the Warmoesstraat during a visit to the city.

One surprising aspect of Amsterdam is that throughout the early years of the Dutch Revolt the city remained resolutely on the side of the Spaniards. It had had its moments of Protestant upheaval early in the sixteenth century. In 1566, during the outburst of iconoclasm, its paintings and religious images were destroyed as thoroughly as those of any other town. Soon afterwards, however, the Calvinists took fright and fled abroad. Catholic merchants now took charge and made a brisk profit from supplying grain and other provisions to the Spanish armies. They paid no attention to the pleas of the rebel Dutch whose cause they were undercutting. In 1578, the city was forced to come to terms with William of Orange. Protestant patricians returned to power, swept out the Catholics right through the city hierarchy and entered the alliance against Spain. This shift was called the Alteration.

Seven years later Antwerp fell to the Spaniards and ceased to be an effective trading rival. This was Amsterdam's greatest opportunity and the merchants rose to it. They were much helped by the many wealthy and enterprising Flemish Protestants – merchants, artisans and artists – who now arrived in Amsterdam as refugees. The rate of growth accelerated and accelerated again.

By the end of the sixteenth century, Amsterdam fleets were adventuring deep into the Arctic in search of trade routes. In epic voyages as far as Australia and Tasmania, they opened up eastern spice routes for themselves and began to displace the Spanish and Portuguese. The Barents Sea, Tasmania and of course New Zealand all acquired their names from journeys starting in the Dutch provinces. In 1602, the Dutch formed an East India Company based on Amsterdam. The VOC, as it was called, established trading posts which became colonies. It signed treaties and conducted wars. By 1669, at the peak of the Dutch golden age, the VOC owned 150 trading vessels and 40 warships. It employed 10,000 soldiers and 1,000 shipbuilders worked in its yards at Amsterdam. That year it declared a dividend of 40 per cent.

The activities of the VOC in the seventeenth century created an empire, the Dutch East Indies, based on what has now become Indonesia. It was to endure until just after the Second World War. The Cape of Good Hope was used as a staging post on the journey east and Dutch farmers – the Boers of subsequent history – settled the hinterland with consequences which have proved even longer-lasting.

The Dutch were also active along the American seaboard and in the Caribbean. A West India company was formed but found itself perpetually involved either in outright war or punishing skirmishes. The Dutch for a short while held a settlement on Manhattan Island, calling it New Amsterdam. They were happy, after some reverses in a naval war with England, to swap this for Surinam on the shoulder of South America. New Amsterdam, of course, was transformed into New York and has since acquired some reputation in its own right. The Dutch held territory in Brazil for a while and lost it – there are some marvellously unexpected paintings, landscapes and nature studies, from this episode. They captured the Spanish silver fleet in 1628. Piet Heyn, the Dutch commander, remains a perpetual inspiration to the young. But in comparison with achievements in the east, western successes were few and the West India company eventually collapsed.

As carriers of trade the Dutch were dominant in all parts of the world from the start of the seventeenth century. The Dutch fleet was by far the largest in existence. Dutch ship design was the envy, at different times, of the Englishmen Sir Walter Ralegh and Samuel Pepys. Despite the romance of distant voyages, though, the Baltic trade remained the most important economically. The arrangement, though often a contested one, was that all ships entering the Baltic should pay the Danes a tax based on the size of their decks. This led the Dutch, in thrifty fashion, to design a vessel with vast and swelling holds beneath a tiny surface of taxable top-deck. The 'flute', as it was called, became an extremely successful craft, reemphasizing the position of the Dutch as master ship-designers.

Naturally enough, Amsterdam burst out of its own bounds. At first it had been a small horseshoe along the river, walled and turreted and giving on to the Zuider Zee. Some of the river water had been diverted into canals, three on either side of the main river and running out parallel to it. In 1609, in a piece of city planning that has determined the look of Amsterdam ever since, it was decided to build another three large canals in a sweeping semi-circle round the nucleus. A talented sculptor named Hendrick de Keyser was appointed city architect and in 1613 the plan went into operation.

All three canals were dug at the same time, starting at the sea end. From outside to inside they were called: the Prinsengracht or Princes' Canal; the Keizersgracht or Emperors' Canal; and finally the Herengracht or Gentlemen's Canal – names that convey the spirit of the enterprise. The first wave of digging took place on the west and carried the canals down just to the bottom of the horseshoe. The second and final wave carried them on round the bottom and half way up the eastern side. There were nearly 100 islands and 400 bridges; and soon canal-houses of unmatched grace and practical utility began to spring up along the sides of the canals.

It is partly their shape which makes them so delightful. Narrow-fronted, since frontage width was taxed, and surprisingly deep, with both a front and a back house joined on by an interior courtyard, they climb up generally through five tall floors, contracting at the top into an ornamental gable with a protruding hoist-beam. As you look along the canals the hoist beams make a predatory row, like so many eagles sticking out their necks. They are still used for lifting furniture, stairs being far too narrow. The gables are varied and ingenious in shape, ranging from a simple, stepped effect to sweeping bell-like curves, with the dark mouth of a trap-door punched into the house-front just below the hoist-beam.

The attraction lies partly in the colour – deep reds of matured brick with sandstone decoration or else, from later in the seventeenth century, the sombre grey of stone-built classical façades. The water of the canals is sometimes still and shiny. Sometimes it slaps a murky brown against the sides of the canals. Trees line long stretches of canal, providing dense bird-filled foliage in summer, in winter the black branches allowing a clearer view of the houses behind. Then there is the effect created by the multitudinous windows. They occupy almost the whole of each house-front, giving an effortless airiness and delicacy to the great architectural semi-circle of the three canals. Water and glass together provide a million bright reflections of one another and of the trees and sky.

The Dutch very seldom draw their curtains and in the evening, at the moment when the lights go on, the canal-houses seem weightless and fragile, almost on the verge of becoming airborne. Then the windows offer tantalizing glimpses of interiors – here a grand salon with gilded ceiling, there a warehouse split into many floors, revealing pot plants the size of half-grown trees and bookshelves that seem to contain unlimited possibilities.

Frequently, at the time when they were built, the lower floors of the canal houses were used as shops or for the display of goods. The family lived in the middle floors and merchandise was warehoused in the attic. Some now have later-looking frontages. Others are a hodge-podge of different periods. Where old buildings have actually gone, the replacements are generally discreet and in an appropriate scale, at least on the main canals. (Between the canals there are some genuine horrors. Banks are the principal offenders.) But mostly the canal vistas are immaculate seventeenth century.

Where a bridge crosses one of the three great canals, and particularly on the tram routes, there is generally a scatter of shops, a little patch of liveliness with bars and cafés and perhaps a flower stall or herring *broodje* man. Then the canal may enter a domestic phase, quiet and rather grand, or, in places, slightly run-down, in spots in multi-occupation. A single canal, within the space of half an hour's walking, will carry you from busy metropolitan grandeur through cathedral close quietness and tree-lined provincialism to the sleazy tat of the city's underside. Water, brick, stone; branch and leaf; windows and gables; epicentre of canal-side Holland, treasure and pleasure-quarry of the north.

The citizen of seventeenth-century Amsterdam most highly regarded by posterity is undoubtedly Rembrandt Harmensz. van

Rijn. His place in Dutch art will be considered later. But for the visitor to Amsterdam, his occasional views of some corner or other of the city, his many etchings and drawings of its street life, the landscape round it and the portraits he made of its citizens form the best and richest of introductions. His own life story, too, as one becomes familiar with it, enriches perception of the old part of the city, much of it known to him, of course, as a place of pristine novelty.

Rembrandt was born in Leiden, in a mill on the Old Rhine. His family name was taken from the river. He studied briefly at Leiden university as little more than a child, then underwent two periods of apprenticeship to painters, one of them a six-month stint in Amsterdam. His first studio was in Leiden and already, at this early stage, he attracted the attention of Constantijn Huygens, polymathic intellectual and secretary to the Prince of Orange of the day: Frederick Henry, younger son of William the Silent. Huygens predicted that Rembrandt and his Leiden companion Jan Lievens would eventually outdo all artists who had gone before. While Rembrandt was still in Leiden, two of his paintings came into the collection of King Charles I of England, most probably through the agency of Huygens.

Rembrandt moved to Amsterdam in 1631 when in his mid-twenties. The first wave of building along the new canals was still intense though nearing its completion. On the west of the inner town Rembrandt must already have been walking some of the canal-side streets the visitor walks today. We know that by the next year he had taken lodgings in the east, just outside the city limits, in a fast-developing thoroughfare called the Bree-straat or Broad Street. He lived here with an art dealer named Hendrick van Ulenborch.

Just at this time, the city architect Hendrick de Keyser completed the stylish Westerkerk which still presides over the new canals in the west. Its tower, several towers of diminishing size stacked on top of one another, culminates in an outsize replica of the crown of Maximilian I of Austria. Amsterdam had lent him money and he had allowed the city to use his coat of arms and crown. His arms are the three diagonal crosses of St Andrew which are to be found on every bollard alongside every canal in Amsterdam. Soon after the Westerkerk was finished the philosopher Descartes lodged right beside it in a charming but now fragile-looking little house. 'In what other country', he wrote, 'can one enjoy such complete liberty?' But he complained that everybody was so engrossed in their own interests 'that I could spend the whole of my life there without being noticed by anybody.'

De Keyser, designing churches and houses at a great rate, was evidently busy. So was Rembrandt. His first Amsterdam commission was an individual portrait. By the following year he had completed one of the group portraits at which he was to excel. *The Anatomy Lesson of Dr Nicolaas Tulp*, a professor whose name meant tulip and who lived in a grand house on the Keizersgracht, now hangs in The Hague. It shows the master-surgeon, surrounded by eager-eyed disciples, in the act of dissecting the left arm of a corpse. The apparent rendering of a real moment involved a good deal of artistic licence since dissection, at that time, started at the stomach, not the arm. But it helped launch Rembrandt as a fashionable portrait painter. Over the next ten or fifteen years he painted or etched churchmen of all persuasions and their wives, leading figures from the city's substantial Jewish community, doctors and lawyers and other professional people. Amalia van Solms, wife of Prince Frederick Henry, also sat for him, though the portrait is not one of his most successful.

Rembrandt's subjects look out at us in their varying kinds and conditions, initially perhaps a little round in the face, though often elaborately dressed and with such detail in the surface of the textiles that the masters of the Flemish fifteenth century come to mind. Soon, though, it begins to seem as if the inner person is on view. The sitters reveal a seriousness which must surely have been a part of the life of Amsterdam. There is human dignity without much pompousness, a strong suggestion of intellect and self-assurance.

Rembrandt at this time was also painting more of the biblical scenes with which he had made his name in Leiden, including a series for Prince Frederick Henry. Constantijn Huygens acted as intermediary. Rembrandt had how gone far beyond his early master, Pieter Lastman, creating works which were intense, theatrical, increasingly Baroque. He was simultaneously building up an intimate portfolio of street scenes, etchings and drawings, showing, for example, mothers with their children, dogs, circus animals, men at work, poor Jews from the humbler portion of the community and many beggars and paupers, representatives of the thousands made homeless and helpless by the wars of northern Europe and the dislocations of early capitalism. These drawings seem to show an ungrudging, non-judgemental humanity. The Frenchman André de Piles, writing much later in the century, records that when Rembrandt was accused of keeping low company he replied: 'When I have a mind to unbend and recreate my mind, I do not care for honour so much as I do for liberty.'

In 1633, the year after Dr Tulp, Rembrandt became engaged to van Ulenborch's niece Saskia. Three days later he drew a betrothal picture of her in a straw hat with flowers. Her parents were prominent Frisians – her father had been in Delft on an embassy from Friesland to William of Orange when William was assassinated. Rembrandt and Saskia were married in Friesland, in the small town of Het Bildt where she had connections. From then on, she was a constant presence in his work – seen as Flora, seen on Rembrandt's knee and sometimes, sadly, ill, even to the point of death. It may be an illusion but those who know the work begin to feel they know the relationship and have some part in its liveliness and intimacy. Saskia becomes a friend in Amsterdam.

Rembrandt and Saskia lived at various addresses. She bore three children but all died within weeks. On 1 May 1639, the couple moved into a large house bought on credit just next to van Ulenborch's on the Breestraat. This had two storeys and a stepped gable. It was built in the year of Rembrandt's birth and later in his lifetime, after he had left it, acquired a third storey and a heavy classical cornice. The house is not specially attractive, but it functions as a Rembrandt museum showing prints of almost all his 250 or so etchings – and showing, too, how they were made. The delicacy of the etchings, seen *en masse*, is all the more astonishing when one considers how roughly Rembrandt could sometimes paint.

Here Saskia gave birth to a child who lived – Titus, shown in his youthful freshness in many Rembrandt drawings. In 1642, a year after Titus's birth, Saskia died here. Here, too, Rembrandt amassed his extraordinary collection: strange and exotic clothing seen often in his paintings, busts of Homer and Aristotle, weapons, all kinds of curios and hundreds and hundreds of works of art – drawings by the great masters of Italy, Germany and Holland and paintings which included contemporary Dutch masters, a work by Raphael and another which Rembrandt attributed to Giorgione. In this house, after Saskia's death, he became the occasional lover of Geertje Dircx whom he had engaged as a nurse to Titus. But Rembrandt and Geertje Dircx fell out. She sued him for breach of promise and pawned jewellery which Saskia had left for Titus. Rembrandt now pursued her angrily to a reformatory where she spent several years. She was finally released against his wishes. Meanwhile he had taken as his mistress another younger woman named Hendrickje Stoffels. Contemporary accounts suggest she was a loving replacement for Saskia, caring for Titus as well as for his father. Together, she and Rembrandt had a daughter named Cornelia. It is hard to recognize Hendrickje confidently in direct portrayals but her presence as a model may be felt in some of the glowing female nudes which Rembrandt now produced.

He ran a school for apprentices in the Breestraat house. Surviving drawings show them gathered round him. His methods caused distress to his late seventeenth-century biographer, Joachim von Sandrart, who complained that Rembrandt had no hesitation 'in opposing our rules of art, such as anatomy and the proportions of the human body, perspective and the usefulness of classical statues'. He made any changes that he felt like in his students' work, no matter how unorthodox, 'so long as in his opinion they were successful and apposite'.

The Breestraat, later renamed the Jodenbreestraat or Broad Street of the Jews, was at the centre of the district where the Jewish community was settling. Menasseh ben Israel lived in the immediate vicinity. He was the teacher of Spinoza, author of a grand religious work which Rembrandt illustrated and subject of a sensitive Rembrandt portrait. Many have argued that Rembrandt's portrayals of the Jews reveal a special affinity or at least a special interest in them. At all events a group of synagogues was springing up nearby. The interior of one of them, the handsome Portuguese synagogue, today reopened as a museum, is shown as it was in the seventeenth century in a well-known painting by Emmanuel de Witte. Its massive pillars and wooden balcony, profusion of giant candelabras and the long red curtains hanging beside the tall windows create a splendidly dramatic effect. The area around the Jodenbreestraat remained mostly Jewish until the Second World War. Then it became a ghetto into which many thousands of Jews from all parts of Holland were concentrated before their journey to death. Thoughts of their unspeakable calamity become bound up with thoughts of Rembrandt.

In Rembrandt's day the Breestraat was just on the edge of town. He used to walk out into the country, east to the village of Diemen, now a suburb, and south along the River Amstel to the village of Oudekerk. During the first fifteen of his almost twenty years here he produced great numbers of landscape drawings and etchings. The Amsterdam skyline becomes familiar in his distant views of it and under his hand the River Amstel and the houses and the incidents along it take on a transforming sense of tranquillity and depth. It is as if he could extract the essence of a scene and offer it to us both in its own time and timelessly.

When Rembrandt came out of his front door and turned left for town, he would have had to enter the city through the massive, brick-built gateway of the St Antoniespoort with its turrets and gable windows and steeply sloping roofs. Amsterdam was still a defensible walled city. Even when the canals were finished, the plan was not complete until a set of massive bastions were thrown around the whole. The St Antoniespoort on the old eastern border still exists. At one time it housed the offices of the Guild of Surgeons. *The Anatomy Lesson of Dr Nicolaas Tulp* hung here along with *The Anatomy Lesson of Dr Johan Deyman*, a later work on a similar subject. At one point the St Antoniespoort was made into a weigh-house – the gate was blocked off at this stage – and later it was used as a museum.

Carrying on past the St Antoniespoort, Rembrandt might have turned left, down towards the Munttoren or Mint Tower. This marks the start of the modern flower market along the far bank of the Singel. On his way he would have passed the Kloveniersdoelen, the hall of the Kloveniers' militia company, now long gone. This might have encouraged him to reflection since it contained a work often regarded as his most important and always as his most spectacular. Painted for the company in the year of Saskia's death, it was a vast, theatrical canvas showing the militia assembling under their leader, Captain Frans Banning Cocq. It is packed with activity and surprises, the portraiture bold but subordinated to the event and the whole, though a daylight scene, illuminated by thrilling shafts of light. This is the picture now known, misleadingly, as *The Night Watch*, and, on the available evidence, admired by contemporaries despite a subsequent legend to the contrary.

If at the St Antoniespoort Rembrandt had angled right instead of left he would have come in a moment or two to the Oudekerk. Saskia was buried here. Today the short walk takes one through the centre of the red light district. Here young women and some not so young sit largely naked in little plush parlours with the legend 'Kamer te huur' – 'Room to let' – as often as not inscribed on the window. Some stand rather than sit, pressing up against the glass, in their disrobed state suggesting not so much sexual activity as athletes ready for the off. It is astonishing to see them for the first time, particularly if you walk inadvertently across the invisible border of the district to find yourself, quite by surprise, at eighteen inches distance from a nearly naked willing woman. Then there are sex shops, displaying, I hope in jest, goods of quite outrageous size and for a wide variety of purposes. There are windows advertising live sex shows and others welcoming the passer-by to the pleasures of group sex. Much of it seems quite friendly, but some of the pictures on magazine and video covers are true grotesques. In the narrow alley-ways there is an atmosphere of drugs and a whiff of potential violence.

The Sex Cinema Amor, located in a fragile and elegant canal-house of the smaller kind, looks equably across the canal at the bulk of the Oudekerk. Around the great church itself there is a cobbled precinct, the street-level windows mostly occupied by prostitutes in tiny parlours. In one corner of the church building there is an office where a neat and tidy lady in a black dress with electric typewriter, pot plants and files on shelves, looks straight across, if she should care to look, at one of the 'rooms to let'. The curtain is often closed, meaning the occupant is, as it were, occupied.

Saskia lies inside the church, under a slate slab inscribed with modern lettering.

A step beyond and you are in the Warmoesstraat, a step across it and you are in Dam Square. Here, in the 1660s, and with Rembrandt still in the Breestraat, the architect Jacob van Campen was commissioned to erect a town hall in the new classical manner. It was planned as a temple to the power and wealth of the great new city. Its high grey sides and the allegorical statuary of the pediment look down blankly on Dam Square. Only the weather-vane appeals. It is a golden replica of a 'koggeschip', one of the little high-pooped vessels used for the Baltic trade before the 'flute' appeared.

This new town hall, once occupied by Louis Napoleon and now a royal palace of the House of Orange, still dominates Dam Square. Like most of Amsterdam, it is built on wooden piles driven through the mud beneath into a firm sandbank. There are

13,659 under the new town hall. While it was under construction, the old town hall burnt down and Rembrandt, who seems to have had a penchant for dilapidated buildings, characteristically drew the old town hall in ruins, not the new one rising beside it. The Montelbaarnstoren is one of the old city towers and practically within view of the house on the Breestraat. A little spire had been built on top of it at about the time of Rembrandt's birth. But Rembrandt chose to draw it as it had originally been. One wonders whether he felt admiration for the new part of the city along the great canals or for the new artisan district beyond them on the west. This was called the Jordaan, perhaps in joking reference to the tribes who dwelt beyond that river, or, more probably, as a corruption of Le Jardin, the name given to it by Huguenot settlers. Many of its street names are the names of flowers.

It was just on the edge of the Jordaan, however, that Rembrandt, devastated by money troubles, soon had to make his home. There is a strong suggestion that he was recklessly extravagant, buying items for his collection regardless of the cost. His biographer Baldinucci, writing in 1686, accuses him of having tried to push his own etchings to 'intolerable' prices by buying them back all over Europe, whenever they came on sale, at a wildly inflated price. The name of one of his most elaborate etchings – *The Hundred Guilder Print* – supposedly derives from this risky-sounding tactic. Rembrandt may also have been dealing directly in art works by others than himself.

At all events, surviving documents show that by 1656 he was borrowing heavily to make the final, long-delayed payments for the house on the Breestraat. One of his creditors was the wealthy and well-connected Jan Six, subject of Rembrandt portraits and etchings. His own house and collection are on public view today.

Rembrandt was now obliged to sell off some of his possessions at auction in the Kalverstraat. Today this is a pedestrian shopping street of the most tinselly kind, running up through the middle of town from the flower market to Dam

Square. The city's historical museum, a fascinating source on the seventeenth century and on much else besides, is tucked away behind the Kalverstraat in a handsome old orphanage. Tucked away even deeper behind the orphanage is the quiet retreat of the Begijnhof, set up in the late medieval period for unmarried women of rich families who wished to do good works. The deep peace of the Begijnhof, with its quaint and individual houses, each with a garden separated from its neighbour by a white wooden fence, contrasts most forcibly with the fever Rembrandt must have felt as he began to drift towards financial calamity. The Kalverstraat might seem to represent his feelings better.

The borrowing and selling did not yield enough. The house in the Breestraat went to pay his debts. Bankruptcy in those days involved disgrace and prison and Rembrandt managed to avoid this by applying for legal cession of estate. This meant he was no longer allowed to handle his own affairs. Titus and Hendrickje were now technically the ones in trade and Rembrandt was their employee. The three went off to live by the Jordaan in a moderately broad street called the Rozengracht or Roses Canal. Today it is rather a characterless tram route. In Rembrandt's time it had its own canal, now filled in and serving as the tramway. The Rozengracht was out beyond the Westerkerk. But though the houses built for Professor Tulp and Captain Frans Banning Cocq were only five minutes' walk away, Rembrandt, Titus and Hendrickje were definitely on the wrong side of the water.

Rembrandt himself was little more than fifty. All his life he had painted self-portraits. In some he may well have been using himself as a subject of study rather than deliberately making any kind of personal statement. We do not know what the real motives were. But many of the self-portraits are so intense it is hard not to read them as a biographical, even a spiritual progression. Those of this period show the famous coarse-featured face with its bulbous nose and puckered chin wearing an expression of stolid suffering. There is good evidence that he was by now less willing to please, more committed to his own vision. But he still had patrons wanting portraits and still painted a large variety of other subjects in his customarily wide range of styles. There was the controversial *Conspiracy of Claudius Civilis*, done for the new town hall and soon rejected, though today regarded as one of the finest of his historical works. There was the vivid group portrait of the Syndics of the Clothmakers' Guild. During the late 1660s he painted the poignant, warmly glowing, red and gold evocation of two lovers known as *The Jewish Bride*: all of these beyond question masterpieces.

Rembrandt now grew old with surprising speed. Soon Hendrickje was dead, not yet forty, possibly of plague. Five years later Titus married. Within months he too was dead. Rembrandt briefly lived alone with his daughter Cornelia but himself died a year after Titus, on 4 October 1669, aged sixty-three. He, Hendrickje and Titus now lay in de Keyser's Westerkerk, poised between the Jordaan and the great canals and under the pompous crown of Maximilian.

FIVE

Dutch Masters

Rembrandt was not alone. Most people who have never been to Holland can probably tick off on their fingers ten or a dozen others whose names and works live on. Frans Hals's sitters look out from some 250 surviving portraits, alert, indulgent, laughing, caught, so it would seem, in moments of real life. Vermeer's female subjects, so often solitary or attended by a single man, preserve their air of still detachment among surrounding objects hushed with significance.

Frans Hals and Vermeer are household names. Behind them come Pieter de Hooch, another painter of quiet interiors, and Jan Steen, Ter Borch and Gabriel Metsu, creators of those scenes from daily life known as genre paintings. The landscape painters include Jan van Goyen and the wonderful Salomon van Ruysdael, his nephew Jacob van Ruisdael, the general favourite of the critics, and Meyndert Hobbema, known above all for one particular painting, a double row of trees receding into the distance near the little town of Middelharnis. There are flower painters like Bosschaert the Elder and still-life specialists like Pieter Claesz. whose cheeses, herrings and pewter mugs seem to express something far beyond themselves. Pieter Saenredam painted soaring church interiors and townscapes. Willem van de Velde the Younger is held by many to have been the finest marine artist ever to put brush to canvas.

Behind these again come scores in every branch of painting. For this was the great age of the specialist. And just as the look of the old town hall of Amsterdam, demolished centuries ago,

becomes with familiarity part of our version of modern Amsterdam, so the work of these painters, whose names at first seem strange and difficult, becomes part of our real experience of Holland. Dutch art, concerned as it mostly is with depiction of the real or seemingly real, comforts by its solidity and the sense of directness it creates. It yields up not just a beautiful and detailed version of some aspects of Holland in the age of the great painters but a mode of perception so singular and delightful that it gets right in the eye and can become a possible way of seeing. This at least is my own experience: the painters of the seventeenth century, more than historical explanation or sociological inquiry, make modern Holland seem directly apprehensible, an extension and development of what they themselves have rendered in terms so clear it is possible to feel, however illusorily, a sense of proper understanding.

The question, though, is where to make a start. A prudent answer, in order to escape the mass and weight, might be with one of the smaller collections, the quite outstanding Mauritshuis in The Hague, for instance, or the fine Frans Hals museum in Haarlem. More of these later. In practice most people will begin in the biggest and grandest of the collections, that of the Rijksmuseum in Amsterdam. Its seventeenth-century works stand as a monument to the experience of the whole of the Dutch nation during that period.

The Rijksmuseum was completed in 1885 to the plans of the same pinnacle-loving architect who devised the Central Station. Rembrandt's *Night Watch* is the centrepiece. It is extremely well-attended by visitors from every nation and best seen the moment the museum opens on a weekday morning, preferably in February. It presides over a wide gallery where Rembrandt himself features in a self-portrait as an old and tired St Paul. St Paul hangs beside the so-called *The Jewish Bride*, perhaps the most tender, even poetic, of all the paintings of Rembrandt's old age. St Paul and the Jewish bride look straight across the gallery at the marvellously alert group portrait of the Syndics of the Clothmakers' Guild. Though Rembrandt was old when he painted the Syndics, he was still restlessly experimenting. We know from X-rays that one of the figures in this composition, the servant who stands modestly behind the clothmakers, was shifted several times before the painter settled on the final composition.

Just near the Syndics hangs the *Anatomy Lesson of Dr Johan Deyman*. In this, the doctor's assistant holds the top of the skull inverted in his hand like a small basin while the doctor unravels the cadaver's brain. It hangs down on either side of the face like an old pullover. The viewer stares at the underside of the dead man's pale feet. It is an odd-shaped work, rather like an altarpiece, all that remains of a larger painting damaged by fire.

Elsewhere among the Rijksmuseum's Rembrandt collection there are portraits and self-portraits, biblical and historical scenes and a little landscape of a small stone bridge under a threatening sky, the trees behind it vivid and vulnerable in a shaft of light. If nothing else, the Rijksmuseum offers a full account of the career and emotional range of the greatest, if most untypical, of the century's great masters.

That is just a beginning. There is a whole wall of paintings by Vermeer, about one eighth of his known output. The wall includes *The Little Street in Delft*. In this, one woman sews in a doorway under a gabled brick façade, while another, visible down a tranquil passageway, has set her broom aside. Everybody knows the scene. Then there is the kitchen maid, blue apron, yellow blouse, pouring out milk from a jug; and perhaps best known of all, the woman in blue smock, map on the wall behind her, reading a letter in the same clear window-light in which the kitchen maid pours out the milk.

There are interiors by Pieter de Hooch. The prolific Jan Steen is prolifically represented. There is, for instance, one of his *Merry Families*, singing and carousing in exuberant confusion. Cheerful, disordered households are still known as 'Jan Steen families'. And there's another of his most familiar works – *Sinterklaas* or *The Feast of St Nicholas*. This falls on 6 December and is the day the Dutch give presents. According to Dutch folklore, St Nicholas comes up from Spain with his assistant Black Peter bringing gifts for children. Good children, like the little girl in Jan Steen's foreground, receive delightful toys and sweets. Bad children get canes – and may well cry, like the poor naughty boy in the background here. Other Steen pictures, such as *The Doctor's Visit* – the Rijksmuseum has one of many versions painted by Steen – can seem distinctly fresh: the malady, well beyond treatment, is clearly sighing love – with the added rider, made clear by symbols well understood at the time, that the young woman is pregnant.

Steen is much enjoyed by the Dutch public and *The Feast of St Nicholas* is probably known to every adult and child in Holland. Nicolas Maes's *Old Woman in Prayer* is another immensely popular work. Here an elderly but firm-faced lady, in lamplight, in a modest interior, prays over her simple supper. Her hands are joined, eyes closed, while on the far side of the table from her (the near side for the viewer) a black and white cat tugs at the table-cloth, appearing quite likely to bring the whole supper crashing to the ground. It is an open, accessible painting, saved from mere chocolate box status by an indwelling clarity.

The list of Rijksmuseum works valuable for their individual quality, for their part in the development of Dutch painting or for their place in popular affections is almost infinitely extensible. The difficulty lies in seeing the paintings sensibly.

It is all very well to say it is essential to go several times and look at pre-selected paintings. But until one becomes familiar with the collection that is virtually impossible. One may decide to visit, say, the genre works of Gabriel Metsu – nearly a room of these, including his instantly effective *Mother with Sick Child*. But how does one get past the late medieval works of Geertgen tot Sint Jans? And then, once past good Geertgen, one may fall a willing victim to Frans Hals's rollicking double-portrait of Isaac Abrahamsz. Massu and his wife Beatrix van der Laen, he at his broad ease under a tree, she more upright, outwardly submissive, but with a pucker in her cheeks and a distinct glint in her eye. Or landscapes may seduce with ferries crossing still rivers and cattle resting under trees. Or it may be the drooping sails of ships in a dead calm; or moonlit scenes; or snow- and ice-scapes peopled by tiny figures, skating, falling over, chatting, playing golf. It is hard at first to make much sense of it. Then little by little, almost without one's noticing it, some order begins to appear among the richness of impressions and one is free to make more purposeful and limited visits.

At this stage the visitor begins, perhaps, to consider the phenomenon a little more deeply. The history of painting itself provides an initial vantage point. It is impossible, for instance, to imagine the eventual emergence of the Dutch seventeenth-century school without the pathbreaking work 200 years before of Jan van Eyck and Rogier van der Weyden, masters of the realistic surface. The part played by the extraordinarily individual Hieronymus Bosch seems not to have been a central one, though the genre elements of his painting and his background landscapes made their contribution to the tradition. Bruegel, as we have seen, took the tradition and amplified it, helping to establish a precedent for a whole range of approaches and a great variety of subject matter.

Eventually, during the wars of the Dutch against the Spaniards and following the destruction of Catholic authority in the north, Dutch and Flemish painting began to develop separately. In Flanders, by the end of the sixteenth century, Peter Paul Rubens was bursting into high baroque, a form of art that seemed entirely appropriate to the palaces and churches it was made for. In the north the tide of energy was beginning to flow in a different direction.

A considerable number of Dutch towns made distinct contributions and one may begin to gain a purchase on the painting as a whole by looking at it town by town. Utrecht is the best starting point, since early on, at least, it stood mid-way between the new Flemish experience and developments in the infant Dutch Republic. This is largely because the city, one-time centre of Catholic power, retained even in its new Protestant guise as close an understanding of Rome as Catholic Flanders.

Utrecht painters almost invariably made the trip to Italy, often staying for years. They led the way in forming a Dutch society of painters there, knew one another by engaging nicknames and experienced the impact of two great painters in particular. One was the lyrical German landscapist, Adam Elsheimer. The other great influence was Caravaggio who impressed by his willingness to depart from Italianate concepts of the ideal, painting dramatic versions of everyday human faces. It was Caravaggio beyond any other, of course, who developed the use of contrasted light and darkness known as chiaroscuro.

From Utrecht and Utrecht-influenced Dutch painters there poured a torrent of elaborately dramatic paintings, full of the new lighting effects. Two of the finest Utrecht artists are Hendrick Terbrugghen and Gerrit van Honthorst. Both are represented in the Rijksmuseum. The lesser known Adriaen Bloemart taught almost all the other Utrecht painters during an exceedingly long career and may have been more central to general developments. There were also landscape painters who specialized in Italianate mountain scenery, replete with waterfalls and gushing brooks, sights not to be seen in the Low Countries except with the eye of faith.

The Utrecht-centred tradition in a sense gave birth to Rembrandt. All forms of painting, wherever they appeared, were mirrored and developed in Amsterdam. Rembrandt's most significant teacher, Pieter Lastman in Amsterdam, had been in Italy for some years with the Utrecht painters and absorbed the same influences that were working on them. It is no accident that Rembrandt used chiaroscuro from very early on in his biblical and narrative painting, refining it into his own deeply moving treatment where central shafts of light pierce the shadows invading the whole of the huge spaces round the actors. There is no doubt that Rubens, too, also reflecting Italian influences, made a considerable impact on Rembrandt at about the mid-point of his career.

Leaving aside Rembrandt, who was always individual, it has to be admitted, whether we like it or not, that there is much in seventeenth-century Dutch painting which is reminiscent of

83

Italian. Indeed, throughout the eighteenth and well into the nineteenth century, this 'grand style' was far more admired than the plainer and more realistic-seeming work we think of today as peculiarly Dutch. Utrecht more than any other city was the channel through which Italian influence flowed.

Haarlem, that great home of painting, comes closer to what we today consider Dutch. It was here, above all, that Dutch landscape painting developed. The tradition of the fantastical mountain scene, brown in the foreground, green in the middleground and celestial blue in the far distance, had been worked up in Flanders and virtually sanctified by Adam Elsheimer in Rome (alas, the attribution of the beautiful 'Elsheimer' *Tobias and the Angel* in the National Gallery in London has recently been challenged). As the troubles with Spain reached their height in the late sixteenth century, many Flemish landscape painters moved north to Haarlem. Roelandt Savery was one of the most impressive. Hendrick Goltzius, another famous name, arrived from the Dutch Rhineland. Both were capable of realism as well as fantasy. Before long native Dutch painters from closer by were moving into Harlaam and working from the city.

This Haarlem generation included Jan van Goyen and the, to me, magnificent Salomon van Ruysdael. Both worked in what is sometimes called a 'tonal' style, subduing the whole of a scene to the same atmospheric mood, expressed through harmonies of colour. By now the landscapes they and their generation painted were mostly broad and low with enormous skies above them. Recently art historians have pointed out that the range of skies is limited, even a little formalized, but the paintings seem no worse for that. It is exhilarating to see those skies, cumulus rolling upon cumulus, blues, blacks and greys, all held in the same rhythm that gives unity to the paintings. From this period, too, come powerful evocations of peace, often including rivers, bridges and ferries. There were cattle, sailing craft and trees, and, seemingly almost always, a church spire with its attendant town somewhere in the distance.

The Haarlem landscapists began early and carried on in full spate right up to the third quarter of the seventeenth century. Jacob van Ruisdael is considered by many to have been the greatest. His work is as moody as Rembrandt's and became increasingly melancholic as he grew older. In his luxuriantly complicated trees one may still see the same enthusiasm for proliferating vegetation that Pieter Bruegel brought back from Italy over 100 years before.

The other astonishing aspect of Haarlem painting was its portraiture. Perhaps it was an accident that the talent of Frans Hals emerged here rather than elsewhere. But Hals lived for close on ninety years, always in Haarlem, and in his own person provided a major strand in the development of an art form which achieved exceptional prominence in Holland. One reason for the emphasis on portraits may have been the Dutch interest in the particular as opposed to the general, the detailed statement rather than the overview, the observed rather than the ideal. One consequence is the sense of personal acquaintance the viewer is able to feel with seventeenth-century Dutch individuals.

Hals's early works were mainly genre scenes, with a special enthusiasm for merriment and revelry – an early account says he was drunk most nights as a young man. But he soon became a specialist in the group portraits ordered by bodies like the civic guard and the militia companies, finding lively ways of arranging the group so that all those in the picture got their fair share of the glory within an entertaining composition. He was, of course, the great master of the human smile and bright light falling on lace cuffs and ruffs. He painted many individual portraits, attempting, it seems, to catch a characteristic moment or expression rather than render inner feeling. The results, from *The Laughing Cavalier* in the Wallace Collection in London to *The Merry Drinker* in the Rijksmuseum, are spirited and splendid. His work darkened in his later years, perhaps reflecting a change in the times. But there is firm evidence of financial troubles even worse than Rembrandt's. He was sued at one time or another by a wide variety of creditors. His baker seized his possessions in lieu of cash and he appears to have died destitute or very nearly so.

Some of his surviving work may be seen in the Rijksmuseum but the best collection is in the Frans Hals museum in Haarlem. To reach this excellent gallery you will probably start out from the town's main square, itself familiar in many paintings. In one corner stands the great church of St Bavo. Haydn and Mozart both played on the organ here and Pieter Saenredam painted the sweeping aisles in some of his best work. Beside St Bavo stands the medieval Butcher's Hall, fantastical with pinnacles and gables, regarded as a key building in the development of style. From the other end of the square, an august town hall looks out across the stalls on market day.

A wiggly walk leads from the heart of town to the Frans Hals museum. This was formerly an old men's home and Hals, in old age, painted magnificent group portraits of the Regents and Regentesses of Haarlem's charitable institutions. These sombre works hang in the museum together with the earlier group portraits, flashy and dashing. To see them in a single session is, one feels, to watch the painter move from optimism to a steadier endurance.

The experience of Leiden was different again and here Rembrandt had a direct part to play. While he was still a young man working in his own studio there, he had had as one of his first pupils a fifteen-year-old boy named Gerrit Dou. Dou stayed on and contributed, still under Rembrandt's stylistic influence, to a local tradition of small-scale, highly finished paintings with an enamel-like gloss. Some have seen this as a continuation of the microscopic work initiated by van Eyck, though in Dou's case the obsession may have gone too far for his own good. Once, when complimented on his rendering of a broom the size of a fingernail, he is said to have replied that it would be three more days before he had finished it. Other local painters who worked on a small scale and to a high finish include Frans van Mieris the Elder and Gabriel Metsu.

Over in Delft, twenty kilometres away, Rembrandt also had some influence. His wonderfully talented pupil Carel Fabritius was one of the few not to be overshadowed by the master and was able to develop a genuine style of his own. He painted some portraits in a technique like Rembrandt's but then began to treat his subjects in darker hues against a lighter background. This was the very reverse of Rembrandt's tactic of throwing the central action of his painting under a spotlight while all around a gloomy background gathered. Dark subject on light background is, of course, the way Vermeer was soon to work and it is possible to see Fabritius, who moved from Amsterdam to Delft, as intermediary between the two greatest masters of the Dutch seventeenth century. He may even have been Vermeer's teacher.

Fabritius himself is probably best known for his immensely evocative small picture of a goldfinch in a cage. This hangs in the Mauritshuis in The Hague. With the Rijksmuseum and the Frans Hals museum, the Mauritshuis has to be one of the great centres of pilgrimage. The collection is not enormously large but it sometimes seems to be composed entirely of famous paintings. Some of the most challenging and some of the most beautiful of all Dutch seventeenth-century art is here. The range extends from *The Anatomy Lesson of Dr Nicolaas Tulp* to Fabritius's *Goldfinch* and a charming flower painting by Bosschaert. Still lifes by Willem Kalf and Pieter Claesz contrast with a Ter Borch scene showing a mother apparently scouring a young girl's head for nits. Jan Steen has an exceedingly merry *Merry Company* and, in a tiny picture, a young woman, roguish as can be, sets herself to a dish of oysters, aphrodisiac and signal of intent. In the background a text quotes the appropriate saying: 'Easy come, easy go.' Loveliest of all in the Mauritshuis collection and perhaps the best-known single picture of the whole Dutch seventeenth century, is Vermeer's *View of Delft*, seen across water under a gathering sky.

Fabritius was killed on 12 October 1654, aged thirty-two, by the explosion of the Delft powder magazine, an unprecedented blast which became a byword for horror much like the St Elizabeth's Day flood. Very few of his paintings survive. Vermeer, then about eighteen, lived on to produce his own small output, scarcely forty known paintings, yet all of them familiar wherever European art is studied and enjoyed.

Little is known of Vermeer's life except that he was a member and then master of the Delft guild of painters, that he married and had eleven children, and, like Frans Hals, ran up a large debt to his baker. Two years after his death his wife went bankrupt. He was probably a Catholic. The fragments of biography seem small and bitty.

Because of the presence of Fabritius, Vermeer and a line of genre painters, it is tempting to value Delft more highly than the other towns. Yet Haarlem was extraordinary and an earlier generation than ours would have said the same of Utrecht. And even a town by town account of the main provincial centres leaves out some of the most characteristic of other painters not in Amsterdam. Jan Steen, pub-owner and self-professed reveller, also a Catholic, flitted between Delft and Haarlem without belonging to either. Gerard Ter Borch, after a youth of painting brothel scenes, moved to Deventer, once home of the pious Brethren of the Common Life. He became a member of the burgher or regent class and painted respectable portraits of his new associates. The deaf-mute Hendrick Avercamp, whose scenes on ice are instantly recognizable, came from the town of Kampen and retreated there again from Amsterdam. Aelbert Cuyp, whose scenes of cows and rivers are bathed in uninterrupted golden light – a trick brought up from Italy by the Utrecht painter Jan Both – was a citizen of Dordrecht.

As for Amsterdam itself, the roll-call is enormous. In the Historical Museum behind the Kalverstraat there is a list of the painters who worked there a whole lifetime or spent part of their careers in the city. They range across every style and specialism and include many of the best marine painters, among them Jan van de Cappelle and the Willem van de Veldes, father and son. The father did drawings, often of battle scenes, and from these his greater son worked up the paintings that are attributed to him but which are, in a truer sense, joint works.

The Dutch painters came from all kinds of backgrounds. Fabritius had been a carpenter, whence his adopted name. Jan van de Cappelle was the wealthy owner of a dyeing business. He had a fine town house, a country estate and yacht and his art collection included more than 500 drawings by Rembrandt. Mostly, though, the painters came from the emergent middle class. This, above all, is where the energy appeared to lie.

It is one thing to point to achievement, list the centres of excellence and praise the great painters one by one. It is quite another, far harder, perhaps impossible, to explain why it happened. No answer can be entirely satisfactory. But one can start, at least, by trying to place the paintings within the larger context of their time.

The Twelve Years Truce of 1609 effectively established the Dutch Republic. It also endorsed a mood of growing self-confidence. In retrospect it can be seen that the decade from 1586 – 96 was in many ways the most intense of all, even though the war was at its height. This was the time of the greatest maritime and commercial expansion. It was now that the greatest number of Protestant refugees arrived from the south to settle in Zeeland and the province of Holland, bringing their wealth and the artistic tradition of Flanders. By now the painters of Utrecht were busy and numerous. The landscape painting of Haarlem had begun its breathtaking ascent.

But soon the fiercest and most orthodox of the Calvinist sects began to pose a threat to the development of art.

Prince Maurice was the eldest surviving son of William of Orange. Soon after William's death in 1584 the young prince became captain general and stadholder in five of the six provinces. The name 'stadholder', still full of resonance for the Dutch, originally meant 'place-holder' or 'royal deputy' under the Spanish administration. This was William of Orange's post

89

when he embarked on the course which led to war. The Republic retained the title and in practice the stadholders were drawn from the House of Orange. At times when the Orange princes were forced into eclipse, the post went into abeyance. These are called 'stadholderless periods'.

Maurice was a military man, never so happy as when under canvas. The person effectively in charge of political and economic life was Johan van Oldenbarneveldt – known familiarly to the English who dealt with him as Mr Barnfield. He was Maurice's opposite in most respects – subtle, well-informed, a prodigious worker, flatterer and diplomat. In 1600, however, Oldenbarneveldt quarrelled with Maurice – mainly because, in young prince Maurice's opinion, the older man had failed to give adequate support to a campaign in Flanders.

The quarrel smouldered on and became entangled with religion. During the early part of the seventeenth century two contrasting factions emerged within Dutch Protestantism. It began with a theological dispute between professors at Leiden University, Arminius and Gomarus by name, then widened and widened till the rival political factions of Maurice and Oldenbarneveldt coalesced around the opposing religious views. Oldenbarneveldt and the Arminians, also known as Remonstrants, favoured religious tolerance. Maurice, who probably cared little for the details of the dispute, threw in his hat with the fiercer Gomarists or Contra-Remonstrants. The Contra-Remonstrants believed in predestination and a narrowly orthodox interpretation of Calvinism. By 1616 matters had reached the point where Oldenbarneveldt and the province of Holland declared their intention of recruiting their own militia. In 1618, Maurice replied by seizing Oldenbarneveldt and subjecting the old man to cruel and extended interrogation. Though stripped of his state papers he appears to have resisted all attempts to confuse and incriminate him.

Soon, in Dordrecht, a crucially important Protestant synod was debating the religious disagreement. Maurice's Contra-Remonstrants won, though by the narrowest of margins, and

Maurice promptly took advantage of the occasion to have Oldenbarneveldt's head struck off in front of his palace windows in The Hague.

At this moment the emergent republic could have turned permanently to extremism and intolerance. Painting and culture generally, not to mention daily life, would presumably have developed very differently. In the event, the stricter Calvinists were never quite able to make the Republic a theocracy. Maurice died too soon for that, in 1625. His brother Frederick Henry, the next stadholder, was a more accommodating man, less anxious to take on the burghers of Amsterdam. Their credo was free trade for all and the greatest possible open-mindedness.

There were in fact two tendencies, which long remained central to political events. On the one hand stood the House of Orange and its supporters, often the ordinary people. The other was the faction of the burgomasters and the cities. As the policies of the synod of Dordrecht began to fail, so the burgomasters asserted themselves, setting the tone for the Republic. In Amsterdam the first free press in Europe emerged at this time. There was an immense volume of political and religious pamphleteering, an openness which attracted figures like Descartes and the Czech educator Comenius. Learning flourished; knowledge of the world expanded rapidly. Globes, though expensive, became relatively common. Maps, atlases and studies of distant countries appeared in great profusion. Microscopes and optical lenses brought news of what was closer home. And everywhere the painters painted.

The Orange Court at The Hague was a small-scale affair, though enlivened by the presence of the exiled King and Queen of Bohemia. Elizabeth of Bohemia, known as the Winter Queen because of the brevity of her reign, was a princess of the House of Stuart, and her presence made The Hague attractive to other members of the British royal family, in exile during the Commonwealth. This gave the Orange Court a superficial glitter, attractive to romantic novelists. Taste was generally baroque. Most of the artists patronized by the court were either

Flemish or lesser-known figures from the Italianate school of Utrecht. Rembrandt, briefly, was an exception, painting not only his portrait of Amalia van Solms, wife of Frederick Henry, but also a series of great religious works.

It was the burgher civilization, not the court, which bought the works of the Dutch 'realistic' painters.

One reason for the direction this painting took was the new commercial situation. There was no Catholic church to commission religious art. Instead there emerged a market place for painting very similar to twentieth-century arrangements. Except in the case of portraits, painters generally worked speculatively, then tried to sell their work when it was done. Picture shops were numerous in seventeenth-century Holland – one can be made out in a corner of Dam Square in a painting in the Amsterdam Historical Museum. The burghers bought the pictures for their homes and offices and shops, so far as one can tell because they liked them and because they might one day prove a good investment.

Parallel with their domestic destination, the paintings themselves grew more domestic in tone. Much of what they showed was of natural interest to the townspeople: their own daily lives and activities, familiar household objects, flowers, foods like cheese and herring. The kind of shipping shown by the marine painters was directly familiar to much of the population, in part because the harbours where they moored were often right in town. In landscape painting, the friendly and familiar profile of the distant town, complete with recognizable church spire, is part of the celebration of their own locality for urban dwellers full of love and pride. They seem to have been interested in themselves as well; no previous age had been so thoroughly committed to portraiture.

The thirst for paintings was enormous. The English traveller Peter Mundy, visiting Holland in 1640, gave the country a specially fond place in his writings. In a passage which has become one of the set-pieces of art history, he wrote, with typical gusto:

As For the art off Painting and the affection off the people to Pictures, I thincke none other goe beeyond them, there having bin in this Country Many excellent Men in thatt Facullty, some att presentt, as Rimbrantt, etts, All in generall striving to adorne their houses, especially the outer or street roome, with costly peeces, Butchers and Bakers not much inferiour in their shoppes, which are Fairely sett Forth, yea many tymes blacksmithes, coblers, etts., will have some picture or other by their forge and in their stalle. Such is the generall Notion, enclination and delight that these Countrie Native(s) have to Paintings.

Astonishingly, given the impression of peace and solidity conveyed by the paintings, the Dutch Republic was almost continuously at war. The truce of 1609 excluded Spain's colonial possessions and fighting continued episodically in the Far East, the Caribbean and along the coasts of the Americas. When the truce ended, Spain and the Dutch Republic went to war again in Europe. Spain had relinquished hopes of a total reconquest early in the century. The point was affirmed in the debates of the Spanish Council of State in 1628. Don Fernando Girón, a veteran of the Flanders campaigns, put the issue vigorously: 'The experience of sixty years of war has shown that the Low Countries' wars have been and will continue to be the longest, most expensive, the most bloody and most interminable of any war in History.' Even so, there was virtually annual campaigning for more than quarter of a century from 1621. Then, in 1648, the combatants signed the Treaty of Munster. This gave permanent recognition to the Dutch state along borders practically the same as they are today. It allowed the Dutch to trade in east and west and to retain all territory they had won from Portugal. By providing that the Scheldt would remain closed, it guaranteed that poor, long-suffering Antwerp could never re-emerge to threaten Amsterdam. There was little else the now powerful Republic could have asked for.

The Dutch were not particularly inclined to celebratory paintings of state events. They preferred analogies, or parallel

scenes like Rembrandt's ill-fated *Conspiracy of Claudius Civilis*.
But Gerard Ter Borch, who was present at the signing of the
Treaty of Munster, painted a version of the scene. Though this
was quite small it contained over fifty detailed portraits of the
participants, not excluding the painter himself. Ter Borch tried
to sell the work, it seems, for the enormous price of 6,000
guilders. Being offered less, he kept it.

By now Frederick Henry was dead. His son William II, aged
twenty, became captain general and stadholder of most of the
provinces. He indulged in a few military gestures, attempted to
besiege the recalcitrant stronghold of Amsterdam, then died
unexpectedly of smallpox.

The burghers suddenly had the upper hand and a stadholderless period began. This was perhaps the epoch of the Republic's
greatest artistic achievement. Rembrandt was painting now. So
was Vermeer. Frans Hals, though old, was also still at work.
Genre, portraiture, landscape and marine painting were all at
their apogee. Politically, Johan de Witt became the dominant
figure in the Republic, controlling events through an extraordinary mixture of wisdom and deceit.

Artistically speaking, it was too good to last. The burghers were
becoming aristocrats. Thanks to the windmill, large tracts in the
province of Holland were being drained and readied for
agriculture. The burghers bought country estates in the new
polders and began to seek a new, Frenchified elegance.

At sea, commercial rivalry brought on a succession of wars
with England. One might have thought Johan de Witt's
Republic and Cromwell's Commonwealth would have been
bound by ties of religion and shared political beliefs. On the
contrary, they stood toe to toe in terrible enmity. English poets
and pamphleteers poured out their condemnation of the Dutch
in an orgy of literary disapproval.

The first English war began in the middle of the century, soon
after an English Navigation Act had cut out the Dutch as carriers

of goods to England. It also obliged Dutch ships to strike their flags on meeting English squadrons. Maarten Tromp and Michiel de Ruyter were the leading admirals on the Dutch side and they fought extremely daringly – Tromp with a broom tied to his masthead to signify his intention of sweeping the English from the sea. But in the end it was the Dutch who came off worst. Commercial losses were particularly heavy.

Many in Amsterdam were ruined. Rembrandt, applying three years after the war for legal cession of estate, gave 'losses suffered in business as well as damages and losses by sea' as the reason for his financial difficulties – if true, evidence that he was trading.

The second naval war was fought against a restored British monarchy from 1665. Between the two wars, Johan de Witt had refurbished the Dutch fleet and made it more of a match for the English. The Dutch took Willem van de Velde the Elder to sea with them as a war artist and his version of a celebrated *Four Days' Battle* hangs in the Amsterdam Historical Museum. It is in grisaille, a kind of painting done with pen and ink. Both sides suffered great losses but victory, finally, went to the Dutch. Then, in 1667, the Dutch fleet sailed up the Thames into the Medway. They burned, scuttled or captured sixteen English vessels, including the flagship, the *Royal Charles*. The guns were heard in London. Samuel Pepys wrote in his diary, 'By God, I think the devil shits Dutchmen.'

It was now that the Dutch exchanged the future city of New York for Surinam. But though the peace seemed to be on reasonable terms, never again was naval power between the two countries to be so evenly poised. From this time forward the English were in the ascendant at sea. As the Dutch slipped from the pinnacle of power, so, in painting, the old forthright engagement with reality began to shift and slide.

It is too simple to assume, however, that the era of great painting and domestic architecture was merely a by-product of Dutch success against the Spaniards and the construction of a burgher state, fuelled by discovery and commerce. This does not answer the more inward questions of what Dutch art was really all about. It is at the level of meaning that art historians and critics have had the greatest difficulty.

It is the realism which has caused the problem. For a start, and at an early period, northern art offered a direct challenge to the dominant Italian style. While the Italians were concerned with proportion and harmony, perspective and idealism, the Low Countries' painters mostly offered representations of what they saw with their own eyes. Michelangelo, a contemporary of Bruegel's, was openly contemptuous of this. Another contemporary, Francisco de Hollanda, records the Italian master's belief that Flemish painting would appeal only to those who lacked 'a true sense of harmony'. 'In Flanders', Michelangelo reportedly went on, 'they paint with a view to external exactness or such things as may cheer you and of which you cannot speak ill, as for example saints and prophets. They paint stuffs and masonry, the green grass of the fields, the shadow of trees, and rivers and bridges, which they call landscapes . . .'

Clearly none of this qualifies as art in Michelangelo's view. Indeed, when Bruegel died, his friend the map-maker Ortelius praised the northerner's painting, in a memorable epitaph, as scarcely works of art so much as works of nature.

The English painter Sir Joshua Reynolds visited Holland in 1781 and found he had nothing at all to say about Dutch painting except what the subjects were and whether or not a painting was well done. A typical entry from his notes reads: 'Dead swans by Weenix, as fine as possible. I suppose we did not see less than twenty pictures of dead swans by this painter.'

What then was the point of it? Surely the pleasure of recognition, coupled with admiration for the painter's skill, could not, on its own, account for the deep impression that the paintings have made and continue to make. The novelist Henry James pinpointed the problem after a trip to Holland. 'When you are looking at the originals', he wrote, 'you seem to be looking at the copies and when you are looking at the copies you seem to be looking at the originals.' Was it a canal-side in Haarlem, he asked, or a painting by van der Heyden? The maidservant in the street looked as if she had stepped out of the frame of a Gerrit Dou and could equally well step back in again. 'We have to put on a very particular pair of spectacles and bend our nose well over our task, and, beyond our consciousness that our gains are real gains, remain decidedly at a loss how to classify them.'

One possible answer has seemed to emerge in recent years through genre painting. Many Dutch still lifes contain some reference to the certainty of death – if not a skull beside the scholar's pile of books, then a guttering candle about to burn out. Flowers may stand for brevity of life and often, in a flower painting, there is some minutely observed noxious insect, as ready as Blake's invisible worm to bring its canker to a moment of earthly perfection. This kind of painting is called a Vanitas. Moving on from this point, art historians have begun to draw attention to the importance of popular emblem books. These contained pictures with proverbs or riddles and passages of moralizing text. What, the historians began to ask, if all or most of the genre scenes, like the Vanitas paintings, had inner meanings? Perhaps they were a kind of riddle, a proverb made visible as in the emblem books and, more particularly, a moral guide or warning just like the Vanitas still lifes? Those who began to examine pictures on this basis are sometimes described as iconologists.

Their way of thinking has been associated with some astonishing revisions. One particular painting by Ter Borch shows a young woman in a satin dress standing with her back to the viewer. She is deep in conversation with a seated older woman and a rather galantly dressed gentleman, top hat in one hand, the other raised as an accompaniment to speech. To eighteenth-century eyes this seemed a domestic scene, and the painting was referred to as *The Paternal Admonition*. Goethe, who may have known it as a print, proclaimed it a model of domestic delicacy and moderation. What he did not realize was that in the painting there had originally been a coin in the upraised hand of the 'father', mostly scratched out but with enough fragments remaining for it to be recognized. The contemporary interpretation is that the painting is a brothel scene, the seated figures the procuress and customer.

The missing clue here was the scratched-out coin, its disappearance suggesting later prudery. It is believed now that a number of Dutch paintings similarly acquired false names and interpretations during the eighteenth and nineteenth centuries. Often the missing clue is verbal. Many of Jan Steen's paintings are clearly based on proverbs and sayings. These sometimes appear as legible, painted texts. But one Steen painting in particular illustrates the kind of inquiry scholars have had to make in order to rediscover buried meanings. The picture in question, one of his most elegant and best-known works, is called *The Morning Toilet*. There are no obvious textual clues. But looking through an arched doorway, we see a young woman seated on a bed. She is drawing her stockings on to her bare legs. Beside her there is an open jewel- box and a candle. According to the Dutch museum director Rudi Fuchs, the painting is erotic, a warning against venal love, worked round the popular contemporary saying: 'Neither does one buy pearls in the dark nor does one look for love at night.' He concludes: 'The girl, then, is a prostitute; she is putting on a stocking, conspicuously enough. The Dutch word for stocking, *kous*, had in slang another meaning: vagina.'

When this kind of interpretation convinces, it confirms the belief that there was indeed a verbal base for many of the scenes of genre painting. It confirms the important parallel of the emblem books. And it shows that the paintings often dealt with matters that were close to the bone. One disadvantage of the approach, however, is that it tends to play down the purely pictorial content, subordinating the look of things to the supposed riddling intention. And whether these works should be seen as warnings and moral exhortations, as the so-called iconologists suggest, is another troublesome question.

When Bruegel painted his great omnibus work, *The Netherlandish Proverbs*, he seems to have been recording them as a kind of painted encyclopedia rather than suggesting the viewer should choose to live by one moral code rather than another. Similarly with his painting of children's games. The effect is almost taxonomic, like a botanist or a zoologist listing species and sub-species. It can be argued that when Bruegel painted his alpine panoramas the act was as close to map-making, recording what is seen and known, as it was to idealized Italian landscape painting.

In all of this Bruegel stands as a great antecedent of Dutch realistic painting of the seventeenth century. And the argument can be taken further. For if the act of knowing can be shown to be inseparable from the recording of knowledge, and if Dutch painting can be taken mainly as a method of recording, then a fresh and promising perspective begins to emerge. Genre paintings, in this view, begin to look like acts of observation, statements of how things are, rather than moral homilies. We begin to get a rather different impression of what painters may really have been doing.

In a fascinating polemic, the American art historian Svetlana Alpers has harnessed the work of seventeenth-century explorers, scientists and philosophers to an analysis of Dutch painting that owes little to versions of art history based on Italian models. She begins with the optical lens and microscope, arguing that they allowed vision to operate in greater detail and exactitude than ever before. A reading of the autobiography of Constantijn Huygens leads her to the conclusion that while he was indeed the first to recognize the genius of Rembrandt, he did so when most obviously under the influence of an Italianate admiration for history painting. But in his other life as a scientist, less often given attention by art historians, he no sooner looked down a microscope than he 'called for a picture' to record what he had seen. This, Alpers implies, was the fundamental motivation of Dutch art. Not only was observation inseparable from recording, the two together were fundamental to the great extension of knowledge then taking place.

Though Descartes and Spinoza both produced major works on Dutch soil – so that it would be a rash person who maintained philosophy was lacking in the Dutch Republic – Alpers maintains there is a shortage of written texts to explain the inner nature of science and painting and the relationship between them. For this she looks to England, especially to Sir Francis Bacon and the savants of the Royal Society. The Royal Society was in touch with Dutch investigators. Antonie van Leeuwenhoek, for instance, the first man to use the microscope for systematic study, forwarded his results to the Royal Society and left them a posthumous gift of microscopes in special boxes, each with an object for study placed before it. Much of what English scientists had to say, Svetlana Alpers argues, is relevant to the objectives of Dutch painting.

'All depends on keeping the eye steadily fixed upon the facts of nature', wrote Bacon, 'and so receiving their images simply as they are. For God forbid that we should give out a dream of the imagination for a pattern of the world.' What was necessary, said Robert Hooke in his *Micrographia* of 1664, was observation of the concrete world of things and 'a sincere Hand, and a faithful Eye, to examine, and to record, the things themselves as they appear'. Time and again, writes Alpers, Dutch art suggests that 'meaning resides in the careful representation of the world'.

The great attraction of the argument is first that it seeks to link Dutch art to winning and recording knowledge and, second, the suggestion that Dutch artists accordingly studied the appearances of things with an attitude little short of reverence.

Much of what Alpers says has enraged other art historians, particularly the Dutch. They accuse her of being unwilling to accept the extent of Italian influence and, by this refusal, of diminishing the importance of biblical and historical painting, both intensely admired in the seventeenth century. She has even been accused of misrepresenting historical texts so as to play down the relationship with Italy. And why drag in English philosophy, they ask, when what is at issue is Dutch painting?

Underlying the quarrel is the deeper suggestion that our whole understanding of the seventeenth century will be pushed askew if we come to believe that meaning lies mainly in the extent of observation and realism. To the iconologists, much of the meaning lies finally in the moral messages they think the pictures contain. This coincides with a view of the seventeenth century as an era of sombre moralizing and weighty ethical consideration. They believe that for the painters this approach went hand in hand with their undisputed surface realism and that it is precisely this combination which gives the paintings their extraordinary, seemingly real but often illusionistic character.

The trouble is that the two approaches seem in the end to be mutually irreconcilable. Those who read the books of the contending scholars may well find themselves swayed alternately in different directions and feel, quite properly, that they will never know enough to make a rational evaluation. If that is so, they will be thrown back, as I have been, on their own original responses to the paintings, though made more wary now by knowledge of the difficulties. For me at least it still remains the case that in the stillness of a Vermeer composition or the liveliness of reflection on the surface of a van de Cappelle river there is a communication about the common nature of things so powerful as to be painful. This, if it does not sound too trite, is a good reason why the visitor should go to Holland and – by doing so – put himself in the way of all the other experiences of past and present which that unusual country has to offer.

SIX

William and Mary

In 1672, when the Dutch Republic was at its apogee, a crisis occurred which threatened to put an end to all that had been achieved. For this was the Rampjaar, the Year of Disaster, when Louis XIV of France, denouncing the Dutch as 'petits commerçants', swept down on the Republic with a vast army led by Europe's most skilful generals.

In their moment of despair the Dutch people, ruled now by the burgomasters for more than twenty years, turned with a longing the burgomasters could not resist to a young prince of the House of Orange. He saved his country and, having done so, launched himself on a career of unswerving opposition to French power. He remained stadholder of the Republic but later achieved a half-share in the English throne. His career as an opponent of France pointed towards the notion of a balance of power in Europe, of great importance for the future. So far as England was concerned, the reign of William III ushered in a constitutional monarchy in which the sovereign was obliged to rule jointly with parliament.

The beginning was heroic and the consequences of the whole long-felt, but there was from start to finish something peculiarly disagreeable about this stadholder and king. One person, however, appears to have loved him unequivocally: Mary Stuart, niece of Charles II of England, daughter of James II, William's own wife, and, in the fullness of time, the queen of England and joint sovereign with her husband.

William began the Rampjaar of 1672 with only moderate

prospects and seems already to have shown signs of an awkward temperament. He had had an extraordinary childhood, on both a personal and an official level. And perhaps when one considers his general asperity and some of his future actions, it would be charitable to remember the difficulties and humiliations he experienced during his formative years.

His father was William II, the young stadholder who died of smallpox in 1650. The baby was born eight days after the father's death into an atmosphere of darkness and despondency. The baby's mother, whose nineteenth birthday fell on the same day, was an earlier Mary Stuart, daughter of Charles I and sister of the future Charles II. She had been married at the age of nine and had come unwillingly to Holland in her teenage years. Widowed at eighteen, she disliked Holland and was heartily disliked in turn. Just ten years later, of course, her brother Charles became king of England, departing for his kingdom from Scheveningen in a crowded scene recorded by William van der Velde the Elder – the picture hangs in the history section of the Amsterdam Rijksmuseum. Mary soon followed her brother to the Restoration court, leaving her son behind. Within a year she was dead. The news, when it reached William, provoked a collapse in that unhappy child, now eleven years old, asthmatic and obliged to wear a back brace. Throughout his life his health was a concern to those around him.

The young prince was an embarrassment to the power-brokers of the Republic. For most of the period the burgo-masters – or regents, as they are often called – were led by Johan de Witt, supported in turn by his elder brother Cornelis. The burgomasters reckoned, very reasonably, that a succession of stadholders had embroiled the Republic in unnecessary wars, resulting in high taxation and damage to trade. Accordingly they had decided to rule without one. For a time an Act of Exclusion barred the House of Orange from political office, supposedly in perpetuity. But it proved impossible to maintain the ban. At one point, the prince was formally adopted as 'a child of state'. The move was intended to keep him under the thumb of the burgomasters but it actually operated in his favour by conferring official status on him.

Throughout his teenage years, William was kept under close observation by Johan de Witt, obliged to conceal any ambitions he might have. He had perhaps been helped in this by an education designed for him, and for just this kind of eventuality, by Constantijn Huygens.

This was the same Constantijn Huygens who had served as secretary to the stadholder Frederick Henry, recognized the genius of Rembrandt and helped commission his great religious paintings for the court. After Frederick Henry's death he had been secretary to William II and after William's death to Frederick Henry's widow Amalia van Solms. In due course Huygens was to become secretary to William III as well and held the post until old age obliged him to hand over to a son of the same name. His other son was Christiaan Huygens who became a scientist of world renown. In the early 1640s Constantijn the Elder built himself a country house outside The Hague. The house, which goes by the name of Hofwijck, is an architectural gem. It stands in rectangular oddity, not too big and not too small, in the middle of a rectangular moat. But it has been smothered by the expanding suburbs of The Hague and what was once a place of retreat now has a motorway and a railway line on one side of it, an unpleasing canal and main road on the other. It remains, though, a pretty and unusual house.

Huygens prescribed for the young prince William an education of rigid self-control, based on the maxim that whoever is master of himself is master of all others. But religion was even more important. 'Among all virtues', Huygens wrote, 'the first is the fear of God, which above all others must be continually inculcated, so that it may take early root in the Prince's soul.' By the age of eight signs of self-will and petulance had been made out in the prince and he was sent to Leiden University with a further educational prospectus from Huygens and instructions to his tutors to cure him of this complaint. He attended two church services a day, in Dutch and French, and was obliged to study a formidable list of subjects.

Not surprisingly, the youth who emerged from this education and the attentions of Johan de Witt was known for his reserve. In 1666, the French ambassador at The Hague reported that the prince was 'a great dissembler and omits nothing to gain his ends'. The note of French hostility is obvious. Six years before, when William was still a child, Louis had contemptuously seized the Principality of Orange, the small Protestant enclave in the south of France from which the House of Orange took its name. It is said that William never forgave this injury and that the memory underlay the whole of his political and military life.

In 1665, during the second naval war with England, there was public pressure to make the fourteen-year-old prince captain and admiral general. In 1672, when Louis XIV invaded, the pressure grew irresistible and he was appointed to both positions, initially for a single campaign.

Events moved at a great pace. The French, under Turenne, Condé and Luxembourg, advanced deep into the Republic. All turned on the defence of Muiden. The castle here had earlier been the centre of a famous literary coterie. Now it controlled the sluice gates needed to flood the perimeter of what remained of the Republic. Here the elderly John Maurice of Nassau, former governor of Brazil, stood in desperate resistance, 400 men against 5,000, and finally saved the day. As on other momentous occasions, the Dutch were able in the end to turn the watery nature of the country to their own advantage.

In The Hague, the public had turned against the brothers de Witt. Both were assaulted by crowds. On 4 July, the States General made William stadholder and military and naval leader for life. Within days Cornelis de Witt was imprisoned in the Gevangenpoort, a gatehouse in the centre of The Hague. Rashly, he asked his brother Johan to come and visit him. Johan came, and, as the story has it, read to Cornelis from the Bible while a crowd gathered outside. The militia, supposed to be in charge, was ready to fraternize with the crowd. A troop of soldiers, more inclined to obey their officers, was ordered away to another emergency. William was out of the city on military business.

Predictably, the crowd rushed into the Gevangenpoort, up to the second floor where wealthy prisoners were held, and emerged again with the two men who, for two decades, had guided the affairs of the Republic. The brothers died quite quickly and were then hung naked by the heels, horribly mutilated. The scene is recorded rather too fully in a painting in the Rijksmuseum, again in the history section. William himself showed no compunction and subsequently rewarded those who had led the crowd.

The chamber where Cornelis de Witt was held is today part of a prison museum, visited at the price of an interminable guided tour of instruments of torture. The chamber itself is rather cool in atmosphere, leaving a mixed impression of comfortable wooden beams and aching iron bars. Outside, where the brothers died, there is a statue of Johan de Witt with fleshy lips and prominent lower jaw.

The Binnenhof or Inner Court, the parliament building of the modern Netherlands, is just across the way from the Gevangenpoort. It is full of memories of William and full of darker memories too. It was here that Oldenbarneveldt, Johan de Witt's predecessor, was executed fifty years before by order of Stadholder Maurice. These two deeds of blood, enacted at most 300 metres from one another, struck contemporaries as forcefully as any aspect of the Republic.

The Binnenhof itself is a most harmonious cluster of buildings, flanked on one side by an open piece of water, the Vijver pond complete with swans and island. Just outside the Binnenhof, and from across the water seemingly almost a part of it, stands the formal and classical Mauritshuis. It was built by Jacob van Campen, architect of the Amsterdam town hall, for Prince John Maurice of Nassau and is, of course, the home of one of the great collections of paintings.

In the centre of the Binnenhof there is an ample courtyard and right in the middle of this there stands a medieval hall, the Ridderzaal or Hall of the Knights. It is heavily restored but impressive even so – a roof of mighty timbers like a ship turned upside down and hung with the banners of the provinces. It is here that the reigning king or queen delivers the annual speech from the throne. Dutch schoolchildren are encouraged to see the Binnenhof, and within it the Ridderzaal, as the embodiment of democracy.

Oldenbarneveldt was executed on a raised platform just to the left of the Ridderzaal's main door as you stand facing it. Contemporary prints show crowds gathered in the courtyard and perched on the roof. To the left of the platform again were the windows of Prince Maurice. Here Maurice's grandson William III spent much of his childhood and later had his principal residence as stadholder. The main hall of the princely apartments is now the upper chamber of the Dutch Parliament and on the opposite side of the courtyard, the lower chamber sits in the former ballroom of an eighteenth-century Orange palace.

Despite the death of Oldenbarneveldt in the courtyard and of the de Witts just a little way outside, the handsomeness of the Binnenhof helps create that sense of broad and open dignity, even serenity, which distinguishes The Hague from other cities in Holland.

In 1672, even after the successful defence of Muiden, the crisis remained acute. The young stadholder set an example of personal courage and determination and over several months of complicated campaigning the flooded Water Line kept the French at a distance. By autumn Marshal Luxembourg was complaining that 'nobody would dream of moving about unless he had turned into a duck'. Finally the French withdrew, leaving William firmly in power in a country which had come within a whisker of destruction. He was to rule for the following thirty years, for the first time in Dutch history achieving unity of purpose between the burgher cities and the House of Orange.

His major thesis was that security could only be assured if the Spanish Netherlands (modern Belgium) could be maintained as a buffer state between France and the Republic. France continually attempted to gain possession of the fortresses in the area. William, as continually, struggled to establish alliances strong enough to beat off the French. Each summer he led the allied armies in the field.

He was not a particularly successful general, except in organizing retreat. But he loved battle with deep intensity and thirst for danger. He loved hunting with the same reckless passion and both pursuits enabled him to gratify a preference for male company.

At present, however, he was bent on his life's work of resisting France and this included thoughts of a marriage that would add to his military strength. James, Duke of York, brother of Charles II, heir to the English throne and William's uncle, was himself a Catholic, perhaps friendly to France. But James's daughter Mary had been brought up a Protestant and the Protestant gentry of England began to favour the match. William had been to London in the winter of 1670 and may have seen the nine-year-old Mary – a fine dancer as Samuel Pepys recorded: 'I did see the young duchesse, a little child in hanging sleeves, dance most finely, so as to almost ravish me, her ears were so good.' William returned to England for her in 1677. She was now fifteen and tall; he was twenty-six and short, with a persistent, hacking cough and a stooped back. Mary wept when told he was to be her husband. They married nevertheless and soon set off for The Hague.

According to that entertaining historian Dr Gilbert Burnet, a Protestant refugee in Holland later appointed Bishop of Salisbury by William, the prince had 'observed the errors of too much talking more than those of too cold a silence'. It was his education, Burnet thought, which had placed him under 'an habitual caution he could never shake off'. He spoke little, said Burnet, 'and very slowly and most commonly with a disgusting dryness which was his character at all times except in a day of battle: for then he was all fire though without passion.' He neglected Mary for his male friends. But she appears to have fallen in love with him. Her sense of duty may have played some part in this, but the anguished tone of her letters when separated from him, her dread of the dangers he might face in battle, seem to indicate genuine emotion. This endured through at least one miscarriage, a false pregnancy and years of childlessness. Some thought William's ungracious behaviour sprang from a dread that if she became queen of England he would be her subject, inferior in rank. Dr Burnet claims that he intervened on this matter, successfully dragging into the open an issue William had been too mortified to deal with. Mary's response, according to Burnet, was a passionate affirmation that it was he who must rule and she would be happy to obey. After this, some thought, the relationship improved.

Mary had many friends and was cared for, even loved, by the Dutch people. She persisted in her habit of playing cards on Sundays. She eventually gave up dancing but became a great country walker. Her striking looks, familiar from many prints and paintings, combined in her favour with her energy and enthusiasm. She even learned to skate – despite the scoffing of the French ambassador. 'It was a most extraordinary thing', he wrote, 'to see the Princess of Orange with very short skirts partly tucked up, and iron skates on her feet, learning to slide now on one foot and now on the other.' The French observed her marriage to William with what Burnet described as 'a sort of malicious criticalness', longing to censure and, if possible, disrupt this union of Protestant prince and princess.

There was one pursuit which William and Mary shared wholeheartedly. This was the improvement of existing Orange palaces and, in the most interesting case, the construction of a new one.

For years William had based his hunting expeditions on the little settlement of Dieren on the eastern side of the Hoge

Veluwe, that stretch of heath and forest running up from Arnhem across the centre of the country. In 1684 William bought a piece of land at Appeldoorn towards the north of the Hoge Veluwe. The following year Mary laid the first stone of a new building there. This was to be the palace of Het Loo, chaste in pink brick, more formal than extravagant, elegant but not excessive unless perhaps at some points in its fittings and furnishing. Here more than anywhere else the memory of William and Mary lives on.

The visitor approaches by way of the stables, quite possibly mistaking them, as I did, for the palace. The palace, while dignified, is on a less grandiloquent scale. It has a fairly simple three-storey façade flanked by lower wings reaching forward to make three sides of a square. Over a century later, when Napoleon's brother Louis became king of Holland, an extra storey was built on top and the whole was covered with a grey-white plaster casing. This layer of rendering and the Napoleonic extra storey have lately been removed, restoring the palace to its old proportions and giving it, in the process, a spick and span new look.

Mary loved it. She came here when she could, went walking with her friends and leapt the ditches. William also came frequently, hunting with the German princes he was anxious to enmesh in his alliances. When he was king of England it became an important diplomatic centre.

If you entered at the front door – which, alas, visitors cannot – and carried on straight up the stairs in front of you, you would find William's bedchamber and private cabinet or office to your left. Mary's, built to an identical plan, is on the opposite side of the building to your right. Both sets of rooms have been redecorated to an inventory of 1713. Mary's bedchamber seems almost suffocating in the heaviness of the wall hangings and the floral brocade around the four-poster bed. William's has gaudy orange wall-coverings and there are dynastically orange ostrich plumes above the corners of his blue-draped bed. The private offices of both are far more charming – highly but prettily

decorated and looking out over the miniature hedges and formal patterns of the replanted seventeenth-century gardens. Fountains seem to play at every intersection.

The architect was one Jacob Roman. More important was the decorator, Daniel Marot, a Protestant and Frenchman. When Louis XIV revoked the edict of Nantes in 1685, Marot and other Huguenots fled north, bringing with them a new wave of artistic talent. Marot was a prodigy, a recognized master of the decorative French style by the age of twenty. His service with William gave his ideas exposure and helped set a trend for the elaborate and fanciful.

What this meant at Het Loo can be seen in the contrast between the 'old', pre-Marot dining room, and the 'new', 1690 dining room immediately adjoining it. One is heavy and venerable in feeling, its dark furniture and heavy Antwerp tapestries illuminated now by the flicker of electric candles. The 'new' Marot dining room is white and gold with fluted columns. Brighter heraldic tapestries designed by Marot occupy large tracts of wall. Upstairs in Mary's bedchamber, and in her cabinet, the wall hangings follow designs by Marot. It is his style which dominates in the redecoration, as in Mary's lifetime.

The painted ceiling of Mary's bedchamber, showing the cardinal virtues, clearly reflects the same taste. It is probably the work of Gérard de Lairesse, another interesting figure to rank alongside Constantijn Huygens or Daniel Marot.

Gérard de Lairesse was born in Liège, now in Belgium, in 1640. When he arrived in Amsterdam as a young man, he was drawn, despite his own formal training, to the impulsive power of the elderly Rembrandt. De Lairesse was already a victim of syphilis and a Rembrandt portrait of him shows the ravages of the disease with considerable tenderness. Despite his illness de Lairesse went on to enjoy a brilliant career. (His best work can be seen in the Binnenhof in The Hague and in the Peace Palace in the same city.) Later he lost his eyesight but became, in blindness, the indispensable art critic and historian to his period, author of *The Art of Painting*, in its day a seminal work. He could not deny, he wrote, that he once had a special preference for Rembrandt. 'But at that time', he continued, 'I had hardly begun to understand the infallible rules of art. I found it necessary to recant my error and to repudiate his; since his was based on nothing but light and fantastic conceits, without models, and which had no firm foundation upon which to stand.'

The frothy academicism of de Lairesse and the coolly exuberant decorations of Daniel Marot met in Het Loo, surely the most interesting building of its time in Holland.

Charles II of England died in 1685. Mary's father, an open Catholic, now came to the throne as James II and, after a brisk start, proceeded to mismanage affairs so drastically that the Protestant interest in England intensified their contacts with William. Whether simply in quest of a throne or, as is more likely, hoping to use the throne to lock England into a Protestant alliance, William listened increasingly.

By 1688 he was ready for the gamble. Dangerously late that autumn, when it became clear the French would not attack, he embarked a fleet larger than the Spanish Armada. At the first attempt he was beaten back by storms and hundreds of horses suffocated under battened hatches. But when the 'Protestant wind' next blew from the east, the fleet set out again, streaming along the southern coast to make an easy landing in Brixham. It was a fine feat of logistics, prelude to the first successful invasion of the British Isles since 1066.

The rest, in a sense, is British history, though making a substantial impact on the Dutch. William proceeded in a leisurely fashion. He entered Exeter with 200 Surinamese, fantastically uniformed, at the head of his troops. He waited. Then he moved on London. In due course James was allowed to escape and, after much constitutional wrangling, William and Mary became joint king and queen of England, obliged to rule according to a Bill of Rights which severely curtailed the autocratic powers of the crown. This was the price he and Mary were obliged to pay for their joint throne. William conducted state affairs. Mary considered herself incompetent, though ruling with spirit when William's absences obliged her to.

They were crowned in 1689. In the same year James II reinvaded Ireland and was decisively defeated by King William at the Battle of the Boyne, a victory for Protestantism if ever there was one. Another major incident concerned the loyalties of Scotland. Encouraged by the government, the Campbells of Argyll slaughtered a group of Macdonalds, man, woman and child, after enjoying a week of their Highland hospitality. This was the Massacre of Glencoe and it took place just twenty years after the death of the de Witt brothers. William once again took matters very coolly.

Then there was the question of William's Dutch favourites. William Bentinck, who had been his friend and helper for many years, came to England with his prince. To general irritation, William showered him with favours and made him Earl of Portland. Towards the end of the reign Bentinck was displaced as favourite by Arnold van Keppel, a far younger man to whom it is likely William was attracted. William's sexual preferences were a matter of interested speculation during his lifetime. Certainly he indulged Keppel and finally made him Earl of Albemarle.

For the rest, it was a matter of striking a political balance in London, maintaining the alliance against Louis and annual campaigning, just as before, in continental Europe. Each season, after the campaigning, William would retire to Het Loo for a round of diplomacy and hunting, regardless of the weather or his health.

Mary, for her part, left Holland with grief as great as when she first arrived, protesting that it was a country 'where in a word I had all earthly content and sufficient means to bring me to Heaven, abundant cause to make me love it, and no small reason to doubt if ever I should be happy in my own country . . .'

'I looked behind,' she wrote, 'and saw vast seas between me and Holland, that had been my country for more than eleven years. I saw with regret that I had left it, and I believed it was for ever; that was a hard thought.' In one respect, though, life remained Dutch. Mary brought with her from Holland, along with her regrets, a love for blue and white Delft earthenware which was to have a considerable impact on the great English country houses and on British popular taste as well. Many would put Delft earthenware in the same order of excellence as Dutch seventeenth-century painting.

There is an apocryphal story that Jacoba, doomed cousin of the Duke of Burgundy, was the founder of the art. In plainer fact, the techniques essential to Delftware, part Spanish, part Italian, came up through Antwerp in the sixteenth century. They found their Dutch expression in tiles for floor and walls, in larger decorative plaques, in outsize individual tiles, sometimes a metre wide, and in a host of plates, vessels, pots, jugs, vases, table decorations, models and figures of every conceivable description. The range included even brush handles and violins.

In the early period, particularly in tiles, the Spanish influence was clear, with a strong hint of Islamic patterning to accompany pomegranates and grapes. To these, after their arrival from Turkey at the turn of the seventeenth century, the thoughtful Dutch might add a tulip. Decorative tiles were usually made in groups of four, each contributing to the overall design. Once into the seventeenth century the range is huge. There are tiles with stylized flowers and tiles with realistic flowers. (The painter Judith Leyster is thought to have been the author of a botanical catalogue whose ravishing images crop up here and there on tiles.) There are tiles with fruit baskets, with birds and flowers, with animals, with soldiers. These last show types of guns and how to fire them. Rural activities are illustrated. There are tiles of ships at sea and scenes of ship building. There are sea monsters and dolphins, mermaids and mermen. Perhaps best known of all are those showing children's games. These are common in antique shops and seekers after the seventeenth century should be cautious. They were in continuous production from 1650 till about 1900. In many – raising an issue best discussed in terms of table and decorative ware – the Chinese influence is paramount.

There are two collections with a full range of tiles. One is in Delft in the former home of Lambert van Meerten, a compulsive nineteenth-century collector who finally went bankrupt for his pains. Here there are almost too many and the story of their evolution is not easy to follow. There is a more comfortable display in the great beamed attics of the Princessehof in Leeuwarden, the former home of the Frisian stadholders (normally drawn from the cadet branch of the House of Orange). Here, if one has not already made the realization, one may experience a shock of kinds: Dutch tiles are not just blue and white, as the popular image has it, but a mass of other colours too, of limpid greens and daring reds, clear orange, mauve and yellow. The blue and white is pure and beautiful; the polychrome is often gorgeous.

The tiles were made in many places but the town of Delft became the centre for earthenware. Here, even more clearly than in tiles, the story revolves around the eastern trade with China.

What happened, broadly, was this. The secret of porcelain was unknown in Europe but if earthenware was dipped into a glaze containing tin, then fired to 'biscuit', the first stage in hardening the clay, it would come out with a matt white surface suitable for painting on. At this point it was decorated. Dipped into glaze again – this time a glaze containing lead – it was fired a second time to emerge, ultimately, with a fine lustrous finish. The trouble was that the temperatures required for the final firing were extremely high and of all the colours only cobalt blue was able to resist the heat. As a result, at about 1600, the Delft potters were indeed specialists in blue and white quality ware. And this was just as well.

In 1602 and again in 1604, the Dutch captured Portuguese carracks loaded with blue and white Chinese porcelain and brought them to Amsterdam. The delicate beauty of the china caused a sensation. (The same occurred again in our own time when the wreck of a Dutch East Indiaman laden with china was discovered by divers. This cargo, rather inferior in quality though with a perfect provenance, was sold in Amsterdam for an enormous sum.) Before long the potters of Delft, working with a light clay mixture meticulously washed, were able to turn out earthenware rivalling Chinese porcelain. It was called 'kraak' after the captured Portuguese carracks. Thanks to the East India Company, the range of imported china soon expanded. Delft imitations and variations kept pace. Sometimes the designs were European, sometimes they were Chinese, sometimes an interesting mixture.

The Delft collection in the Rijksmuseum is a good starting point. Mercifully, it is not huge but it illustrates the range and contains some of the loveliest Delft work surviving anywhere. Several of the finest pieces, with those beautiful gradations of blue from gentle whisper to a darker edginess, show sea scenes of purely Dutch inspiration. Another high point is a landscape tile, a huge rectangular plaque by Frederick van Frijtom. This is regarded as both an artistic and a technical triumph, despite some scarring where there was difficulty in achieving even firing. The scene is classical, with bridge and river, travellers in woods, ruins, a distant city. Other work by van Frijtom, some elsewhere, shows typical Dutch scenes – ferry crossings reminiscent of Esaias van de Velde's paintings, church interiors like Saenredam's.

Of the handful of great Delft masters whose marks are clearly recognized, van Frijtom specialized in the European style. Samuel van Eenhoorn achieved extraordinarily graceful shapes with Chinese decoration – the prettiest of his works in the Rijksmuseum is a blue and white bottle, a jug without a lip. Even more interesting historically is the work of Adriaen Kocks who became a specialist in tulip vases – huge great constructions shaped like obelisks or pagodas and made of a succession of stacking ceramic boxes each a little smaller than the one below it. Spouts sprouted from every corner and flowers could be placed in them.

Adriaen Kocks was also expert in a new technique. Starting out with a blue and white vessel, in what had previously been virtually a finished state, the potter added a polychrome design in the more fragile colours, reglazed the pot and fired it a third time, at a lower temperature to spare the pigments. This so-called 'mixed technique' yielded a whole new range of brilliant polychrome. The potters learned how to add gold as well, creating yet another a type of work called 'Delft doré'. Examples of both polychrome and doré can be seen in the Rijksmuseum and to my eye they are often more beautiful than the blue and white. There springs to mind a little pair of model cows, with floral flanks, blue mane, blue and white legs and gilded horns. The most riotous use of colour in the Rijksmuseum collection is in a wall plaque showing, in an interesting mix-up, black people dancing among orientals.

By the late 1650s Japanese motifs were also reaching Holland. The Dutch, uniquely for a European nation, had been allowed to trade with the Japanese mainland from a base on the island of Deshima in Nagasaki harbour. At a time when supplies of porcelain from China were jeopardized by political upheavals, Japanese porcelain made in the Arita district became available to the Dutch traders. They recognized its excellence and began to ship it through the port of Imari (Imari and Arita are both names of great significance to lovers of ceramics). Delicate imagistic touches, sprays of flowers, branches, rocks, slender ladies known as Long Elizas – in Dutch 'lange lizsen' – now enter the Delft repertory.

Delftware, drawing on Holland, China and Japan, was at its height when William and Mary built Het Loo and decorated their English palace of Hampton Court. Mary's preference for blue and white helped fix blue and white in the popular subconscious as the essence of Delft. Het Loo was full of it. Adriaen Kocks was now commissioned to make a series of blue and white vases for Hampton Court. Fine tile-work, based on designs by Daniel Marot, was ordered from Delft for the Hampton Court dairy, establishing a line from Paris to London by way of Het Loo. The impact was considerable. William Cavendish, Duke of Devonshire, ordered forty 'pagoda' vases for his great house at Chatsworth. William Blathwayt, William III's war minister, made a substantial order for his house at Dyrham Park in Gloucestershire. A large piece now in the Victoria and Albert Museum in London appears to have been made for the Marlborough palace of Blenheim.

All this was grand and courtly. Dutch potters meanwhile settled in England and produced humbler, more domestic wares. Nor should the humbler Delft of Holland be forgotten. For most of us it must be the individual surviving plate, with a storm at sea or a bridge over a canal, or a tile with a tulip or a child playing, which in the end is the best measure of Delft.

The fashion for Delft was Mary's best memorial. She died in 1694, aged thirty-two, worn out with the sensations of old age. Some thought that William only cared for her because she had brought him a crown. They were surprised when he collapsed with grief. Recovering, he picked up his old life with his favourites, his fervent hunting at Het Loo, his military crusade and the struggle to finance it through the British parliament. 'It is impossible', he wrote in a letter, 'to credit the serene indifference with which they consider events outside their own country . . .'

He died in 1702, little lamented, after a fall from a horse. It was the 'disgusting dryness' that coloured memory of him.

At one time it was conventional to say that William's reign in England had been unfortunate for Holland, making the Republic a second-class power and a dependency of England's. It could equally be argued that after William died the Republic was in a more realistic situation, no longer obliged to act as the great nation it had only briefly been. Maritime power had passed to England. There was no prospect of dominating on dry land. Holland continued to commit its forces, though rather timorously, to the alliance led by England. It enjoyed the benefits won by the victories of the Duke of Marlborough and profited by the new balance of power established across Europe. This allowed business to proceed as normal.

Dutch trade was still enormous by comparison with any country other than England. Drawing handsome profits from the East Indies and the Caribbean, the Dutch settled down to a period of solid wealth. When trade eventually diminished, Amsterdam became the principal financial exchange of Europe. There was some social stress but by and large the first three quarters of the eighteenth century were peaceful. Reckoning on the number of gold bars in merchants' strong rooms, the historian Johan Huizinga said this, not the seventeenth century, should be counted as the golden age.

Dutch art of the eighteenth century, once written off as the shadow of a former greatness, is surprisingly complete and satisfying, part of a richer pattern than many are prepared to recognize. Again, as on so many subjects, the Amsterdam Rijksmuseum makes the general point. One Rijksmuseum painting in particular elaborates it.

This is *Jan Gildemeester's Picture Gallery*, painted in 1794 by Adriaen de Lelie. It shows an elegant Jan Gildemeester and his friends in a gallery where every picture on the wall appears to be from the seventeenth century. The message about the importance of the earlier Dutch masters is clear. But the ease and relaxation of Gildemeester and companions is quite as striking as the deference to the past and may well seem less challenging and sombre than seventeenth-century work. Decorative art, begun so strongly by Gérard de Lairesse, now reached its highest point in the work of Jacob de Wit. *Trompe-l'oeil* ceiling paintings are still called *witjes* or 'little whites' in a friendly play on his last name. Cornelis Troost became a master of pleasant portraiture and conversation pieces and did agreeable theatrical scenes as well.

The real surprise is to find that all the styles or types of seventeenth-century art are still in evidence and in good shape. The sons and grandson of Frans van Mieris, for example, continued to paint the highly finished small genre scenes so typical of Leiden. Jan van Huysum was a magnificent flower painter, offering bouquets that were more higgledy-piggledy than before. Adriaen van der Werff, described in 1721 by the art historian Arnold Houbraken as the greatest of all Dutch masters, was far more highly prized than Rembrandt ever had been, working on a small scale and with a touch of the romantic. Little of this work is as incisive as earlier painting but much of it is extremely pleasing.

Delft earthenware continued strong as well, until its market was destroyed by the arrival towards the end of the century of cheap and comparatively indestructible 'creamware' from Stoke-on-Trent in England. The response to Stoke-on-Trent, in Holland as elsewhere, was to increase the manufacture of top-class porcelain, the process having finally been discovered by the Europeans. The main Dutch porcelain factories were all in the Amsterdam area, at Weesp, in a former gin distillery, then at Loosdrecht and after that at the Amstel porcelain factory. All these turned out charming work, of a lightness and floral stylishness which could well stand as a symbol of Dutch art in general during the eighteenth century.

As for politics, the Dutch elected to live without a stadholder from William III's death till 1740. It was a period of decentraliza-tion with the burgomasters still in power. After this came two more Williams, divided by a regency.

Amsterdam had remained a leading centre of political and religious freedom and many of the great works of the enlightenment were published here. The stadholdership of William V, from 1766, was marked by the emergence of French- and American-influenced radical thought, leading in turn to the emergence of a pro-French political grouping called the Patriots. The Patriots were opposed equally to the House of Orange and to the burgomasters. In 1787 they gained control of most of the country but on the way to this success insulted William's wife so that her brother, the Prussian king, was irritated enough to intervene. William recovered his country and some of his dignity. He lost control again in 1795. Now the ballroom of his new palace in the Binnenhof was converted into the debating chamber of a revolutionary, pro-French assembly. (This is the ballroom, now equipped with green leather desks and a very pleasant atmosphere, where the lower chamber of the modern nation meets.) William V departed from Scheveningen to exile in a modest fishing boat. The Dutch Republic became the Republic of Batavia, nominally independent but in reality an appendage of France. In 1806 Napoleon turned it into a kingdom under his gentle brother, the twenty-eight-year-old Louis, giving him just enough time to start on a reform or two, add the extra storey to Het Loo and shift his main place of residence restlessly between The Hague, Utrecht and the new town hall in Amsterdam.

Louis was turned out by his brother in 1810 and now Holland became a part of France, swept up in Napoleon's military disasters. The country was centralized administratively but the episode was over in just four years. In 1814, by its own choice, the former Dutch Republic became a monarchy. This was the birth of the modern state and it meant, among other changes, that it was necessary to start all over again with a long line of Williams, numbering them from one to infinity as if there had never been a stadholder.

SEVEN

Monarchy to Mondrian

The monarchy encouraged into being by the victorious allies in 1814, though briefly interfered with by the Nazis, endures very comfortably today. Hardly a voice is raised against it. But for both Holland and the monarchy, there have been some interesting changes on the way.

The new nation of 1814, for instance, included both Holland and the Belgium of today. It was deliberately fashioned around memories of the Dukes of Burgundy and the unity achieved in the Low Countries under Charles V. But revivalism proved inadequate and the two halves split apart most painfully from 1830. William I, who remained king of Holland, could not bring himself to accept the Belgian secession for a decade, hankering for military reconquest. Later, relations were embittered by a dispute over the River Scheldt. The intricacy of the matter can be measured by the weight of dusty volumes on 'the Scheldt Question' still to be found in second-hand bookshops.

Eventual acceptance of the secession meant, however, that Holland was able to concentrate on its own affairs. It soon became clear that repairs were needed to the structure of the state. Poor King William I, though professing himself 'born a Republican', still had a tendency to autocratic behaviour. This caused irritation. More importantly, the regent class had been virtually reinstated by the constitutional arrangements of 1814. This made the base of the state extremely narrow.

William I abdicated in 1840 – the first of several royal abdications. Under his son William II the reform movement gathered pace. It was 1848 that finally proved crucial for Holland, as it did for much of Europe. Anxious about what was happening elsewhere, William gave his support to the idea of a new constitution and a new one was evolved in a remarkably short time. It remains in force today. The main provisions are not unusual. There is a directly elected lower chamber which initiates legislation. The upper chamber is elected by the Provincial States and its duty is to keep an eye on legislation from the lower chamber. But, significantly, the constitution also provides guarantees for many other lower level bodies. Some think it is the belief in multiplicity which has allowed Holland to develop the representative and responsive form of government it practises today – locally as well as nationally.

J. R. Thorbecke, the liberal politician personally responsible for the constitution, is celebrated in Amsterdam by an attractive little square named after him. It runs down out of the larger Rembrandtsplein, familiar because of the multitudinous café tables set out there in summer. The Thorbeckeplein has an open-air arts and crafts market on Sundays and a mass of bustling night clubs. The great man's statue looks down the Reguliersgracht, a waterway which cuts across the three great seventeenth-century canals and which has often seemed to me, particularly in spring, the prettiest single canal in Amsterdam. Thorbecke deserves the view.

The new constitution, said Thorbecke in a key phrase, 'does not know one absolute will'. Because Holland lacked Great Power status it did not matter if it also lacked the capacity for swift and decisive action. 'In 1848,' wrote the historian Ernst Kossmann, 'for the first time, liberty was seen as a luxury made possible by the very lack of power . . .' This concept is critical to an understanding of contemporary Holland. The country had seen itself as the natural home of justice ever since the early days of the Republic. Sometimes this inclined it to smugness, sometimes to a quite surprising radicalism. Holland's vision of itself as a just society was considerably helped along by the small-nation argument behind the constitution of 1848.

Though Thorbecke was trying to open the system to a variety of views and interests, it took another seventy years to bring the vote to all the people. There were other gaps in the apparatus of fairness. In the East Indian colonies, the Dutch were busily reducing the local population to the condition of serfs through what was called the culture system. In exchange for lower taxes, this obliged them to put one fifth of their land and, soon, even more of their labour at the disposal of the Dutch authorities. It was an unjust system, made worse by abuse. Its inventor, the Governor-General Johannes van den Bosch, had previously tried to cure unemployment at home in Holland by exporting paupers to compulsory labour in the eastern fenlands of Drenthe, still at that time a dismal region of heath and swamp.

There was poverty now in the Dutch towns. Investment was cautious and, though the population grew, no industrial revolution occurred. After all, the country still had windmills and canals left over from its earlier activities. Agriculture became more important until, almost without anybody noticing it, the economy was primarily agrarian.

This was paralleled by the emergence of a new group of painters who came eventually to be called the Hague School. They drew their inspiration from the countryside, particularly the polder landscape and the lives of fishing communities and peasants on the land. They were generally without interest in political or social affairs and rigorously excluded the modern life of the towns from their work – an approach, one might have thought, which would have made for a hollow romanticism. In fact, they are seen today as strong precursors to much that has happened since in European art. What marks them out is a painterly integrity, a resolute commitment to the image which becomes more apparent the more their work is seen. Ultimately, their concentration on the image led towards the cul de sac of 'art for art's sake', obliging their successors to take a different route. But if the Hague School had not existed, it is clear that neither van

Gogh nor Mondrian would have painted as they did. And in the Hague School itself some fine painting would have been lost.

The movement climbed from slow and unrecognized beginnings in the 1850s to international acclaim in Europe and the United States. It only then gained recognition in Holland. For the last twenty years of the nineteenth century, the Hague School was entirely dominant in Dutch art.

At first the Hague School painters had nothing particular to do with The Hague. Josef Israels, later to become a central figure, made his name in Amsterdam. Paul Gabriel and the excellent Willem Roelofs lived as far away as Brussels, though Roelofs, a keen painter of polder light and landscape, came up to Holland every summer. Many of the next wave first met in Oosterbeek, a little town which was to figure unhappily in the Second World War. It is situated on the bluff above the Rhine just west of Arnhem. The heath and forest of the Hoge Veluwe to the north, the huge trees round Oosterbeek itself, the Rhine and the smaller rivers combined to give it an idyllic air. In summer, the painters worked outdoors in the woods and 'baptized' new arrivals in a brook under trees they knew as 'Wotan's Oaks'.

By about 1870, though, most activity was concentrated on The Hague. It, too, still had a peaceful, partly rural atmosphere. The dunes, which have mostly been built over now, came right up to the edge of town. The fishing port of Scheveningen, today a packed resort, was practically on the doorstep. As the art historian Ronald de Leeuw has observed, with a touch of amusement, 'the shrewder landscape painters were careful to select houses near a railway or tram station so that they could set off on painting excursions as soon as the weather was suitable'.

Some of them became extremely prosperous. The Hague possessed an artists' society called Pulchri Studio and Queen Sophie, wife of King William III, often joined in its discussions. (She also befriended the historian John Lothrop Motley whose portrait hangs in her reassembled room at Het Loo.) The queen's interest did no harm to sales of Hague School paintings.

Almost all their work had a strong atmospheric quality, an individual tone extending across the surprisingly wide range of subjects that they dealt with. Landscape was central but there was also portrait and figure painting, architectural painting, just as in the seventeenth century, and quite a quantity of genre painting too.

There used to be a belief that the Hague School painters had returned to their Dutch roots through the mediation of Constable and the Norwich School in England. These painters supposedly passed on their enthusiasm for Dutch art to the landscape painters of the Barbizon School in France and so, through them, circuitously back to the Hague School. This is perfectly plausible since all these influences were indeed at work. The Norwich School admired the Dutch masters. So did the Barbizon painters, by inheritance from Norwich. Hague School members admired such Barbizon painters as Millet and Courbet. But many of the Hague School group had arrived at their appreciation of the Dutch seventeenth century independently, copying the great originals in Amsterdam and The Hague as part of their training. J. H. Weissenbruch, the Hague School landscapist possibly most admired today by critics, was quite specific on the point. 'I remember that in my youth', he wrote, 'the paintings of those old Dutchmen took my breath away by the way they made nature speak to you. If anyone taught me how to look at nature it was our old masters.'

The list of Hague School painters is quite a long one. But soon the contribution of individuals begins to stand out and the viewer develops an eye for particular painters.

Weissenbruch's landscapes generally contained water, often with boats and windmills. There are some interiors and townscapes and a quite lovely view of Dordrecht, that favourite painters' theme, by moonlight. Then there were the three Maris brothers – Jacob, Willem and Matthijs. Jacob was mainly a landscapist, but he also worked with figures and interiors. One of his paintings, *The Truncated Windmill*, shows a mill in close-up with its top chopped off, giving it a surprisingly modern look. Willem almost invariably painted cattle on the edge of water while loudly proclaiming the subject was unimportant, all that mattered was the tone. Matthijs Maris was quite extraordinary, painting alarming and uncomfortable pictures, weird brides in veils with a touch of the Scandinavian madness shown in Bergman films. Later, he drifted into self-imposed exile in rented rooms in a slum district in London, occasionally turning out dream pictures now increasingly admired.

Josef Israels is another of the most important. Heavily influenced by Millet, his speciality was sombre, solitary figures, poor people in dim light, often in the presence of death. Sometimes his struggling characters are placed on darkened heaths, for all the world as if they were out of Thomas Hardy novels.

My own favourite is Anton Mauve, though he was a difficult character, anxious, often depressed and always over-sensitive. He had had an early training as an animal painter and some of his most beautiful scenes, in silvery grey with a hint of pink, show beach scenes with horses or donkeys. Of all Hague School paintings those I can call to mind most clearly are by Mauve, one showing the broad backs of three well-dressed men on horseback making their way down to the beach for a morning ride, another a group of donkeys tethered on the dunes.

They loved the sky and often used it as a starting point. They loved the sea as well and from about 1870 it features very prominently. Hendrik Mesdag, a Groningen-born painter who had started out as a banker, came to paint very little else. He was another interesting character. He lived in a handsome house in The Hague but kept a hotel room in Scheveningen on permanent rental, with a sea view of course, and painted there almost every day. He collected the works of the Barbizon School and of his Dutch contemporaries and his collection grew so large he had to build a special gallery for it next door to his house.

In those days most big towns had 'panoramas', paintings in the round that were exhibited rather in the spirit of the fairground. Mesdag was invited to make a panorama of Scheveningen and agreed to do so for a large fee, hoping to create a major work of art. He set to work briskly with his wife, also a painter, and with two assistants (one of them, G. H. Breitner, later became a considerable artist, leader of the so-called Amsterdam Impressionists). Unlike most panoramas, Mesdag's still survives and in beautiful condition. It is a complete environment, a circular rendering of Scheveningen in 1880, with beach and fishing fleet on one side, a little wooden pavilion on an artificial dune for the spectator to stand in and on the other side the village of Scheveningen. It is a curiosity but in its freshness and seaside atmosphere, its delicate greys and wider range of blues, undoubtedly a work of art.

Vincent van Gogh saw it while still a young art dealer and was most impressed. He was in general a friend to the Hague School.

When it comes to van Gogh's own development, there is no doubting the importance of the Hague School. Nor is there any getting round the fact that of his ten brief years as an artist half were spent in Holland. It is of course the works of his last two years, in Arles and finally in Auvers-sur-Oise, which are the best known, swerving as they do between an overpowering sense of life expressed through the fragility of peach blossom or the tenderness of grass and an intolerable pressure as he moves towards his death. All these later works have an evident relationship with French art and the Louvre in Paris did at one time plan to classify van Gogh among the French painters. But reconsideration of his career led the museum to conclude that he belonged more truly among the Dutch.

To run through the details quickly: van Gogh was born in 1853, the son of a Protestant clergyman. The family had connections with the art business and at the age of sixteen he became a junior clerk with Goupil et Cie., important Paris art dealers with branches in The Hague and London. Vincent spent four years with Goupil in The Hague, then a year and a half in London till finally, after some rapid oscillations, he was sent to Paris on a permanent basis in 1875. He was by now increasingly disenchanted with art dealing and was sacked in 1876. But seven years in the trade had given him a first-rate knowledge of contemporary painting. His admiration for Millet was intense; and he had of course pondered and approved the work of the Hague School painters.

At this point, however, he was in the grip of growing religious enthusiasm. Returning to England he took a job as a school teacher in Ramsgate, then found another post in Isleworth, on the edge of London, where he could also preach. The poverty of the London slums challenged and confirmed his faith. He read intensively, came back to Holland and worked in a bookshop in Dordrecht, then spent a year in Amsterdam preparing to study theology at the university. This stifled him; he abandoned the course, spent three months more at a college for missionaries in Brussels and eventually, in November 1878, he went to preach and minister in the Borinage, the coal-mining region in the south of Belgium.

It is well known how his identification with the miners, his willingness to embrace their poverty and suffering, led to his dismissal the next year with an accolade for his devotion and a buffet for excessive zeal. The end of his missionary work, one more in a series of apparent failures, led to a crisis for van Gogh and he emerged at the end of it with a new commitment, this time to a career as an artist. He was unlike the Hague School painters. His commitment sprang from a fierce social conscience, stirred by the fervour of Dutch Protestantism and affirmed by the poverty of miners, slum-dwellers and peasants. As readers of his letters will know, he threw himself into this new undertaking with his usual passionate recklessness. No major artist has been better documented. He wrote tirelessly to his younger brother Theo who had remained an art dealer and who supported Vincent as well as he could – though what he sent was often very meagre. There were other letters, too, to friends and family.

Leaving Belgium, van Gogh went to live with his parents in Etten in the south of Holland and here he drew and drew, awkwardly at first but with increasing command. He fell in love with his widowed cousin, Kee Vos, was abruptly rejected and finally, when he followed her to Amsterdam, was sent brusquely packing by her father. By the autumn of 1880 he was taking occasional lessons in The Hague with Mauve who was married to another of his cousins. Early in 1881, though so hard up he could not pay for food or furniture, he took a studio of his own in The Hague and found having it, as he wrote to Theo, 'wonderful beyond words'.

Van Gogh's career was so short and his progress so rapid that every moment seems critical. The Hague period, which lasted for two years and through a second studio, was marked by major developments. He had already done an impressive drawing called *Worn Out*, showing a man seated on a chair, his arms across his knees, head resting on them. It has the strength of Israels, though with simpler line and more of a cutting edge. Now he drew another piece called *Sorrow*, using a naked model whose long and awkward breasts, thin legs and miserable posture, head once again on folded arms, has less of the sentimental in it than most work by his contemporaries.

Looking at van Gogh's drawing from this period we come to recognize the model, much as we recognize Rembrandt's Saskia. She is Sien Hoornik, a prostitute who came to live with him in his studio. She already had one child and she moved in after giving birth to another baby. Van Gogh cared desperately for the baby and struggled to achieve a reasonable relationship with Sien, despite the anxieties of his own family, Sien's heavy drinking and pressure on her from her brother to return to prostitution. Van Gogh drew her repeatedly, showing a sharp profile and a peevish expression.

There is an elderly man who also becomes familiar, appearing in a variety of costumes, sometimes with the numbers 199 visible on his shoulder. He was an inmate of the local poorhouse, one of the unfortunates known as Orphan Men, and the identification number on his shoulder has led to the rediscovery of his name: Adrianus Jacobus Zuyderland.

Matters were going badly in van Gogh's tutelage with Mauve.

One evil day, meeting van Gogh by chance in the dunes outside The Hague, Mauve told him their relationship was over and accused him of being a 'vicious character'. Stunned, as it seems from his account, van Gogh walked away alone, as he was so often to be in the remaining years. Though realizing he could never confine himself to the style of a single painter, he had admired Mauve intensely.

By September 1883 his relationship with Sien was also impossible. He set out for the gloomy heaths of Drenthe and here, aching with loneliness, tears welling up in his eyes whenever he saw a woman with a child, he did a series of highly personal small paintings and drawings of peasants at work.

Defeated in the end by loneliness he retreated again to his parents, now at the small country town of Nuenen, not far from Eindhoven. This was a hard time for everybody. A letter from Theo to his parents makes it clear that none of the family considered Vincent normal. He was difficult, abrupt, irascible, his behaviour over-intense in all its phases. The dominie's house in which the family lived, with its calm eighteenth-century exterior, wide windows and black shutters, offers a totally contrasting sense of peace, bringing the words 'old Dutch' to mind, much as one might speak of an 'old English garden'. There is a busy road in front of it today, but the peace emerges in a painting by Vincent, now in the van Gogh Museum in Amsterdam. There is another there as well showing the little church with its high pointed roof, tall little spire and taller trees around it, the congregation peacefully emerging after the service.

Vincent was now preparing himself to take one of those leaps in art which sometimes affront contemporaries but which seem afterwards to have been proper and necessary, almost inevitable. This leap was made manifest in *The Potato Eaters*, now widely regarded as the great painting of his Dutch years; and in retrospect it is easy to see how the work he did in the next few months led up to it.

Today Nuenen is a dormitory town for Eindhoven, serving the Philips complex. When the van Gogh family lived there the district was mainly occupied with textiles. The weavers worked at home on looms which practically filled their largest rooms, creating problems of perspective for anyone trying to draw them. Van Gogh drew them intensively and painted a series, of varying success, in which the weaver and the loom have become virtually inseparable, a single dark creation. The best of these paintings is in the Kröller-Müller Museum in the Hoge Veluwe. This has a quite superb van Gogh collection.

At the same time there were studies of peasants working, a theme van Gogh was to transplant to the brighter fields and lighter skies of France. He did a series of peasants' heads and hands. These were the preparatory works.

At its simplest level *The Potato Eaters* of 1885 is a picture of a peasant family eating their evening meal in lamplight. It was a familiar Hague School subject, but instead of sentimentalizing the peasants, or making them monumental, van Gogh portrays them almost as grotesques, with bulging cheeks and bulbous upturned noses, heavy lips and cavernous shadows under eyes. Using a technique derived from Israels, van Gogh worked out from a dark base, intended to throw any slight lightening of tone into greater prominence. But the dark surroundings and khaki-coloured skin of the peasants make the scene more shocking.

Van Gogh knew he would face criticism – as he immediately did from one of his closest friends, another striving painter – and took up advance defences in his letters to Theo. He seems to have felt free to paint like this because of his identification with the peasants. He hoped to show the nobility of toil and the overwhelming character of the peasants' struggle with nature. The painting, in its superficial ugliness, paradoxically reveals the strength of his commitment to his subject and also the extent to which he would use exaggeration to express his vision. The final study for *The Potato Eaters* is in the Kröller-Müller; the finished picture is in the van Gogh Museum in Amsterdam. They are still decidedly uncomfortable.

By now, inexorably, a fresh series of unfortunate events had occurred in van Gogh's personal life. Living next door to the vicarage was a family with a single daughter, Margo Bergeman, rather older than Vincent. She fell in love with him and he responded. But soon, because of 'evil things' said about them, Margo took poison. Though van Gogh visited her in hospital, this was the end of their relationship. In the spring of 1885, his father had died. Next he began to have troubles with the Catholic clergy. Van Gogh had rented rooms for a studio from the Catholic church and was now living in them. Local priests rebuked him for his familiarity with the peasants and offered his models money not to sit for him.

Not everything was bad, however. He visited the newly opened Rijksmuseum in Amsterdam with a friend who has left a wonderful account of how van Gogh was unable to tear himself away from Rembrandt's *The Jewish Bride* and how he revelled over paintings by Frans Hals. We know from his own account that he found he could read the great Dutch masters in a new way. Contact with their work confirmed his feeling he was taking the right direction; and it was time to move.

His path through Paris, his meetings with the Impressionists and Post-Impressionists, his new enthusiasm for Japanese prints – all these had a visible impact on his work which can be marvelled over in the Kröller-Müller and van Gogh Museums. By the time he reached the south of France his paintings had lost the early darkness of Millet and the Hague School. They blazed now in bold yellows and retreated into blue abysses. Gauguin came to visit him in Arles; they quarrelled: van Gogh cut off part of his own ear. Periods of madness now began, full of terrors and potential violence. Mostly his work was unaffected but during one confused episode, painfully for the viewer, he introduced from memory Dutch peasants labouring in a dark northern landscape surprisingly relieved by the Mediterranean verticals of cypress trees.

In 1889 and 1890 van Gogh spent time as a patient in a mental hospital in Provence, then moved north again to Auvers-sur-

Oise, to live in an inn under the eye of Dr Paul-Ferdinand Gachet, friend to the Impressionists. During these last years he painted many great but terrifying pictures – death as a reaper in the cornfields, massed corn in swathes and stooks with crows making their grievous way through heavy sky. This period is well represented, too, in the Kröller-Müller and van Gogh Museums.

In 1890 he shot himself in the chest, dying a day and a half later. His last recorded words, as his brother Theo tried to rally him, were the terrible refusal of hope: 'La tristesse durera toujours.' They hung his most recent paintings in the room where his body was laid out and filled the room with a multitude of sunflowers and yellow dahlias.

Piet Mondrian was the next of the Dutch painters who may be said to have shifted the whole course of painting, even if just a little. Like van Gogh, though with very different consequences, he came from a background of committed Protestantism. He was as dedicated as van Gogh to the practice of his art and in consequence was often lonely. In almost every other way, however, he was dissimilar. Throughout his long career the stress was on discipline and order; the many steps which led him from Hague School realism to a completely abstract style of painting all depended on a meticulous, if unusual, intellectual progression.

Mondrian was born in 1872, making him just nineteen years younger than his tragic predecessor. Where van Gogh's father had been a clergyman, Mondrian's was headmaster of Protestant elementary schools, first at Amersfoort in the centre of the country, then at Winterswijk close to the German border.

His father's position as head of a denominational school was more significant than it sounds. For after 1848, the question of education was central to the national debate and the solutions arrived at have in practice determined most of the social structure of contemporary Holland. The elder Mondrian was deeply involved in the arguments.

Broadly, the liberals wanted to offer the mass of the population the opportunity to 'improve themselves' through education. They wished to set up state-run schools, Christian but not specifically Protestant or Catholic. The religious interests, in what was partly right-wing resistance to the growth of the secular state, insisted that state support should go not just to 'neutral' government schools but to private Protestant and Catholic schools as well. The principle, and, when the principle was conceded, the level of support for the religious schools was a constant battleground. Mondrian's father was implicated, first as a follower of the political leader Groen van Prinsteren and, after him, of Abraham Kuyper. Kuyper wanted to scrap the existing system and start again on a basis of out-and-out pluralism, a determined insistence on diversity. He finally achieved power early in the present century; but already, during Mondrian's childhood, Protestant propaganda was flowing in and out of the family home in the form of leaflets, prints and lampoons. There was a strong campaigning atmosphere.

As a child, therefore, Mondrian had had a ringside seat for the tussle which was to shape his country and, though he moved away from doctrinaire religion, he in his turn took a highly ethical and eventually utopian view of society. It is likely that the austere tradition of Protestantism lay behind his ultimate decision to paint within a rigorous set of self-imposed limitations. But this is to run almost fifty years ahead of the story.

Young Mondrian was educated in the ideals of the Hague School, partly by his father who was a qualified drawing teacher, partly by his uncle Frits, a painter who had trained under Willem Maris. Frits specialized in oil sketches made on the spot and young Piet Mondrian followed him in this. He took lessons from another professional painter, Braet von Uberveldt, who lived near Winterswijk and had a large collection of his own, including a mass of Hague School reproductions. Mondrian borrowed and copied them. He too qualified as a drawing teacher.

His earliest work was mostly oil sketches and still lifes. In his thirties he settled into landscape painting, fairly conventional works marked out from the Hague School only by a tougher attitude to composition. Sometimes he created a deliberate and unresolved tension between the foreground and the background of his pictures.

Slowly Mondrian began to abandon the use of realistic colour schemes, painting his landscapes in broad swathes of any colour he felt appropriate. There is a wonderful painting, almost entirely red, of trees along a river under a rising moon. A few years into the present century the influence of van Gogh began to strike home with the Dutch painters. They coupled his vividly expressive use of colour with the dabbing technique of Seurat to create a style known as luminism. Encountering this among his fellow painters on summer visits to the island of Walcheren in Zeeland – Middelburg is the capital of Walcheren – Mondrian developed his style again, achieving monumental versions, halfway to abstraction, of such traditional Dutch subjects as windmills, lighthouses and sand dunes.

Because his life was outwardly so quiet, and because one knows of him primarily as the chaste painter of rectangles, the effect of his work from these two periods – of luminism and subverted landscapes – may come as a surprise. It offers sweeping brilliance of contour, form and colour. My own first sight of a large mass of paintings from this period, in the Hague Municipal Museum, left me, for a moment, quite dumbfounded.

In 1909 Mondrian joined the Theosophical Society of Amsterdam, questing for unity beneath the surface of appearances. For the rest of his life, a partly oriental way of thought, refracted through the European prism, was at the centre of his preoccupations. The doctrines were also close to neo-Platonisn, with nature cast as an obfuscator obscuring the essences of things. The task of the painter was to recognize the universal and achieve the reconciliation of opposites, especially of vertical and horizontal. Dutch landscape with its flat horizons and the straight strokes of trees and churches has virtually no other accents. Perhaps this was a starting point for him. But mainly Mondrian's career appears to be a slowly gathering rejection of what he thought to be the accidental and temporary nature of the visible world.

The real start was through Cubism. After seeing Cubist works at an exhibition in Amsterdam in 1911, Mondrian made haste to leave for Paris. Much of his work, like that of Léger and Picasso in this period, now became ochre in colour, oval in form, based on a deconstruction of external objects. But this was not enough for Mondrian and he soon passed through Cubism to enunciate a set of doctrines in which the work would have no recognizable starting point, no reference to external observation. The inner reality, Mondrian came to think, lay in the straight line and the right-angle, in the primary colours yellow, red and blue and the three non-colours, black and grey and white. This is the familiar Mondrian of the rectangles.

These notions came upon him little by little during the First World War. He had left France to visit his sick father and was trapped in neutral Holland by the German assault on Belgium and the battles in the fields of Flanders. During the war years he worked through a famous set of paintings based on a pier with breakwaters extending from it into a sea with breaking waves. These are the so-called plus-and-minus-sign compositions (these signs, like vertical and horizontal, are also important in theosophical symbolism). And then at last, with almost fifty years of his life gone, he launched himself into the purely abstract world of his rectangles, a form of art which he called 'neo-plasticism'.

In 1919 Mondrian returned to Paris. Twenty years later the approach of another war drove him to London, then on again to New York city and his final works – the fine, high-spirited *Broadway Boogie-Woogie*, a square checkerboard of tiny rectangles in primary colours, rather resembling the map of an underground system; and, last of all, the diamond-shaped, unfinished *Victory Boogie-Woogie*. He died in February 1944, having made one of the longest and most influential journeys in the history of painting, opening up for others a highway to the abstract. He held the utopian belief that he was offering a set of universals which could lead to the reform of human society.

It is the early Mondrian paintings which are most clearly Dutch and the ideas and imagery of neo-plasticism which were to prove most important for international culture, not just in painting but in graphic design and advertising, in architecture and, even more impressively, in modern furniture. For when Mondrian arrived at these concepts he did so as a member of a group whose work has since proved seminal, in Holland and beyond, to developments across the range of the visual arts and their functional application. The group was called De Stijl, quite literally 'The Style'.

It came into being in 1917 through a magazine of the same name set up by the painter Theo van Doesburg. As well as Mondrian and van Doesburg, the group included two other painters, Bart van der Leck and Vilmos Huszar. Mondrian always acknowledged that the particular idea of rectangles had come to him from van der Leck, an engaging artist who embraced the right-angle only briefly. Most of his paintings – a number can be seen in the Kröller-Müller museum – retain just enough of their original to be witty and graceful. In the end he retreated stage by stage to realism.

Van Doesburg was a tireless propagandist and took the ideas of De Stijl to Paris and to the Bauhaus in Germany. Eclectic and mercurial, finally more of a critic than a painter, he carried the magazine with him in new directions. Mondrian, with some bitterness, resigned from the group in 1925 and, though it was he who seemed to fall away, he was in fact the only one of the De Stijl painters who persisted in working within the original concepts.

De Stijl had originally included architects as well but in the end the most important moved outside the group, particularly into public housing where some De Stijl ideas soon gained a wider circulation. By far the most important individual inside the group, apart from Mondrian, was the cabinet maker and part-time architect Gerrit Rietveld. (He had studied at night school and did not have a full architectural training.) This brilliant man, whose influence can still be felt, produced the famous 'red/blue chair', made almost entirely out of rectangles like a neo-plastic painting, and decorated in bright primary colours. This became the symbol of the De Stijl movement.

Rietveld's last work, fittingly, was the van Gogh Museum in Amsterdam. He died while the project was under way. One of his associates took over and also died; it was finished by a third. The building that resulted still gives a lot of pleasure. At some cost to the display of pictures, the museum marches upwards through ascending rectangles to achieve a liberating play of space and light – not quite De Stijl but some kind of parallel to the excellence of the unfinished *Victory Boogie-Woogie*.

The period from the start of the Hague School to the height of De Stijl was only about seventy years. The changes in art were enormous. These were also years of remarkable change in other aspects of Dutch life.

Throughout the middle of the nineteenth century the country had remained stubbornly old-fashioned, economically backward and much praised by foreign visitors for its quaintness. Now, in response to growth in the Ruhr, Rotterdam began to grow to handle the new traffic. Further north, a new canal, still used today, was cut through the fields and dunes from the North Sea to Amsterdam. Throughout the Randstad activity and population grew.

The tardiness of this industrial revolution meant that some of the worst experiences of England, Germany and Belgium were avoided. Much of the housing, though, was dreadful. In the agricultural east, to the shame of the Netherlands, turf cutters still lived in what were virtually holes in the ground and continued to do so right into the present century – anyone who wishes to be shocked by their lifestyle should visit the

Openlucht or Open Air Museum near Arnhem where examples of rural buildings from different parts of the country have been brought together in an otherwise illuminating display. Conditions in the major towns were sometimes little better. The slums in Amsterdam were vile. Though a number of enlightened pieces of legislation were put through in the 1870s, mainly concerned with child and female labour, conditions favoured the growth of socialism and revolutionary feeling.

A Calvinist minister named Domela Niewenhuis articulated the miseries of the poor and became a considerable socialist leader. Eventually, responding to an apparent desire for martyrdom and isolation, he led the last remnants of his flock into a powerless anarchism. His place at the centre of socialism was taken by Pieter J. Troelstra, a Frisian who, in 1903 and again at the end of the First World War, stood at the centre of possible revolution. On both occasions, however, socialist fervour gave way to a stronger longing for stability.

In the Dutch East Indies, meanwhile, the culture system had been modified, thanks to an extraordinary novel exposing its cruelties. This book, *Max Havelaar*, was published in 1860 by a writer named Eduard Douwes Dekker but using the self-pitying Latin pseudonym Multatuli, 'I have suffered much.' It awakened a great sense of guilt, and there now prevailed in the East Indies for several decades a set of so-called 'ethical policies', made less effective by the behaviour of Dutch residents on the spot.

At home, it remained an article of faith that the country could and should behave in an ethical fashion. The American millionaire, Andrew Carnegie, impressed by an international peace conference at The Hague in 1899, put up the money to house what was intended as an international Court of Arbitration. This vast building, part Flemish-pompous, part English-boarding school, stands near the centre of The Hague, a monument to an idealistic venture which never worked, but which was clearly an antecedent of the League of Nations and the United Nations after it.

Neutrality was also a firm policy, firmly endorsed by Queen Wilhelmina. Her parents were William III and his second wife, Queen Emma. Her older half-brothers had died and she herself came to the throne in 1898 after a period of regency, interrupting the sequence of Williams and ushering in what has been an unbroken line of queens until the present day. There were disadvantages in the policy of neutrality, however, as the Dutch discovered during the Boer War when obliged to watch impotently as the British overcame their 'kith and kin' in the long struggle in the Cape. In the First World War the policy worked: like Switzerland, Holland was saved from the horror and destruction that ravaged all her neighbours.

Soon after the First World War Holland began to emerge as something of a model industrial state. Fright at near revolution in 1919 combined with general idealism combined to produce sound welfare legislation and a drive for better housing. Meanwhile a policy of virtually separate existence for each of the religious communities was receiving its final touches.

The system originated with the separatist school structure Mondrian's father helped to bring about. By 1920 all schools, whether state or private, had achieved equal status through a careful balancing of public funds. Catholics and Protestants now had their own all-through school structure and there grew up around the schools a complete life support system for each denomination. A Catholic would normally go to a Catholic school, attend a Catholic university, play for a Catholic football club, work for a Catholic employer, buy vegetables at a Catholic greengrocer, listen to Catholic broadcasting and die in a Catholic hospital. The same went for the Protestants and finally for the Socialists as well – a development which weakened the movement by giving it respectability.

Each of these separate communities was thought of as a *zuil*, a pillar of the state, and so the system acquired the name *verzuiling*, hard to translate in English except by the fearsome word 'pillarization'. Though it is in many ways schismatic, one of its main effects has been to allow Dutch life to develop in a more varied form than in many other countries. Particularism and separatism, echoing centuries-old divisions, had been harnessed to create a new stability. Such was the state of affairs when the Second World War broke out.

EIGHT

Lessons of War

Coming south out of Groningen, just on your left between the cemetery and the prison, there stand six sculpted hands, each taller than a man. The hands are grey and cast in metal, clenched or outstretched, contorted, not quite right. A seventh hand, its absence marked by an empty plinth, was never made because of the sculptor's death. Even this absence adds to the force of the city's memorial to its 3,000 Jews, almost all of whom lost their lives during the Second World War.

This is the aspect of the war in Holland most foreigners know most about: how the Jews from outside Amsterdam were crowded into the Jewish quarter in the capital, how all were subjected to humiliation and petty persecution and finally deported to the east in cattle trucks and boarded-up freight trains. Even before they set out on their last journey, British broadcasts to Holland were reporting mass gassing of Jews in Poland. But 20,000 out of a Jewish population of 140,000 were hidden away in cellars and attics by ordinary Dutch families, ready to risk their lives for them. The Dutch were among the few in occupied Europe who tried to protect the Jews. Many of the hidden Jews were caught before the end. The war had proved too long. Outer detail and personal response, from the perspective of an adolescent girl, are set out in Anne Frank's diary. This unforgettable account tells how she, her family and friends, went into hiding early in July 1942. The epilogue tells how Anne, her mother and her sister, met their deaths early in 1945, having survived almost until the end – three of the 106,000 Jews from Holland who were annihilated.

These terrible events must be central to any account of the war in Holland but they are better seen as one strand in a confused and contridictory pattern, full of courage and lack of courage, impossible moral choices, indignity, disaster, hope, hope dashed, hope finally triumphant. In retrospect, the difficulty of the choices and the consequent confusion of values become a second central strand to be added to the story of the Jews. Even this, of course, is to leave out the actual events of war, which included the sudden collapse of Holland at the start, Allied failure at Arnhem in 1944 and the consequent prolongation of the war. This led to the desperate 'Hunger winter' which preceded liberation.

The first the Dutch knew of their own particular war was the sound of bombers droning overhead as if towards England in the early morning darkness of 10 May 1940. They crossed the country, flew out to sea, then doubled back again to bomb the ring of airfields round The Hague. Next, still in an early morning sky, parachutes appeared, followed by gliders disgorging more paratroopers. Meanwhile German troops and armour swarmed across the border in the east. At one point a group of German prisoners was marched across the border by uniformed Dutch police. Everybody who saw them was delighted – until the Dutch policemen were revealed as German officers in disguise. The uniforms they were wearing had been purloined during the previous months by Dutch Nazi sympathizers and smuggled over the border in preparation for this trick.

The point of the paratroop attack on The Hague was to capture Queen Wilhelmina. If she proved sympathetic to the German cause, she was to be treated regally; if not, she was to be shipped to Germany as quickly as possible. But the Dutch around The Hague fought furiously and this part of the German plot was foiled.

The Germans were totally successful, however, in one key element of their surprise attack. This was the capture of the Moerdijk Bridge over the Hollandse Diep just south of Dordrecht, vital for moving tanks and heavy weapons into the

Randstad. The Randstad, known as Fortress Holland, was considered impregnable because it could be defended by a flooded water-line, just as so many times before. The possibility of an airborne attack does not seem to have been entertained. Certainly it was ignored by the Dutch high command on the morning of 10 May. Though a strong indication of the attack had come from their own military attaché in Berlin, nobody had warned the troops guarding the Moerdijk Bridge. They were still struggling into their uniforms some while after German parachutists had landed at either end of the bridge.

Outside The Hague, even in its vicinity, life continued during that first day with almost surreal normality. Milk, bread and vegetables were delivered as usual. But the military situation was hopeless. Princess Juliana, heir to the throne, left for England with her German-born husband Bernhard on 12 May. Next day, Queen Wilhelmina set sail on a British warship hoping to be put ashore in Zeeland. Matters became so threatening that she was taken to England instead. On 14 May, the cabinet followed. Many people felt a stab of betrayal. It took weeks, even months, for those left behind to see the reasoning behind Wilhelmina's action.

Further to the north, the Dutch were fighting with great spirit. The Germans had come pouring across Groningen and Friesland but at the Alfsluitdijk at the mouth of the IJsselmeer they were met by a defence they could not break. In Rotterdam, too, fighting was fierce; the Rotterdam bridges were as vital to German plans as the Moerdijk Bridge had been. Here, on 13 May, the German commander was ordered to threaten the destruction of the city and if necessary carry it out. On 14 May, negotiations were actually in progress when the Germans bombed the city, killing some 900. Flames spread through the city centre on the wind.

Immediately after the raid, the Germans threatened the destruction of Utrecht. That afternoon, the Dutch commander surrendered Fortress Holland. This ended the action at the Alfsluitdijk where Dutch forces were still maintaining their defence. For most, the five-day war was over. But in the south a few French troops had joined the Dutch. Fighting continued in Zeeland till 17 May when the Germans shelled Middelburg, capital of the island of Walcheren, destroying much of the centre of one of the loveliest of all Dutch cities. Poor Walcheren – the war was to end with more destruction here.

Two thousand troops were dead, and a similar number of civilians. But the real difficulties were only now beginning.

In political terms, Hitler had simply swept aside the neutrality of Holland. He needed the country, to protect the Ruhr and to launch a possible invasion of Britain. Nobody, he told his generals, would raise the question of neutrality 'after we have conquered'. He had made firm plans for invading Holland in the autumn of 1939 but the project had been delayed several times. Not knowing of these plans, the Dutch made strenuous efforts to observe the niceties of neutrality. They were apprehensive of Germany but not particularly hostile. The Kaiser had taken refuge in Holland after the war. Wilhelmina and her daughter had married Germans. There was close commercial and cultural contact. There were close links with England, too, but at least until war began commitment to neutrality made the Dutch almost equally suspicious of both sides.

This began to change after their defeat in 1940. But it was not a simple matter. The Germans considered the Dutch fellow Aryans and at first hoped for their support and possible conversion to the Nazi cause. A Dutch Nazi party, the NSB, was already in existence. It was not very large and its share of the vote was declining by the start of the war. Anton Mussert who headed it seemed to the Germans unsuitable for national leadership. Instead, they directed themselves to the mass of the population. They were courteous and correct, reserved in their behaviour. They even paid for their lodgings – to begin with.

Some began to think the Germans not so bad at all and that it was democracy which had let them down. This feeling, not at all surprising given the temper of the times, still persisted in some quarters even after the appointment of two unsalubrious

Austrian Nazis to control Dutch affairs. The effective head of state was Arthur Seyss-Inquart, later to die as a war criminal. He had been closely involved in the German *Anschluss* into Austria. The head of security, a post soon to gain a ghastly importance, was Hans Albin Rauter, from the 'radical' wing of the Austrian Nazi party. He too met the same fate as Arthur Seyss-Inquart.

The Dutch Nazis formed a Waffen SS. Eventually, many of its members were to die fighting for Germany on the eastern front. Sympathy for the Germans might have been still more widespread if the country had not been so strongly divided into its separate religious communities and had the Dutch not had so thoroughgoing a history of democracy. The religious communities and the numerous political groupings were hard for any mass ideology to penetrate. The strength of the family, too, may have provided an extra defence. But the danger of an over-warm response was certainly there to start with. It diminished sharply from the autumn of 1940 when the Germans confiscated all gold in private hands. Ominously, too, the Jewish President of the Supreme Court was dismissed by Seyss-Inquart together with all Jewish civil servants.

The majority of civil servants were still at their desks, by now trapped in a web they could not retreat from. Orders issued in 1937 had told them to stay on in the event of enemy occupation provided their actions were of benefit to the nation. But if most of their actions favoured the enemy, then they had to resign. The vagueness of the instruction illustrates the difficulty of framing it, let alone the impossibility of interpreting it. But since all actions tending towards civic order must in some sense benefit an enemy as well as the nation occupied, they were from the start in an invidious position. Some were to stay on right through the war, cooperating almost totally with the Germans. They issued edicts against sabotage and helped their masters to recruit forced labour. By the end they became assassination targets for the resistance. But at the start they had believed they could be an effective buffer between the Germans and the people. It took a long time for people to realize that the German war machine was not open to reason or argument. Only the poet Menno ter Braak, who killed himself on news of the surrender, seems fully to have understood what was about to happen. The fact that others did not led to many of the worst tragedies of the war.

The misfortunes of the Jews raise the issue in its starkest form. Early in 1941, Dutch fascists began to parade in uniform through the Jewish working-class districts of Amsterdam. There was fierce street fighting and in one scuffle a Nazi was killed by a young Jew. Rauter, the security chief, reported to Himmler that the dead man's jugular vein had been bitten through and his blood sucked in ritual murder. Next, acid was thrown on a group of pro-Nazi police. Following this attack, 425 young men were rounded up in the Jewish district and taken away.

Worker response to the arrests was swift. The Communists called a strike and, to their surprise since they were few in number, the strike became effective throughout Amsterdam, stopping the port and bringing city transport to a halt. The decent working people of Amsterdam seem to have believed that a democratic protest in favour of the Jews would make the Nazis think again. The result was the reverse. On the second full day of the strike German troops fired on workers in Zaandam and the next day the strike collapsed. It was an intimation that the war was total.

Another 230 Jews were arrested four months later. At the end of that year the families were told that all of both groups had died in concentration camp. There now followed many petty humiliations combined with regulations designed to ruin the Jews financially. They were forbidden to go down certain streets – to them it seemed as if all roads to the green of the countryside were banned. They were forbidden to practise a long list of professions. They were forbidden to go to the cinema. They were forbidden to ride bicycles. The shops they could use were restricted. They were obliged to wear large, six-pointed yellow stars. Their businesses were first registered, then taken over.

During 1941, Hitler decided to terminate the affair by genocide. The following year, the policy was applied in Holland, beginning with a deportation of Jews, officially to labour camps. Civil servants and workers had already been naïve enough to try to help their comrades against the Germans, on one hand by continuing to work, and, on the other, by striking without much understanding of the likely consequences. Now a group of highly placed and equally well-meaning Jews fell into the trap of cooperating with the Germans in the hope of softening the blow for their own people. The institution that the Germans formed and worked through was called the Jewish Council. Its two leaders were a respected industrialist and an Amsterdam history professor and it was they and their staff who took responsibility for the paperwork, first of repression, then of deportation. It has to be said again and again that they, like the civil servants, perhaps deserve pity more than condemnation. Theirs, in a real sense, was a tragedy of totalitarianism, based on a misunderstanding of its nature.

How complex and impossible it was may be deduced from the diary of Etty Hillesum. This extraordinary work, in some respects more moving even than Anne Frank's, remained unpublished till 1980. The diary is long. Unlike Anne Frank's, it tells comparatively little about external events and it is sometimes hard to make out what is happening. But once cut down and published, its value was quickly recognized and it has now been widely translated. What makes the diary so painful is that it tells of a quest for spiritual understanding which leads the diarist to accept, almost in a state of exaltation, that her personal destiny must lie in the concentration camps.

Because the work they were doing was useful to the Nazis, members of the Jewish Council were themselves at this stage exempt from deportation. In July 1942, at the height of the danger, a friend found Etty a job there as a typist in the cultural section. She saw immediately what was happening and put it bluntly in her diary: 'Nothing can ever atone for the fact, of course, that one section of the Jewish population is helping to transport the majority out of the country. History will pass judgement in due course.' Within a fortnight, she had made her own decision, asking to be moved to the transit camp at Westerbork where the Jews were finally gathered before deportation. This camp was in the north-east Netherlands and had been used during the 1930s to house the flood of Jewish refugees escaping, so they thought, from Nazi Germany. From Westerbork, a year later and after giving what help she could, still in her twenties, Etty too found herself on the train to Auschwitz. A letter sent from the camp by a friend says she was cheerful to the last, trying to encourage others as the train left.

For Etty, submission had come to seem preferable to resistance or evasion. The illuminating quality of her diary springs from the account it gives of how she reaches this position. At a practical level she feels it almost a matter of pride to refuse to accept that persecution can touch her. When a young Gestapo member bullies her she feels pity for him. Later, she goes to a chemist's shop to buy toothpaste. Jews have by now been banned from many shops and a voice from behind her self-righteously asks 'Are you allowed to buy that?' She gives a polite answer and goes home reflecting that her questioner is even now perhaps congratulating himself on showing idealism in the battle to save the Dutch from contamination by the Jews. Humiliation involves two, Etty says, the aggressor and the victim. There is, she implies, some kind of victory when the victim refuses the role.

One can see how this approach might allow a person to submit outwardly while inwardly retaining dignity. In Etty's case there was more and it sprang, surprisingly, from her love life. She had become involved with an extraordinary character named Julius Spier, a Jewish refugee from Germany who had been trained in psychoanalysis by Jung but based his interpretation of character on palmistry. He seems to have been a magnetic personality, not regarded as a crank in the intellectual circles he moved in.

Spier taught that psychological health could only be attained by acceptance of suffering. Etty follows him in this. She then translates her own anxiety and love for Spier into a wider humanity. At this moment, early in 1942, the first Jews are being deported and they are mostly those who have arrived as refugees from Hitler. Thinking of Spier, Etty writes in her diary: 'My whole being has become one great prayer for him. And why only for him? Girls of sixteen are being taken to the labour camps as well. We older ones shall have to take them under our wing when it is the turn of us Dutch girls.' By volunteering to go to Westerbork she both submitted to suffering for herself and tried to alleviate it for others.

The camp at Westerbork has been destroyed. In the place where it stood there is a large green space, park-like in effect, inside a rambling woodland full of nature trails. On one side of the open space stand the great saucers of a radio telescope. On the other, there are still remnants of the railway siding from which ninety-three trains departed to the death camps. The rails have been broken off and, like the radio telescope, point upwards, though obliquely, to the sky.

Many have regretted the submissiveness of the Jews and perhaps find it easier to understand those who fought for their own survival. Here the Frank family, with their clear-eyed understanding of what was happening, their careful preparations for hiding and their astonishing powers of mental resistance in concealment provide an example to wonder at. The Frank diary offers all too clear a picture of external events as they moved towards their conclusion.

The rooms where they and their friends were hidden, in the traditional canal-side 'achterhuis' or back-house, are now a memorial open to the public. It is close to the Westerkerk and those who visit it may remember how Anne loved the sound of the Westertoren bells till they were taken away to be melted down with all other available metal for the German war effort.

The number of those in hiding – known as *onderduikers* or 'submergers' – was swelled as the war went on by the addition of many thousands of Dutch males trying to escape forced labour in factories in Germany or in the construction of German military defences in Holland. The concealment of so many of these young men, along with the 20,000 Jews already in hiding, was one of the most outstanding achievements of the Dutch during the war.

Another was the strength and vigour of the underground press. It flourished mightily, with house-to-house circulation of everything from mimeographed summaries of BBC news from Britain to genuine newspapers. Some of today's leading papers began during this period. They were distributed by women and teenagers. Whenever one thinks of Holland during the war one is forced to ask the question: would I have had the courage to allow my son or daughter to participate in this? And the role of women in the resistance was absolutely vital.

The underground press has been much discussed in post-war writing. Less attention has been given to another unusual feature of Dutch resistance – the publication of literally hundreds of clandestine books. There are several substantial collections of these in existence and handling them, if one is lucky enough to do so, is an odd experience. It is hard to believe these innocent-looking volumes could, and in some cases did, lead to the death of their creators, caught in an activity the occupying power felt deeply threatening. Some I have seen are fairly crude, full of cartoons of laughable Germans and equally laughable Dutch folk struggling to keep their spirits up. Others are bibliographical treasures, not in any obvious sense works of propaganda but at the same time a defiant insistence that fine book production would continue, whatever the obstacles. The makers of these books were consciously creating works of art as a means of offering an insult to tyranny. It is a perfect illustration both of the rebelliousness of the Dutch in their dealings with the Germans and their willingness to take any risk to assert the values of the civilization they believed in.

Active, aggressive resistance was slow to start, however, and this has often led to surprise, even to veiled criticism. The explanations are straightforward. For a start, the advancing Germans had captured all documentation on individual citizens. It was comprehensive, including not only police files but, for example, church and synagogue records as well. This meant that the German police and the Dutch recruits for whom they provided training – the much-feared 'Green Police' and the extremely sinister 'V-men' – had thorough information on almost the whole population. There was no experience of occupation and little military knowledge. Many of those who first ventured on resistance behaved too openly and were swiftly captured. The flat terrain is obviously a poor one for concealment. Having no mountains to retire to, resistance fighters were obliged to swim among the people like Mao Tse-tung's guerrillas. But there was always a risk of informers among the most sympathetic-seeming group. Worst of all was the dilemma: was it morally right, particularly for a nation long committed to neutrality, to embark on a course of action that would lead inevitably to reprisals and civilian deaths?

All these were constant underlying factors. As a matter of plain and disastrous fact, parts of the resistance were also penetrated by the Germans early in the war. This happened in an extraordinary manner and led to some of the oddest incidents of the Second World War.

The story began with the appointment to The Hague of a German Abwehr officer named Colonel Hermann Giskes, a shrewd and, so it would seem, amusing character. Giskes hoped to capture a resistance radio station and turn it round, or 'play it back', sending communications of his own without the British realizing. If this could be achieved, the Germans would be in direct contact with the unsuspecting British, learning the secrets of their resistance operation and perhaps even managing to manipulate the situation by passing on occasional pieces of misleading information. To do this, it was of course essential to capture an agent and his transmitter without the British knowing. Up to this point, the German police had preferred to use the capture of agents for publicity and show trials. Finally, however, when the police succeeded in capturing an agent and his transmitter shortly before a transmission began, meaning that London could have had no knowledge of what had happened, Giskes succeeded in taking control both of the operator and his transmitter.

The operator's name was Hubert Lauwers and Giskes had no difficulty in persuading him to transmit to England. He had been captured with all his codes so resistance seemed pointless. Also, he believed that he would be able to warn London by the mere act of transmitting. This was because each radio operator had his own fail-safe, a characteristic method of transmitting including a recognizable pattern of small errors, say on every sixteenth character as was the case with Lauwers. If these errors were absent, it was a signal that the operator was acting under duress. London would abandon the station or respond with extreme caution.

Lauwers transmitted his message without errors and, quite unaccountably, London failed to recognize the signal of distress, reacting as if a genuine transmission had been received and continuing the dialogue. When in due course the London operator asked for a dropping zone to parachute in supplies, Giskes provided details of a suitable location. Then he and his men waited in the dropping zone, uncertain who was fooling who, scarcely daring to believe they would really receive supplies and not, instead, be bombed to pieces. To their delight, the supplies were genuine. Giskes had succeeded beyond his wildest expectations. And so the 'Englandspiel' began.

Quite shortly the Abwehr began to receive parachuted agents

as well as supplies. Posing as Dutch resistance fighters, they gave them a friendly welcome and helped them transmit to London the apparent proof of safe arrival. Then they revealed their true identity. In this way, between the spring of 1942 and the autumn of 1943, Giskes captured 54 agents and rounded up 400 Dutch resistance members. He transmitted false reports of sabotage success to London and on occasion the Germans appear to have arranged genuine sabotage against themselves to lend support to Giskes's stories.

Two of the captured agents finally escaped through Switzerland, and made their way to London with their tale. At first they were disbelieved and actually thrown into prison. Not till early 1944 was it fully understood in London what had happened. On April Fools' Day 1944 Giskes transmitted his last message to his opponents in the secret war. 'IN THE LAST TIME', it began, 'YOU ARE TRYING TO MAKE BUSINESS IN THE NETHERLANDS WITHOUT OUR ASSISTANCE STOP WE THINK THIS RATHER UNFAIR IN VIEW OUR LONG AND SUCCESSFUL COOPERATION AS YOUR SOLE AGENTS STOP . . .'

Giskes, honouring a promise made to Lauwers, tried to save the lives of the captured agents and succeeded in doing so till late in the war. A change in the higher command finally cost him his influence and only seven of the men survived. He himself was held as an internee till 1948 and was finally declared to have acted 'in accordance with international law and the unwritten laws of humanity'. When he later wrote an account of his experiences, it contained, bizarrely, an epilogue by Lauwers arguing that he was not, as many thought, a traitor. But why London failed to understand he had been captured remains a mystery.

Giskes emerges as a humane adversary, holding the values that would have made some sense of the initial Dutch response to occupation. He was an exception. With each year the occupation became more brutal and the hatred it aroused still greater.

Dr Louis de Jong, formerly director of the Netherlands State Institute for War Documentation, has pointed out, however, that most people inevitably lived in the middle ground between active collaboration and active resistance. They were forced into an unwilling accommodation which must to some extent have been of advantage to the German war economy. But the unwillingness grew and grew. At the Philips factory at Eindhoven, turning out electronic components for German military use, the workers worked so slowly that the Germans nicknamed Philips 'Fortress England' and contemplated deporting the whole of the labour force.

Matters were brought to a head in April 1943 by a German order for the internment of all former members of the Dutch army. This coincided with a German drive for more forced labour, reprisal shootings of civilians in response to growing sabotage and the mass shooting of captured resistance fighters. A second strike broke out, this time with absolute understanding of what might be involved. Farmers joined in, refusing to deliver milk to factories. In horrific retaliation, seven workers were executed and their bodies put on show in the Philips factory. Altogether, eighty were executed during that first week of May 1943 and another sixty were killed when troops fired on crowds.

Most people still lived in the middle but the middle itself was now the sworn enemy of Nazism. Resistance fighters began to go further. As fleets of Allied bombers rumbled overhead towards targets in Germany, the assassination of Dutch Nazis began. For every one assassinated, police in civilian clothes murdered three prominent civilians. Hostages were taken and killed. If a German was killed, reprisals were atrocious.

By early summer of 1944, the Dutch in their desperate predicament and the surviving Jews in hiding, now fewer in number, looked hourly to Britain as the starting point for the Allied invasion. It came on 6 June, D-Day, and the hopes it awoke emerge clearly from Anne Frank's diary. She thought she might be back at school in September. But soon the

invading forces were slowed down in Normandy. On 1
August, with the issue still unclear, Anne Frank made what
proved to be the final entry in her diary. On 4 August, after
two whole years, armed German police and Dutch Nazis broke
into the Frank's Prinsengracht hiding place.

Despite their slow progress, the Allies, too, were desperate
to end the war before the winter. By 4 September, they had
taken Antwerp and on the following day wild rumours swept
through Holland that Allied troops were entering the country
from the south. Members of the NSB in Amsterdam rushed to
the Central Station to escape eastwards. For a dazzling and
deceptive moment, on a day now known as Mad Tuesday, the
Dutch believed they were free and rushed into the streets to
celebrate. When they discovered their mistake the disappoint-
ment was in proportion to the joy they had experienced.

Among the Allies, a military debate was just concluding.
General Eisenhower proposed to attack on a broad front; Field
Marshal Montgomery favoured a 'pencil thrust' aimed at the
Ruhr. There was fierce quarrelling on the conduct of the
campaign. But Montgomery at last received Eisenhower's
agreement to his intended pencil thrust. It was not entirely
clear that the operation, code-named Market Garden, would
get the military support it needed. But once Montgomery had
permission, obstacle after obstacle, it seems, began to be
wished away. Piecing together the many accounts of what
followed, the reader is left with the impression that haste and
desire for victory obscured the difficulties of the attempt, to the
point of self-deception and recklessness. The need to end the
war overrode what might have been better judgement.

Operation Market Garden was intended to open a corridor –
to 'roll down a carpet' – due north from the Belgian border
across the three Great Rivers of Dutch history. Once across the
last of them, the Rhine at Arnhem, the way would be open to
the Ruhr. This was to be achieved by three things happening
simultaneously. The British XXX Corps under General Brian
Horrocks – known as Jorrocks and reckoned the Beau Sabreur

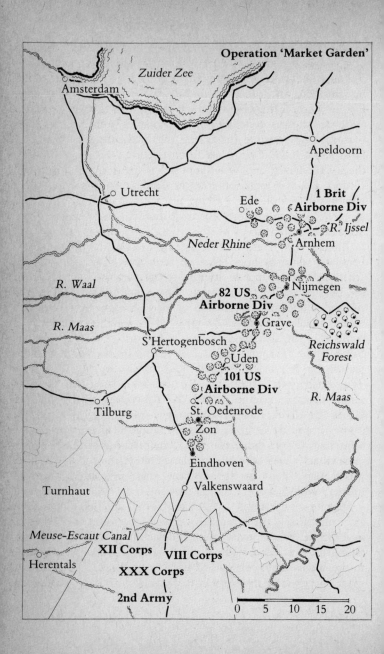

of the British Army – would open up the land corridor northwards, passing directly through Eindhoven with an armoured column. Meanwhile American airborne forces would be landed to take all the bridges between Eindhoven and the Rhine. These bridges crossed canals as well as rivers. British airborne troops, together with a smaller number of Poles would be responsible for taking the final bridge at Arnhem. Horrocks's XXX Corps had to cross all the bridges soon after they were seized and was supposed to reach Arnhem on the second day of Operation Market Garden. In this way, three complicated actions were taking place simultaneously and these three became four when the British forces at Arnhem were divided after they had landed.

Operation Market Garden began on Sunday, 17 September. Problems came at once. General Horrocks could not keep to schedule in his desperate attempt to open up the corridor from the Belgian border to the north. The American airborne forces succeeded in capturing most of their bridges but one was blown and had finally to be replaced by a Bailey bridge. Nor could they at first take the last and most important of their bridges, the soaring span at Nijmegen. It is argued that the reason for delay at Nijmegen was that too much importance was attached to capturing a particular hill as a headquarters rather than the bridge. When the Americans finally did get across the River Waal, it was in open daylight, in unsuitable canoes, raked by German gunfire. Enough of them reached the other side to take the north end of the bridge, opening the way to Arnhem. This was one of the boldest actions of the war, given scant credit in the British press, perhaps because of military envy.

Despite the efforts of XXX Corps and the American airborne troops, the column, as is well known, arrived too late in Arnhem. There, a tiny British detachment had succeeded in taking the north end of the bridge, had held it from the Sunday to the Wednesday, and had finally been killed or captured to a man. Meanwhile, the main part of the British forces had been cut off at the small town of Oosterbeek, once summer haunt of the Hague School painters. They and the 250 or so Poles who finally managed to join them were finally forced to retreat back across the Rhine at night, taking advantage of a heavy rainstorm. It was the ninth day of the action. Only 2,300 got across. Six thousand, left behind, were captured. In all, the British 1st Airborne Division suffered 8,000 casualties.

It is the action at Arnhem in particular which has captured popular imagination. Soon after it was over Montgomery wrote to General Roy Urquhart, commander of the British airborne forces. 'There is no shadow of doubt that had you failed,' he said, 'operations elsewhere would have been gravely compromised. You did not fail and all is well elsewhere . . . there can be few episodes more glorious than the epic of Arnhem, and those that follow after will find it hard to live up to the standards you have set.' The heroism of Urquhart and his men is undisputed but with the passage of time the nature of what happened has become more clear. The attack on Arnhem was a failure with terrible consequences; and little by little military experts and some of those involved have begun to ask why.

This is no place even to attempt a review of the growing literature. But a few of the explanations must be briefly canvassed. It is claimed, for instance, that the planners ignored intelligence evidence that a German Panzer corps, crack troops, heavily armoured and likely to be formidable, was in the immediate area of Arnhem. Certainly they did not tell the men who were actually going to do the fighting. John Frost, the battalion commander who seized the north end of the bridge and held it for three days, knew nothing of the presence of the Panzers – until, that is, he captured one of them and realized with a sinking feeling what he was up against.

Frost and others blame the air force for refusing to land men at both ends of the bridge – as the Germans had done at Moerdijk in 1940. Almost all the critics are united in the belief that the location of the dropping zone eventually agreed, at its furthest point eight miles from the bridge, was a major factor. It was simply too far from the target. The drop itself was conducted over two days, and not on one alone, as was arguably possible. This allowed bad weather to intervene. Half the attack force had to be held back to protect the dropping zone for the second day. Frost thinks this, too, was critical.

General Urquhart was one of a number cut off by apparent radio failure. He drove forwards to find out what was happening and, as a result, was lost, presumed dead, for thirty-six vital hours. In his own account of the battle he provides a stout defence of his actions. A more recent study has claimed that his radio was in fact working but was being used in an attempt to communicate with forces on a different network. Hence Urquhart's frustration and his course of action. Radio failures, at all events, have been blamed for much of what went wrong. Information from the Dutch resistance, sound as it proved to be, was generally discounted because of the knowledge that the resistance had been partially penetrated. It is also the case, according to John Hackett, one of the commanders in the battle and later a general, that the Dutch Staff College had a standard exercise in which young officers were asked to conduct an advance from Nijmegen to Arnhem. The answer that got no marks at all was a move straight up the road of the kind that XXX Corps was asked to undertake.

The Dutch resistance now tried to spirit away as many as possible of the troops who were left behind at Oosterbeek. The civilians of the little town had helped unstintingly during the battle. After it, they hid as many soldiers as they could until the resistance was able to move them further away. Eighty were smuggled across the Rhine in November. Another attempted crossing was ambushed and many lives were lost. Hundreds of servicemen were hidden for long periods in private houses in towns and villages across a wide arc of countryside. One of these was acting Brigadier John Hackett, known to his friends as 'Shan', but to the elderly ladies who now protected him, always, apparently, simply as Mr Hackett. He had been seriously wounded in stomach and thigh at Oosterbeek, sent across the lines to Arnhem hospital along with other casualties, and was smuggled out, still desperately ill, by a local resistance leader. In his quiet house of refuge with the old ladies and their family, Hackett seems to have experienced deep personal happiness. His book *I Was a Stranger*, one of the most sensitive narratives to have emerged from the Second World War, pays a full tribute to the humanity and courage, the constancy and sense of duty of the Dutch. The Dutch paid tribute to the courage of the airborne troops by renaming the bridge at Arnhem after John Frost.

The Hotel Hartenstein at Oosterbeek, elegant and gleaming white today, is scarcely recognizable as the building from which General Urquhart conducted his courageous defence. It is now an Airborne Museum, offering exhibits and a slide show that reinvoke the battle. Not far from the hotel lies the war cemetery, with massed graves on a wide greensward surrounded by tall trees. Survivors, local people, friends, supporters and dignitaries come here each year in pilgrimage. Among the Christian graves with their simple verses and forlornly comforting inscriptions, there are a number of headstones for fallen Jewish soldiers, some of them glider pilots. One of these reads: 'He died so that others of his race might live.' Throughout this part of Holland there are war cemeteries, too many of them, and not far to the south, at Overloon, near Venray, on the site of another battlefield, is the Dutch museum of war and resistance, dedicated to the idea that none of this should ever come about again. Tanks whose crews were killed in the action stand among the birchwoods and in the museum itself there is an eloquent account of the sufferings of the Jews and the struggles of the resistance.

But Operation Market Garden was not the whole of the military story. During that autumn, there was fighting on the west coast too. The channel ports had been destroyed and the

Allies were desperate to open Antwerp to shipping. But the Germans still held both sides of the mouth of the Scheldt estuary, just inside Dutch territory. The Canadians took the southern side, then could not make their way across into the island of Walcheren on the northern side. Walcheren, like any other piece of Holland with water all around it, is like a shallow soup bowl rimmed with dikes. The Allies bombed the dikes and slowly the land flooded, but not enough to drive the Germans out. It was a little like the slow advance of the waters to the relief of Leiden in the sixteenth century. The Allies bombed the dikes twice more in other places and finally ground forces made their way on to the badly damaged island.

The advance now stopped for the remainder of the winter and Holland entered its most terrible phase of all. Resistance was bold and effective but large-scale reprisals always followed. Wherever a resistance act occurred, local people with no involvement were killed and their houses burned. And there were other problems, potentially even graver, affecting still more people.

On the evening of 17 September, the day of the Market Garden landings, the Dutch government in exile asked the railway workers to help by going on strike. They did so, and though the landings came to nothing, they remained on strike. The first German response, from September until November, was to prohibit the movement of food to the Randstad. The hunger began at once and even when food movement was allowed again, supplies were pitiful.

Relief kitchens in Amsterdam were serving a poor gruel to up to 160,000 a day. The winter became bitterly cold. Many were starving and soon the weakest began to die. There was neither electric light nor fuel. Trees were hacked down in the parks. Blocks of wood between tram lines were ripped up and burnt. Untended sewage systems disgorged faeces into the streets and corpses piled up in the churches with no one to bury them.

Now, in desperation, people from the Randstad set out for

the farmland of the north carrying in suitcases or pushing along on prams and trolleys or bicycles with wooden tyres everything they had which they could possibly barter. Some farms were kind and welcoming, beggared themselves to help. Others put up signs saying 'No Bartering'. Cafés were closed. Icy rain fell continually. Some collapsed on the road. Others, who had found food for their families, had it confiscated as they struggled back towards the cities. Pieter Gerbrandy, prime minister in exile, now tried once again, unsuccessfully, to persuade the Allies to move directly to the rescue of Holland. He could not accept, he wrote to Churchill, that there would be only corpses left to liberate. Those who could find them now ate sugar beet and roasted tulip bulbs like chestnuts. It is believed that 15,000 died of hunger during that long winter.

Rescue, when it came, arrived from Germany, not from the south. Canadian troops advancing northwards inside the German border were diverted to liberate the Dutch. But even now there were fresh catastrophes.

It happened that the Germans had succeeded in pressing into military service a group of some 800 Soviet prisoners of war from Georgia. In February 1945 they were sent to share the defence of the northern island of Texel with 400 German troops. In April, receiving orders to embark for the mainland, they turned on the Germans and killed most of them. The alarm was given, more German troops came in. There now began a battle, lasting days, fought from farmhouse to farmhouse, from barn to barn with absolute ferocity. A group of Russians and Dutch helpers managed to reach England in a boat and begged for help. None was forthcoming. The Georgian leader, Loladse Schalwa, was killed with nine of his men trying to escape from a burning farmhouse. Photographs from a few months before had shown him cheerfully jumping his horse over fences set up among sand dunes. A few survivors held out in the lighthouse on the northern tip of the island, a place of sea birds and rabbit warrens, and there conducted a long defence. Captured at length, they were obliged to dig their own graves before being machine-gunned. Yet even so, and despite a menacingly phrased threat that anyone who helped them would be executed and their houses burned, 200 men survived, hidden in island homes.

The protection of the Georgians in the dying days of war may be seen as a symbol of the spirit of resistance. The final event was a tribute to pettiness. Retreating, the Germans flooded the Wieringermeer, a polder only recently won from the sea in the north-west of the IJsselmeer. It was an act that fittingly symbolized the spirit of Nazi endeavour in Holland from the latter part of 1940 until Liberation Day on 5 May 1945.

But how, one may wonder, can it all be summarized, made easier to understand? There was such complexity, so many events, so many lessons. Grief and loss perhaps come first to mind. The wounded and traumatic war-works of the painter Constant in the Stedelijk Museum in Amsterdam can serve as a reminder of this. Part of the sense of grief and loss lies in the history of the Jews. Here the diaries of Anne Frank and Etty Hillesum offer their contrasting perspectives.

It has been left mainly to novelists to tackle the themes of moral confusion and collaboration. Willem Frederik Hermans's illusionistic novel of 1958, *The Dark Room of Damocles*, tells of a man who believes himself a resistance hero, spurred on by a leader very like himself. When his actions are questioned at the end of the war the other self is nowhere to be found and our doubtful hero is shot as a collaborator. Harry Mulisch's novel, *The Assault*, tells of an incident in which a Nazi-loving Dutch policeman is shot by the resistance. He falls in front of the house next door but the neighbours rush out and place the body in front of the home of the child-protagonist. This act of treachery, leading to the annihilation of all his family apart from himself, returns continually to haunt him. One day, much later in life, he meets the daughter of the house next door. Why in front of our house, he asks? Why us? The unexpected reply is that they chose the house to the right because the house to the left was secretly protecting Jews. Confusion upon moral confusion.

But there is something more positive by way of monument and that, though not particularly glamorous, is present every day in the life of contemporary Holland. It is the high value placed by all on the continued operation of a political system which, with its multiplicity of parties and a general refusal to toe the line, may sometimes seem to observers fragmented and divisive. For the Dutch, however, it is proof they are right never to offer blind obedience to authority and never to give in to authority which cannot make a reasonable case. At noon on the first Monday of every month, air-raid sirens sound in the Dutch cities, first the all-clear and then the alarm. This is simply a test but the shocking noise may serve as a reminder of the horrors of war and the importance of political liberty.

NINE

The Dutch in public

Sir William Temple was British ambassador to the Dutch
Republic three times in the later seventeenth century. The
account he wrote, particularly one passage in it, is still used as a
key to interpreting the country. Holland, concluded Sir William, with notably jaundiced eye, 'is a country where the earth is
better than the air and profit more in request than honour; where
there is more good sense than humour, and more wealth than
pleasure; where a man would choose rather to travel than to live;
shall find more things to observe than to desire; and more
persons to esteem than to love'.

The Spanish Duke of Baena was also his country's representative at The Hague three times, first as a young man in the 1920s,
then on two separate occasions as ambassador after the Second
World War. He loved and admired the country and wrote about
it as a series of paradoxes. A passionate sense of liberty, he
argued, went along with a petty tyranny of social conventions.
The Dutch would behave with an accountant's thriftiness in
their private affairs yet give most generously to a humanitarian
cause. They were republican monarchists. Their life apparently
was serene and quiet yet in their deeper nature they were full of
strong feelings, even of obsessions. They were profoundly
religious, wished to get along with one another, yet lived in a
constant friction of argument. There was, he said, a deep
contradiction between their puritanical background and a
sensuous nature.

Much has happened since the Duke of Baena wrote his

engaging, garrulous account and even more, of course, since Sir William Temple's day; yet he and Sir William both pose questions that may usefully be tucked away in the back of one's mind when contemplating the condition of contemporary Holland.

Considering that the country has only 14 million inhabitants it is astonishing how much most people know about its recent history. Having abandoned neutrality at the end of the Second World War and become a member of the North Atlantic Treaty Organization, Holland gained a special fame in the mid-1980s as the last and most reluctant member of NATO to allow American nuclear missiles on its soil. All have heard of Amsterdam as a drugs capital, even if that image is going out of date. There were the squatters battling with the police, and particularly the Provos, those entertaining street politicians so dedicated to happenings. Their answer to transport problems was to build up a fleet of white bicycles which people could pick up wherever they encountered them and which, when they had done with them, they could simply abandon. Then there was the South Moluccan episode when a group of whom few had heard outside Holland and the Pacific seized a train and a school in a spectacular hostage-taking. This was a protest to confound every stereotype, for Holland was generally considered a model in its treatment of minorities. It was above all a land where nobody was meant to be poor or disadvantaged and all its people were meant to be of equal worth.

The emergence of Holland's reputation as a just society able to teach moral lessons, though one with accompanying tensions, implies a long journey from 1945. At that time Queen Wilhelmina's autocratic ways were matched by an exact class structure in which most people knew their place or, if they didn't, were swiftly put in it. The omens for change were not at first encouraging. The confusion of values that had set in during the war and the difficulty of distinguishing between what had been collaboration and what had been sensible, even unavoid-able behaviour, made de-Nazification extremely difficult. There were a handful of trials and then the door swung gently to. There remains a feeling that possibly too much has been swept under the carpet.

The struggle over the Dutch East Indies, where the independence movement was already strong and determined by 1945, has perhaps left still greater scarring. At first British troops and former Japanese prisoners of war, acting in the name of the Dutch, were responsible for horrifying acts of repression. Then the Dutch themselves, in the so-called 'political actions' of 1947 and 1948, attempted to put down the Indonesian independence movement frontally. The ferocity of these two campaigns has remained a dismal memory for the Dutch. Nor were the 'political actions' successful. The first was effectively halted by Australian protests. The second was stopped after eight months by America's threat to cut off Marshall Aid to Holland and by the intervention of the United Nations Security council. The Dutch had aroused a worldwide storm of anti-colonialism.

This was the nadir; and it is from about this period, rather than the end of the Second World War, that the Dutch moral ascendancy, if it is not too much to call it that, began.

Looking back, one can see that many of the threads were already poking out of the history of the past, ready to be pulled together in a new pattern. It is worth enumerating them.

First, there is an exceptionally long democratic tradition, linked from the start with the communal struggle against the sea. This struggle, which still persists, remains a unifying factor. Then one must consider the effects of the survival of the independent provinces into the Dutch Republic, despite all the earlier centralizing intentions of the Dukes of Burgundy and the Spaniards. This has played a part in the way democracy is handled.

During the Republic the provinces had to achieve complete unanimity before any decision was taken by the States General. If a matter was in any doubt it had to be referred back to the provincial State involved. This system led to countless delays but ensured that the voices of all the provinces were heard and that no opinion was disregarded. Though a stronger central state was introduced during the Napoleonic period, there remained a clear sense that the country was made up of its individual parts rather than being any kind of dehumanized monolith. This concept was built deeply into the pluralism of the 1848 constitution. In effect, it was a reiteration of the old idea from the days of the Republic that everything, but everything, must be properly discussed and argued out. This in turn is echoed by the modern system of proportional representation and the proliferation of political parties, some of them tiny, which has arisen from it. People do feel they matter individually and that their opinions are important. Political life is disputatious, not dull.

Full thrashing out of issues, however, can still lead to delays as surely as it did during the Republic. Earlier in this century a report on economic affairs in the East Indies ran to thirty-five volumes and was still incomplete long after the circumstances it reported on had changed. Following a present-day election, it may take a full two months before a new government is negotiated into being amid a welter of possible alliances. Politicians from countries with a first-past-the-post system find this eccentric, even irritating. Yet it has the remarkable merit of preventing small majorities from laying down the law for large minorities, a phenomenon America and Britain are all too familiar with. Some say the success of Holland's centrist governments is evidence that small countries at least have little need of strong or extreme leadership, just as Thorbecke implied in 1848. It may even be the weakness of Dutch governments, combined with an efficient, even-handed public administration, which has allowed the people to get along so well.

Compared to the mass parties of Britain or America, Dutch politics is a kind of licensed individualism. There is also great liberty at a more personal level, particularly liberty of conscience. The origins of this approach go back to the religious and philosophical life of the sixteenth century and to the emergence of the Devotio Moderna. After that, thanks to Erasmus, it was expressed in a persistent strain of humanism. On the one hand

Dutch humanism values individual rights in general. On the other, it encourages each individual to find his own salvation in a private compact with God, preferably based on the Bible. Who could interfere in such a sacred enterprise? It seems to the Dutch not just natural, but a moral imperative, to allow each person to go to God – or to the Devil – in his own way. This is one of the basic concepts underneath *verzuiling*, the separate development of each of the pillars of society. For 400 years the notion that each individual must find his own moral solutions has coincided happily with that central ambition of the burgomasters and their society: to make no judgements and to take no sides in any dispute that might interfere with the free flow of trade. The live-and-let-live tolerance for which Holland is famous has profoundly ethical and profoundly materialistic aspects.

Two other matters should also be entered in the list – society's attitude to wealth and, since this is a related question, Dutch attitudes to order. Wealth has always seemed proper and respectable in Holland. There has never been any disdain for trade. At the same time, from the sombrely clothed burghers of seventeenth-century portraits right up to the present day, there has been a persistent refusal to make a display of opulence. A senior television executive in what is effectively the public service, so not himself a mogul, told me it would be impossible to run a Rolls-Royce in Holland because normally polite drivers would make it their business to cut you up at every corner and try to get in front no matter what the traffic situation. If champagne was to be drunk at a reception – and people drink plenty of it, he said – it would have to be Luxembourg champagne. Cuts of salmon would have to be the poorest on the fish. So great is the desire to avoid ostentation that I have heard of a successful businessman refusing newspaper interviews, no matter how useful they might be, in case his rivals thought he was claiming special merit.

This strong sense of modesty in public behaviour, particularly over questions of wealth, has gone hand in hand with a general sense of social restraint and the acceptance of a need for order.

Order collapsed, briefly, during the Patriot revolution of the eighteenth century, but it was soon restored. During the Napoleonic era the supposed revolutionaries made enormous efforts to treat their opponents in a civil and well-regulated fashion. Belief in order was tested once again by the slum conditions of the late nineteenth century and in the aftermath of the First World War, but the bourgeois values of peace, profit and quiet soon overcame the whiff of rebellion. Social justice was instead pursued through liberal legislation, even in times conservative in temper. One of the most striking aspects of Dutch society has always been the unequalled level of help given to the poor. From a very early period the lay women of the Begijnhofs – those oases of medieval peace in many cities – had worked as voluntary nurses and helpers of the needy. By the seventeenth century Amsterdam and other cities had an elaborate system of charitable homes for orphans, the old and the poor. Frans Hals's portraits of the regents of the old people's homes of Haarlem are a reminder. In the Amsterdam Historical Museum there is one whole gallery devoted to paintings connected with poor relief in the city. They make it clear this was a serious matter.

Taken together, a responsive system of politics, the protection of individual rights, the tolerance, the willingness to talk, the sense of responsibility for all, respect for money but refusal of conspicuous consumption – these and all the other threads and pointers from history have provided a basis for a radical transformation of society during the last half-century. One of its central features has been a softening and blurring, almost a disappearance, of class structures.

The starting point was the desire of Catholic and socialist coalition governments in the early 1950s to spread wealth and opportunity right through society. The new British welfare state, though it has since been far less successful than the Dutch in reducing social division, was a major influence and inspiration.

In Holland, schools had always been at the forefront of politics; schools were to prove of great importance in the new social order. Today the educational system remains academically selective with a complicated range of schools and colleges offering differing degrees of emphasis on academic and practical achievement. But the parents are free, within some limits, to choose which level of education to aim for. Even more important, all children except for the tiniest minority attend schools which draw pupils from right across the range of the local community. Some observers believe the school system has done more than anything else to remove the barriers of class in Holland and to open closed doors of opportunity. Foreign families with experience of Dutch schools provide a chorus of praise for Holland as a country for children to go to school in.

In trying to account for the growth of classlessness others look to the pillars of society, to *verzuiling* with its separate Catholic, Protestant and, today, 'neutral', not socialist, structures. Their strength and omnipresence seem to have meant that relationships were forged on grounds of religion, not social class. Recently there has been a marked growth of secularism. Catholics and Protestants have come together, for example, to form the Christian Democrats, one of the three main political parties. Socialists and Catholics have combined to form the largest of the trade unions. Voting patterns and choice of school seem to be less and less conditioned by religious standpoint. There are one or two areas where *verzuiling* is actually increasing but in general it is diminishing in importance while the greater classlessness to which it has contributed endures.

Others again look to the way problems of economic inequality have been handled. The concept here is *nivellering*, a word which becomes familiar since it is quite as central as *verzuiling*. It means quite simply 'levelling' and though the debate today is whether or not levelling has gone too far – destroying financial incentives, persuading people out of further education because they do not believe it will lead to high enough rewards in the future – the extent to which it has been applied is quite remarkable by the standards of all other countries in the world outside Scandinavia.

One of the two main weapons has been a 'progressive' taxation system, taking more and more from the wealthy in a proportion rising according to the degree of their wealth. The other has been a system of generous grants and subsidies. Unlike British arrangements, the combination seems generally to work. Some perfectly respectable statistics from the mid-1980s show that across 95 per cent of the working population the difference in declared income after tax was about the value of one paperback novel a day. On the other hand, one does see with one's own eyes many discreet differences in wealth. Cars, though they are seldom spectacular or flashy, are a good indicator. The explanation is partly that there is a flourishing black economy among those who can conceal their earnings from the tax inspector. Self-employed plumbers, for example, seem to do very well.

The top five per cent, big business managers and so forth, appear to stay even more magically exempt – to the indignation of many of the others. The impression remains that *nivellering* has involved slightly more levelling up than down and that there is still solid wealth tucked away. You hide it, though, if you value your peace of mind. A recent study of the very wealthiest suggests that they are often unrecognizable because they continue to lead normal, hard-working lives. A surprising number are university professors.

Grants and subsidies are very much more generous than in some other countries. For a start, there is a minimum wage. People in employment have to get at least that and if they are sick or unemployed they get subsidies not far short of it. Because of the debate about incentives, the level of subsidy and the age at which it should begin are controversial. Old people, however, receive almost exactly twice as much as, for example, British pensioners. This means they seldom become dependant except when they are ill. They remain quite forceful economic beings, able to make their own decisions and, if they should wish to, give handsome presents to their grandchildren. When they have state-provided help at home, the helpers are trained to

dust high shelves but not the lower ones, so leaving the elderly a potentially satisfying task that will not be too awkward. It is this kind of well-organized, methodical humanity which seems to me so particularly Dutch.

Holland provided the first sheltered workshops for the handicapped. The Dutch were also pioneers in returning the mentally handicapped to the community – and not on grounds of public parsimony either, as one suspects to be the case in Britain and America. Health care for babies is extremely good and thorough. One social worker of my acquaintance believes this alone may have done as much as any financial *nivellering* to break down the distinction between social classes. (Rickets, by the way, is called 'the English disease' in Dutch – a label to weigh in the balance against anti-Dutch phrases embedded in the English language: Dutch treat, Dutch courage and so forth.)

Dutch people are now among the tallest on earth – a tribute to genes, diet and health care. Women strike the visitor, at least the short male visitor, as particularly tall.

There is also a strong belief that everybody is entitled to good housing. Early in the twentieth century the architects of what is called the Amsterdam School were at work in the southern parts of the city, creating solid but rather playful housing where the handsome façade might not relate entirely to what was happening inside. Their work, much visited and admired, was a kind of domestic sculpture in brick. Then came the impact of De Stijl – more matter of fact, inclined to the right angle and simple materials.

J. J. P. Oud, who had been one of the original De Stijl group, became city architect of Rotterdam when he was only twenty-eight. His credo was that there should be 'no more masterpieces for the individual, no more exquisite mansions with fine touches of handicraft and luxurious decoration, but mass production and standardization with a view to providing decent dwellings for the masses'. This way of thought, enlightened for its day, led finally to some fairly unappealing system-building after the Second World War – Rotterdam itself has a number of dismal-looking blocks for workers as well as some fine experimental building and the world's first pedestrian precincts.

Today, however, the so-called 'social' approach to housing has led to a continuing building programme which has indeed provided 'decent', and more than decent, dwellings for almost everybody. Mostly this is expressed in newly built suburbs around the towns, made accessible to all, without class barriers or ghettoization, by heavy subsidy and careful planning of integrated estates with all types of housing close to one another. There is no stigma attached to social housing. The partly agreeable and partly over-safe-seeming suburbanization involved in applying the housing policy is one of the most noticeable aspects of contemporary Holland. The exception is Amsterdam where housing shortages endure.

Like good housing, the treatment of crime may be another index of social health. As early as the seventeenth century, active attempts had been made in Holland to reform criminals, not just to punish them. This was a revolutionary concept. Treatment of offending adolescents during the nineteenth century was extraordinarily enlightened compared to practice elsewhere. The crime rate was so low that the Dutch abolished the death penalty in 1870. By 1886 there was a system of parole. Even today, when the crime rate has climbed to the same league as that of other northern European nations – threatening the notion of Holland as a uniquely stable and law-abiding society – there remains a strongly marked reluctance to send people to prison except as a last report. The number of cells is fixed and none is shared. This means the number of people in prison is static. When 'demand' increases there is a waiting list.

Given the level of provision, from the relative comfort of its prisons to its handsome old age pensions, the 'caretaker state', as it has come to be called, is expensive to run. A lot of the money comes from high taxation which seems little resented. The Dutch evidently feel they are getting a good bargain. The fact that they are major producers of natural gas has helped carry the cost. Over past decades farm production has expanded hugely, making Holland one of the world's leading agricultural exporters. The great multinationals, Shell, Unilever and Philips, have all been doing very nicely, thank you, and Shell has been able to ride out the oil crisis apparently undamaged. *Nivellering* has been taking place against a background of high prosperity, though one increasingly threatened by international developments.

The high level of welfare, fine 'social' housing, excellent health care (about half of it provided privately), an open education system, good provision for old people, a drive towards equal incomes and perhaps even the effects of the 'pillarization' of society had combined by the 1960s to abolish the most extreme distinctions in Dutch society. Attitudes, aspirations, even the way people spent their money, were remarkably consistent right across Dutch society. The old urban proletariat seemed to have disappeared and an entirely middle-class society had taken over. It was true that a Hague accent remained grander than a provincial accent. There were some districts of daunting working-class housing from the nineteenth century still surviving. But the class structure was breaking down to an unprecedented extent for Europe. People had their rights and their rights were seen as equal. Society in general seemed willing to share in the pursuit of peace, prosperity and equity, the enduring bourgeois goals. Within this framework, Holland had become one of the most obviously just societies in the world.

This achievement, it seems now, served also to blow the starting whistle for events of an interesting and extremely individual kind, both entertaining and in some ways disquieting.

What happened is mostly common knowledge. First, in the early 1960s, there was a series of disturbances, some apparently involving hooligans, others perhaps political in origin. Alarmed, the government commissioned a report and for the first time there was public mention of 'provocateurs'. A group of young activists delightedly accepted this as a name for themselves and so the Provo's were born. One aspect of the movement was a rejection of prevailing attitudes to property and housing, those cornerstones of the Dutch sense of identity. Amsterdam had always had its housing shortage and this combined now with a rapid formation of new households – young people wanting to live separately from their parents, perhaps in groups, perhaps with a girlfriend or boyfriend or a partner of the same sex. There was a growth in the number of people living alone. The number of new households made housing even scarcer and, for the Provo generation, squatting quickly became both a way of life and a political commitment.

The squatting and the new approach to politics proved immensely attractive to young people outside Amsterdam, not just in Holland but from abroad as well. Add to this a tolerant attitude towards soft drugs on the part of the city authorities in Amsterdam, and an intoxicating youth culture was born. This, after all, was the age of flower power in California and hippies everywhere. There was an adventurous readiness to experiment with new ways of living.

The highest point of the youth culture was probably when the Provo's transformed themselves into the Gnome Party, or Kabouters. In June 1970 they actually won a handful of seats on Amsterdam's city council. But almost at once the movement began to fall apart. That August, after a two day battle, the hippies were cleared from their perch on the National Monument in Dam Square and now the direction for the youth culture was mostly downhill. Squatting became more violent, with a growing tendency towards pitched battles between police and squatters. The biggest problem was the arrival in some force of hard drugs dealers. What had once been friendly began to be dangerous. Young people felt that a long dream was ending.

Since those days a worried but still comparatively tolerant Amsterdam has continued to put up with soft drugs. These are sold openly in cafés. But hard drugs, originally treated as a public health problem, have become by definition a law and order matter. One consequence is that the hard drugs dealers, pursued from their habitual haunts, appear suddenly and menacingly in unexpected quarters. Another is that Amsterdam can no longer be considered the drugs capital of Europe or even a particularly heavy user compared to London, Milan or other major cities. Squatting has also been reduced by new and more stringent laws.

Holland has football violence, though, and this is a worry for the authorities. Interestingly, they are not bothered, or not particularly, by Amsterdam's long-established red – light district which originally grew up because of the presence of so many sailors. In earlier days in Holland, sex for any other purpose than procreation was considered a bad idea by Catholics and Protestants alike. For people of the middle and upper classes it was an ideal for their sons and daughters to be married as virgins. Working-class people in the cities and on the farms seem to have been more free, delaying marriage until a pregnancy became apparent. But the Dutch, in line with their live-and-let-live practices in other matters, have never had much difficulty with other people's sexuality. Their own, it is fair to say, has been unleashed to a considerable degree since the Second World War. So the Amsterdam red – light district, lurid though it became in the 1960s and remained in the 1970s, was hardly seen as a problem even in the cautious 1980s. Dutch people have lived alongside it and do not get as excited at it as the tourists. Anyone who wishes to see bondage exhibitions or humans copulate with animals is absolutely free to do so. The Dutch attitude may be judged by the fact that there is a single organization representing both prostitutes and their clients.

It would be sad, however, if all that remained of the excitement and good times of the Amsterdam of the 1960s was a fading memory, a surviving red – light district and an enduring problem with hard drugs. The phenomenon, in fact, went far deeper. For as well as concerning themselves with their own particular issues, this generation worried about questions reaching out across the whole of society. Amsterdammers and others all over the country came together in anxiety about the state of the environment, the nuclear issue, the treatment of ethnic minorities, the position of women and a whole slate of moral and political matters. It seemed as if the Dutch, having successfully settled the questions of public care and private wealth, were now free to turn themselves to a range of issues so contentious that in many countries they do not get a proper hearing. But full and open discussion is, of course, a Dutch speciality. It may be that the answers found so far are not always convincing. There have been successes and disasters. But what seems impressive to the observer is the willingness to tackle great issues head on.

The situation of women is one of the most interesting because of its contradictions. Here is a nation which seems to be one of the most progressive in the world. Yet about the same proportion of women go out to work as in Spain, Ireland or Greece. Raise this question with most women and they do not see any problem. They believe that home and family are more important than any benefits an extra wage or wider experience of the world could bring. Nor do most women seem to feel any need for independent earnings. When you see Dutch women in their homes you begin to realize that the importance they and their families attach to them really is no myth. It is not just a matter of cleaning and making the house beautiful – though that, unashamedly, ranks very high. It is to do with the home as the fundamental place of being, retreat and fortress of the family.

To Dutch feminists, this seems old-fashioned, even servile. They argue that women are locked into this way of thinking by their own recent history. Dutch families, both Protestant and Catholic, were large till the present generation. Children now in school seem to have countless aunts and uncles. But the size of the family has begun to plummet and women will soon be able to find more time for themselves and be able to act more independently. This gives the feminists some hope, but they also argue that there are many negative forces in Dutch society conspiring to keep women at a remove from power or business success. They say the discrimination is covert, not apparent, an unspoken compact among men that they will be damned if a woman is going to take their job or be promoted above them. What in the end is so interesting is that the government, even while abused as being part of a system that withholds dignity and fair treatment from women, actually helps fund feminist causes. There are, for example, women professors of emancipation and feminist theology at Dutch universities. The government has had a minister of emancipation. But how far this results in action is a more tricky matter.

Another great question concerns the role and treatment of ethnic minorities. When the independent state of Indonesia was created out of the old East Indies, many Indonesians came to Holland as immigrants. The way they were absorbed into Dutch society, while also retaining a strongly rooted culture of their own, was treated for decades as an object lesson by other European nations. The Indonesian restaurants which sprang up everywhere have also added a good deal to the pleasures of Dutch life. From the beginning, though, there was a special problem over the South Moluccans. There were people from a group of islands which had proved friendly to the Dutch at the time of Indonesian independence. The islands were captured by the Indonesians in a military operation and many Moluccans came to Holland as refugees, believing they had a promise their homeland would one day be restored. Whatever the nature of the understanding, the Dutch were clearly unable to honour it even if they had really wanted to. And so the South Moluccans finally erupted with their celebrated seizure of school and train in the mid-1970s. This seems to have been a final gesture of despair. Today, the group speaks more wistfully of its homeland and remains engaged in fruitless discussions with a Dutch government whose only interest is delay.

The Moluccan issue soon turned out to be only the tip of a fast-growing iceberg. Holland, like West Germany, gave a welcome during the boom years to hundreds of thousands of workers, particularly from Turkey and Morocco. Mosques are now commonplace in Amsterdam and whole districts have a distinctly North African feel. Since then times have grown harder. The 'Mediterranean peoples', as they are sometimes called, receive equal benefits to those of Dutch citizens; and this has led to some hostility. There is still a basic assumption that it is correct and proper to be welcoming. Racism is poorly regarded. Yet more and more you hear the refrain, 'I know what I'm about to say is not exactly liberal, but . . .' and out comes a criticism of Turks or Moroccans justified on economic grounds. There have been incidents of racist behaviour by the police, though many Dutch people are still surprised and shocked by these, an indication they are not routine; there are growing complaints from the guest-worker minorities; and the observer must wonder what will happen next.

But this is nothing to the plight of the Surinamese. Surinam, that small and steamy nation on the Caribbean corner of South America, had been managed over the centuries as a plantation system. Dutch savagery to slaves was often shocking to outsiders. Slowly, matters improved and in 1975 the country gained its independence. Following an offer of Dutch citizenship, great numbers of Surinamese now came to Amsterdam. And here many of them had the misfortune to be caught up in one of the great architectural and planning débâcles of northern Europe.

Down on the south-east extreme of Amsterdam, the house-builders had been at work on what was effectively a satellite city designed to house 100,000. Its name is the Bijlmermeer and it consists of huge hexagonal blocks of flats, solid and decent, but with various features that have led to something not far from disaster. The Bijlmermeer was intended as a pedestrian city. To get to your flat you have to walk either over open ground, with paths winding through a kind of free-growing shrubbery. Or you must approach by walkways which link the blocks at first floor level. People arriving by car have to leave their vehicles in large covered car parks on the periphery and then continue on foot through the walkways. Nobody can tell by looking from their own front door or window who is where or who has entered which block by which walkway, stairwell or path through the shrubbery. Even the shopping centres are in cavernous spaces underneath main roads.

One of the main troubles was that while it was being built the Bijlmermeer grew more expensive than it was meant to be. The rents had to be raised and the flats proved hard to let. Most were standing empty when the Surinamese arrived. Sooner than put them in barracks, a well-intentioned government housed them in the Bijlmermeer. Some are now dispersed about the country but many remain, a country people living like an urban proletariat. Seven out of ten on the Bijlmermeer are Surinamese, more, it is said, than the whole population of Paramaribo, capital of Surinam. The authorities repaint, they put up mirrors so that you can see who may be lurking round the corner, they provide lock-up garages in some of the car parks. I have even seen sculpture on some of the walkways. Yet it is a place where cars and private postboxes are ripped open as a matter of course. Drugs are sold widely among bored and unemployed young people. The feeling is one of danger. There are no women visible anywhere after dark.

I happened to visit the Bijlmermeer with an architect who was one of the first to warn, as far back as 1972, that there was a disaster in the making. Since then, a quantity of less threatening low-rise housing has been built around the edges, softening the effect. A new commercial area has sprung up nearby, including the headquarters of a number of banks, gleaming and reflecting back their bright materials to the sky. My guide the architect was now predicting that by the end of the century the Bijlmermeer would be a fashionable address.

Despite the gravity of its subject matter, the nuclear issue, by contrast with the Bijlmermeer, has been a positive experience for Holland. In opposing the siting of Cruise missiles on Dutch soil the Dutch gained a heady unity of a kind not seen since Liberation Day in 1945. Inevitably, as a member-state of

NATO, the government had to surrender in the end. Perhaps it intended to from the beginning. But more than any other nation the Dutch had made a statement about nuclear war and what many saw as the American threat to peace in Europe. 'We may be the little boy in the family,' says a friend, 'but it's good the little boy's feelings should be heard. I'm proud of my country at a moment like that.'

Art has been a public issue, too, largely because at one point the government operated a system which proved so open-handed that it became a matter of ridicule. Effectively, the government decided to support bona fide artists, if unemployed, by buying up an almost unlimited quantity of their work. It soon had basement upon basement filled with paintings. The scheme was discontinued but it is still possible for individuals to rent leftover paintings from the authorities and, if they like them, buy them on reasonable terms. Not all are bad. I have seen some spectacular paintings from the public stock hanging on private walls.

The dominant painters ever since the war, to divert a moment from the argument, have included Constant, who showed its horrors so movingly, and two others in particular – Karel Appel and Corneille. Soon after the war, they moved to Paris, there falling in with painters from Denmark and Belgium and forming the Cobra group. (Its name is based on the initials of the capitals of each of their home countries.) Much Cobra work is a brightly coloured expressionism which has never gone out of fashion. Younger artists such as Jan Dibbets have since widened out the range, working in a variety of materials and styles. The work is rich and lively and, as so often in Holland, there is a top class museum where one can go to see what is happening. This is the van Abbe Museum in Eindhoven, physically an old-fashioned gallery, though somewhat reconstructed and full of the fruits of an extraordinarily adventurous buying policy. The much admired Stedelijk Museum in Amsterdam also concentrates on modern art and has a fine collection but has not taken its stance so firmly in the present.

From painting, back to public matters – and one in particular which is central to public affairs today as it has been throughout history: the question of land and water. As soon as the Second World War was over, the breaches in the dikes round Walcheren were mended in a spectacular feat of marine and hydraulic engineering. Fleets of vessels dumped into the gaps huge concrete caissons which had already been used to make an artificial harbour during the Normandy landings. The dikes round the Wieringermeer polder in the IJsselmeer, broken by the Germans, were mended, too, and all the lost land eventually brought back into production. Next, new land was added in what is claimed to have been the largest reclamation project ever undertaken. This involved the creation of a whole new province, Flevoland by name, won from the southern half of the IJsselmeer.

On the negative side of the balance sheet, however, were the destructive and terrifying floods of 1953, with 1,800 drowned and a far greater loss of land than during the whole war. The Dutch determined this should never happen again if it could humanly be avoided and so, piece by jigsaw piece, a vast set of water defences were built round the complex mouth of the Rhine delta in the south-east corner of the country. These defences acquired the name of the Delta Works and were finally completed in 1986. They are the largest ever built by man, enormous in scope, complexity and cost, lending themselves so naturally to schoolbook diagrams and demonstrations of man's cleverness that you wonder if they will really work.

But on the way there had been some major readjustments. The point at issue was the destruction of sea-water habitat by the last of the dikes, planned to shut the widest stretch of open water at the delta mouth. The environmentalists succeeded in demonstrating the ecologically damaging effects that would flow from the plan as it stood and, finally, at considerable cost the dike was replaced by a storm-surge barrier. This elaborate construction now lets sea-water through in ordinary weather and only closes at moments of great danger. The change of plan is proof, if proof is needed, of the Dutch ability to argue, sometimes bad-temperedly, until all opinions have been weighed and, in the end, for the Dutch state to act responsibly, even magnanimously.

The environmentalists were also making a case against a long-established plan to win another large piece of land from the IJsselmeer, just up to the north-east of Amsterdam and filling in the gap between the Flevoland polder and the mainland. This scheme was a widely accepted national objective, proof of continuing vigour in the fight against the sea. A challenge to the plan could be interpreted as a slap in the face for a cherished part of history. Yet the environmentalists have made a strong case, based on the likelihood of a falling population and the reality of agricultural over-production. Who wants an airport in the IJsselmeer, they ask? Who wants more motorways to link it to the city? If environmentalists finally win the battle, it will show astonishing flexibility in a nation which has made land reclamation a sacred task for centuries.

Yet even while such experiments and adjustments are in progress the Dutch somehow manage to retain a streak of conformism. One of the most striking aspects of Holland is that while many individuals are capable of highly idealistic and individual behaviour, almost every child is brought up with the injunction to be '*normaal*'.

One interesting question in the land of the eternal paradox is just where the royal family fits into this set of contradictions. To look at Queen Beatrix's hairdo and clothes you would think she was dedicated to the notion of the *normaal* and the pursuit of the bourgeois virtues. The monarchy is an extremely civic institution. Dutch kings and queens are inaugurated, not crowned, and go about their business, busily, in what outsiders sometimes feel a very humdrum fashion. And yet and yet . . . During the long line of queens, from Wilhelmina's accession in 1898 till the present day, the House of Orange has proved itself capable of behaviour at least as unusual as that of many of its unhumble subjects.

First we have Wilhelmina, imperious, old-fashioned, quite incapable of accepting contradiction, the very embodiment of a P. G. Wodehouse aunt. Her daughter, Juliana, was made to sit on a golden chair while invited playmates gambolled on the floor. The other children had to call her Mevrouw – Madame. Come the war, a married woman and heir to the Dutch throne, Juliana surprised the governor-general of Canada by her habit of sitting on the floor.

In other respects as well, Juliana grew up just as Wilhelmina must never have intended. She made court protocol her enemy. She said in a television interview that if she had not been a queen she would have been a social worker. The informality and obvious concern have always made a strong impression. At the same time she has seemed sometimes to lack a normal defensive skin and a capacity for restraining her behaviour. On the fiftieth anniversary of her wedding day she was to be seen on television waving and waving from a balcony with an extravagance which was endearing but not far short of eccentricity. During a television interview on the same occasion with her husband Bernhard, she kept pushing and shoving at him, to the embarrassment of viewers, coyly asking him to tell the nation why he had married her.

Juliana and Bernhard had four daughters – Beatrix and Irene, Margriet – named after the marguerite, the symbol of resistance – and finally Maria Christina. The scrapes that parents and children have been involved in have been quite spectacular and have generally added to the gaiety of nations. Some, particularly the first, have also been a little sad.

The troubles began soon after Juliana's inauguration in 1948. Her daughter Maria Christina had been born blind the previous year and though her sight had been restored by an operation there were continuing difficulties. Juliana was extremely religious like her mother; and a faith healer named Greet Hofmans was little by little absorbed into the royal household as helper and comforter. Maria Christina's sight improved and Greet Hofmans's influence increased. The greatest scandal came when she tried to protect a convicted war criminal from execution. Stage by stage Greet Hofmans came to be seen as the Rasputin of the House of Orange and finally, in 1956, the queen was obliged to dismiss her after an official inquiry. It was a saga which had done great damage to the monarchy.

Next, it was the children's turn. In 1964, to the dismay of Protestants and constitutionalists, it was discovered that Princess Irene had become a Catholic. Contrary to her mother's wishes she planned to marry Don Carlos Hugo, a pretender to the Spanish throne. Next she disappeared – to Paris, as was generally believed. Her parents followed her there, amid great international publicity and suggestions that Juliana's abdication was inevitable. Irene had kept ahead, however, and was already in Spain with her intended prince. It was Bernhard's task to fetch them back from Madrid. Irene returned to an enormous and quite unexpected display of public support, even of love. She married her Catholic prince, was banned from the succession but remains a popular figure. Even after her marriage broke down and she was living with a well-known television personality, people would say of her admiringly that she had twice the dress sense of the whole of the House of Orange put together.

Margriet created the next excitement by marrying a commoner. Some may take this as a mark of virtue in a bourgeois monarchy and it is one of the refreshing aspects of the House of Orange that they are not obviously a part of any royal 'set'. This may make it harder for them to find the kind of marriage partners expected of royalty. Margriet married a Cuban-born social worker in New York and Beatrix, of course, caused a surprise of her own, particularly given Holland's wartime history, by marrying Claus von Amsberg, a German diplomat and another commoner. Their marriage in Rembrandt's Wester-kerk in Amsterdam was the occasion of a lively riot.

That was in 1966. A son was born – Prince Willem Alexander – and all was now sweetness and light between the nation and its House of Orange. Indeed, a decade passed before the next scandal. Now, it was Prince Bernhard's turn. This hardworking prince and 'goodwill ambassador' for Holland had done his best to keep out of what Wilhelmina once described as the 'cage' of royalty. He held high positions in the armed forces and a number of major directorships. All seemed well until a senate committee in the United States reported its finding that a 'high Dutch functionary' had personally received $1.1 million from the American company Lockheed Engineering. The finger pointed at Prince Bernhard and an ensuing Dutch commission found that he had 'far too rashly' involved himself in transactions creating an impression that he was 'open to favours'. Over purchasing from Lockheed he had taken initiatives which were 'completely improper' and placed him, so the commission reported, 'in a suspicious light'.

This was the end of the affair except that Bernhard now resigned his posts. It is a tribute to Dutch tolerance, perhaps also to Dutch admiration for a businessman who knows a bargain, that when he next appeared at an official function, wearing a suit and not the familiar uniform, people felt really sorry for him. He remains in retirement a familiar, even a reassuring figure, his popularity undiminished. He had demonstrated, after all, and particularly during the Second World War, his own overriding loyalty to the nation and the royal family he had married into.

Beatrix is popular as well. She has a most engaging smile and seems, if one may judge by television, to have a ready sense of humour. She finally had four sons, as many sons as her mother had daughters. The nation thinks them a lovely set of lads. But even so, when Juliana abdicated in 1980 and Beatrix was inaugurated queen in Amsterdam, there was once again a spirited riot.

It is clear that over their royalty, as well as every other aspect of their public life, the Dutch are full of paradoxes and surprises. But wherever the nation has actually got to, and however fractious the public debate, it is impossible not to be impressed by the great advances made since the Second World

War. Under its 'republican monarchy', a modern nation has emerged with a passionate attachment to justice and tolerance, to conformism and individualism, extremism and moderation. And public life is often entertaining.

TEN

Dutch interiors

Dutch interiors today, and the temper of domestic life as well, seem to have made their way direct from seventeenth-century painting to the present. Take cleanliness, for instance, and the point will become clear.

Vermeer with his brooms and women sweeping is one of many painters who show cleaning operations in progress. The bucket becomes as familiar as the broom in the art of the period. The notion that cleaning is a serious activity is offered quite plainly, long before other European nations had even considered the possibility of banishing domestic squalor. The Spaniards who accompanied young Prince Philip on the grand tour of his future possessions in 1549 commented on it emphatically. From that point to the present day references to cleanliness are a commonplace of the literature. There is the story of the grandee who arrives on a visit to find the maid washing the floor. To his astonishment she picks him up and carries him to the other side. There is the British ambassador, Sir William Temple, surprised and slightly grumpy to find that spitting indoors at banquets was regarded as a misdemeanour. Even though Amsterdam is dirty and graffiti-ridden and some of the other cities seem to be going the same way, domestic cleanliness remains a real priority. The family caught with their house in a mess would be an unhappy family indeed.

The cleanliness goes with a sense of domestic order which can, at worst, seem fussy and pedantic. At best it gives Dutch interiors today the poise and serenity of a de Hooch painting.

This may be a trap for women but it certainly has consolations. And while it has often been said that the Dutch are primarily a bourgeois nation, to me at least they appear overwhelmingly domestic.

Lighting is responsible for part of the effect. As one wanders the canals of Amsterdam in the evening, inevitably scrutinizing the life they reveal through undrawn curtains, one is struck by the variety and subtlety of lighting. This is partly a matter of arrangement, but partly, too, a function of money. The Dutch place their homes at the centre of their lives and are not afraid to spend to make them beautiful. One could argue, fancifully, that love of good lighting is expressed in Rembrandt's chiaroscuro or the illuminated night scenes of Honthorst or Terbrugghen. But there is straightforward testimony in art to another Dutch trait which survives as surely as respect for cleanliness. This is the love of flowers.

All who have wandered the streets of Holland will have been aware of the huge size and variety and number of house plants which crowd the windows of Dutch houses, twine round any available upright and seem quite likely to block out the light of day. There is a tendency in smarter floral circles in The Hague and Amsterdam to rein back just a little on this thicket-like effect and try for a cooler and more chaste impression, to concentrate on just one or two extremely superior plants. But all without exception participate in that other great Dutch passion – the enjoyment, even adoration of cut flowers. There are flower shops on every corner. No one would dream of letting a big occasion like a birthday go by without cut flowers. Nobody would go out to dinner without a bunch of flowers. A man, going to visit another man for a meal, would take a bunch of flowers for the house. Most houses always have cut flowers behind the barricade of pot plants at the windows. For the New Year's Eve concert in the Concertgebouw in Amsterdam, the density and gorgeous colours of the flowers are in themselves as thrilling as any performance that could take place in front of them. All adults, so it seems, can arrange cut flowers with a swift, sure touch and, if they can't be bothered, the lad in the flower shop will do it for them. There is nothing strange about flowers, nothing cissy in appreciating them. They are a delightful part of life in Holland.

House plants and cut flowers reached their present ascendancy through a number of odd and interesting stages. The early voyages of the Dutch led to great enthusiasm for new species from overseas. The tulip arrived from Turkey, by way of Vienna, round about the start of the seventeenth century. Its exotic possibilities intrigued the Dutch and soon they became adept at developing new varieties. Growers took care to protect their specimens. There is a story that the first man to produce a lilac-coloured hyacinth, mutating from the red, kept the bulbs hung up inside a bird-cage to keep them safe from mice.

As was inevitable, the price of unusual bulbs, particularly tulips, began to shoot up. In one of the strangest excesses of a generally prudent nation, speculative deals on tulip futures rose to a crazy level. A painting by Pieter Bruegel the Younger, now in the Frans Hals museum in Haarlem, shows tulip growers and prospective purchasers in a grand country-house setting. There are generals with swords and sashes and elegant ladies. But every figure in this painstaking and quaintly attractive work is in fact a monkey dressed in human clothes. A house in Hoorn, according to the legend, was sold entire in exchange for three tulip bulbs.

The collapse, in 1637, was as sudden as it was catastrophic. Many were ruined, including that fine landscape painter Jan van Goyen.

Gradually the trade returned to more realistic ways. The Dutch continued to produce their bulbs and the wonderful spring display of colour between Haarlem and Leiden has been annually renewed now for 300 years. At the Keukenhof, a kind of flower theme park at Lisse, just near Haarlem, growers set out their best bulbs under the trees and in large greenhouses, demonstrating the astonishing range of shapes and colours attained by modern plant breeders. It is a floral entertainment which may have a touch of the banal but which is beautiful as well. No gardener should miss it.

The quest for the exotic was joined at the end of the nineteenth century by a new enthusiasm for mass colour. Now, in addition to the bulbs, there developed the beginnings of the modern market for cut flowers. The fact that these are reared under glass means that today the full experience of colour must be sought in the greenhouses as well as in the fields.

A visit to a flower grower can be impressive. I remember on one occasion standing amid seven acres of glasshouse forested with enormous orchids. My guide, one of the owners, happened also to be the chairman of the Dutch orchid growers' association and spoke with enthusiasm. Sometimes, he said, he got exhausted and fed up and when this happened all he had to do was straighten up and wander round the greenhouses and he would feel well again in minutes. Though he worked all day with orchids, he still had them in the house for pleasure. Two other things emerged from our conversation. The first was that orchid growing was a business, hard and demanding and with virtually no room for error. The second was that it was also more than a business – that the pursuit of higher standards and so, ultimately, of higher profits was seen by the orchid growers' chairman as an activity of value in its own right. Far from being questionable on grounds of materialism, I realized as I talked to him, success in commerce is regarded as a sign of grace. The pursuit of profit is the path of virtue; and this has ever since seemed to me one of the keys to Dutch society.

I also learned that in order to thrive each kind of orchid requires the climate of its place of origin. Mountain orchids, for example, need warmth at midday but, reasonably enough, prefer a chilly night. Tropical orchids require a more even temperature. The chairman was running eight separate climates in his greenhouses, all by means of a computer. This looked after temperature, humidity, intensity of light, the feeding of the plants. But if a thunder storm should break out, it would take too long to close all the windows over the whole seven acres.

So in bad weather it was still real farming, all hands ready at a moment's notice to deal with the emergency. And the worst perils? Red spiders and the bumble bee.

Most orchids are sold direct to the retail trade, often individually as a luxury item. Most other cut flowers pass through flower auctions into the hands of flower merchants and exporters. The largest of these auctions is at Aalsmeer near Schiphol airport. It welcomes organized tours and is almost as popular as the Keukenhof and tulip fields.

This is appropriate. The scale of the operation beggars belief. In vast hangars trains of trolleys laden to the brim with literally millions of flowers pass first under the eye of the inspectors – quality control being all – then run through the auction rooms themselves. These – there are several of them at Aalsmeer – are built like theatres with steeply ascending tiers. Flower-growing is a fiercely masculine business and the buyers are almost always men. They sit ranged round the theatre at little desks. Their appearance is casual but tough and self-reliant. As the trolleys chug through, the lots go up on a large computerized board and an arrow showing the price swings round a clock face from high to low, true Dutch-auction style. The first to press his button wins the lot.

Straight after the auction, it is hurry, hurry, hurry, as the dealers, all based in the huge auction building, pack up their purchases to move them off by lorry or by plane from Schiphol. They go all over Holland, Germany and France, to Britain and the United States and a multitude of other destinations ranging from improbable Trinidad to astonishing Singapore. The most popular flower is the rose, followed by the chrysanthemum and the carnation. The tulip struggles to hold its place at number four.

Contemporary attitudes to flowers and the home can be predicted from Dutch painting. One other important attribute of Dutch life, being non-visual, has to be experienced in person. This is straightforwardness of speech, a directness which can rock foreigners on their heels even when, as is generally the case, no harm at all is meant. The Dutch express themselves quite frontally, sometimes without finesse. They are inclined to make personal remarks and may be surprised if you decline to reply in kind. Foreigners who resort to polite evasion are considered neurotic or hypocritical. Seen in these terms the straightforwardness has some logic behind it. But on occasion the bluntness can go a surprising distance. An English friend recalls an encounter with a woman she had met just once before but whom she recognized and to whom she offered friendly greetings – only to be devastated by the reply, 'I'm sorry I didn't recognize you, but you're not the kind of person I would normally remember.' This sort of behaviour is described as *bot* – blunt and then a little more besides.

Against this aspect of behaviour, one must set a far longer list of virtues. I have found sharpness of thinking and social concern at almost every turn. There is a quickness which runs counter to the stereotypes.

It would be easy, having once begun, to build up a list of general observations, to offer a set of snapshots of Dutch life, particularly of the Randstad where most people live. These would show a friendly, open-faced nation, a trifle blunt but very fond of flowers, willing to go to work quite early so as to be back as soon as possible to pursue family life in homes to which they devote the greatest possible attention. They particularly enjoy whatever they think cosy or *gezellig*, though this important aspect of Dutch life involves sociability, even conviviality, as well as domestic pleasure. *Gezelligheid* may be found among friends in a restaurant but the restaurant will have to have flowers and candles. All this could be presented as typical. Few would claim that a small country town, particularly one in Friesland, should be presented as a symbol of the Dutch and the Netherlands. Yet on one occasion, having been invited to just such a town, I felt, almost as soon as I arrived, that this one part, if properly understood, would serve as well as any other to illuminate the whole.

The town was Wolvega, an hour and a half's drive north east of Amsterdam, my hosts Meneer and Mevrouw Koning, house-builders. I make my way through the outskirts of Amsterdam in the 4 p.m. rush hour, out finally through the tangle of motorways and across the new polders of Flevoland in the IJsselmeer. They are cruelly bare except for scattered man-made woods, the fields laid out in large, mechanical-looking rectangles to make a match for modern farm machinery. Almere and Lelystad, the new towns of the new polder province, are visible to the left, angular, manufactured, both needing a lot more time before they accommodate to the contours of human beings. The men from both these towns pour into Amsterdam each morning, leaving behind a race of women known as 'green widows'. Large swathes of oil-seed rape to right and left offer a brilliant, feverish yellow. I pass a road sign warning of leaping deer. Is this a kind of hopeful propaganda, or have deer really been introduced to the polder's artificial woodlands by planners intent on a rich ecology? Birds of prey were lured there – with bird boxes – to keep down the mice which had arrived of their own accord.

Within half an hour the province is behind and the traveller enters the earlier North East polder, dating from the 1940s. Here the trees are taller, the farms more settled. You see that within a generation or two it will wear the long-settled look which elsewhere speaks so emphatically for Dutchness. Soon the Noord Oost Polder is behind as well and the countryside grows older yet again – original swampland long reclaimed for pasture, original open water, man-made canals and water left by earlier peat digging. A few kilometres of the province of Overijssel, then into the southernmost outposts of Friesland. There are great piles of reeds in bundles waiting to be taken away for thatching, then an old farm with the words 'Werk Lust', 'Joy in Work', written on the façade in large brick letters. This is serious countryside.

Wolvega is not a tourist town, though Peter Stuyvesant of transatlantic fame was born here. It has a pretty church with a clapboard tower, surmounted by slated spire. It has a windmill – 'Only one, I'm afraid,' as a member of the Koning family had said to me apologetically on a previous visit. The former mayoral residence has a handsome neo-classical look. But, for the rest, it is not spectacular – a street of modern-looking shops, a couple of industrial estates turning out lorry bodies and furniture and a few smaller products. It has no hospital or 'academic' high school – for these, the people travel further north. But though there are only 12,000 inhabitants and everybody seems to know everybody else as in a village, the feeling in the middle of Wolvega is quite 'towny' with small houses and a few larger ones standing straight on to the pavement. For the most part Wolvega consists of newish suburbs, clean, pleasant, the housing varied within limits and definitely comfortable. When I came here last, Mr Koning drove me around town to show me the kind of houses his firm builds – a life's labour laid out for review along the streets. The houses are open in aspect and attractive. With their plain brick construction and neat gardens, and masses of flowers in the windows, they look both clean and utterly dependable, the way of life secure, the values certain and securely held.

All around Wolvega lies open farming country, suggesting, when you first arrive, the same dependability. Mr Koning, as it happens, has bought his firm from two previous owners named Middendorp and de Boer. This is the name of his company today and it means, in rough translation, Mid-Village and Farmer. With the addition of a catchy name for 'suburb', it would be appropriate as a shorthand for Wolvega.

I reach the town at 6 p.m., the universal suppertime of Holland. The Konings greet me with delightful warmth, he quick and weather-beaten, unflagging in energy, a touch of the middle-aged Picasso in his appearance, she at first more formal, hanging back a little, as Dutch women often do. She soon reveals an amused approach, begins to make her presence felt in the group, prompts others if they forget their own best lines. Though it is often perilous to contradict a commonplace, I must affirm in the name of the Konings and their friends, and of my other Dutch friends and acquaintances as well, that there is plenty of laughter in Holland, a willingness to see the funny side. This often goes with passionate commitments to all kinds of causes. Officialdom can be solemn and self-important, the bureaucracy can drive strong men and women crazy, people can be at pains to cross too many t's and dot too many i's, but if other writers had not put it in my mind, I would never in a thousand years have classified the Dutch as stolid.

The Koning house reveals the advantages of being a builder when you happen to want a house. It is double-solid, with serious walls and a weather-resistant air. Downstairs all is spacious and generally open-plan. There is a large hallway walled off from the rest. The office is also walled off in the conventional manner. But dining room, living room and substantial kitchen make a 'z' around the closed-off spaces, so that the open-plan offers privacy as well as an easy flow from area to area. There's a sense of space upstairs as well, with the bedrooms ranged around a large, comfortable landing.

These arrangements lead one immediately to feel there may be another commonplace to challenge – the supposed Dutch love for miniaturization. Many Dutch houses are tiny and this accounts for the toy-town impression created by some of the older cities. But could this, one reflects, be mainly because land, having been won from water, was overwhelmingly expensive?

Another aspect of the Koning house is the careful attention paid to objects. Running up the open stairway, there is what amounts to an exhibition of old builders' tools, suspended neatly against bare brickwork – picks, planes, mallets. In the hallway a huge pot of plants stands on an old builders' weighing machine. Umbrellas stand in a churn brightly painted in the floral style of Friesland, and more plants stand in a basin on top of another churn. In the main living area there's a fine old Frisian clock, with pendulum and brass weights and, above the face, a little painted picture of sailing boats on water. Christiaan Huygens, scientist son of Constantijn the Elder, invented the pendulum clock in 1657. At about that time, largely as a result of their seventeenth-century expansion in the east, the Dutch appear to have been the first nation to take up the collection of interesting or beautiful objects on a serious basis. This was part of that great expansion of knowledge which Svetlana Alpers finds so clearly reflected in the paintings. The results can still be seen today in the fact that many towns have ethnographic museums, generally featuring eastern exhibits; the tradition is also at work in modern houses like that of the Koning family.

There is nothing ostentatious and nothing extravagant but the whole effect is extremely pleasant.

After we have eaten we go on a family outing. The Konings start work early. Mr Koning begins a tour of building sites at 6.30 a.m., half an hour before his workers arrive. Mrs Koning starts the administration not much later. When the day's work is finished and supper over, the Dutch generally like to do something else quite definite, sport or gardening or working on their homes. In this instance it is an expedition.

Those involved are myself, the Konings, their twenty-three-year-old daughter Sieni and a young woman friend of hers. Sieni has stayed at home and is a doctor's assistant. Anja, the other Koning daughter, is out of the country. She has already made her way round Europe and New Zealand and plans to take on the United States quite shortly.

Whatever family you meet, there seems always to be a traveller in it, as if the security of life at home made for a certain restlessness. These travellers are the Dutch one meets in any quarter of the globe, bright-eyed, seriously interested, daring enough to be influenced by what they see and hear. It is as if they are raking the world for useful lessons, even if these should happen to be in Oriental philosophy or unusual forms of social organization. And the travellers will not be despised or treated as extraordinary if they come back displaying new attitudes. The fact that Mondrian, the so-called father of abstract art, depended so heavily on theosophy, would not be considered too surprising in Holland. Mondrian was also interested in anthroposophy, a comparable way of thought. Its founder was the Austrian Rudolf Steiner. Today in Holland there are sixty Steiner schools.

Anthroposophists occupy high positions in the professions and perhaps the most striking single building of the 1980s was put up by a bank with a number of anthroposophists on its board. This, the NMB headquarters, is in south-east Amsterdam hard by the Bijlmermeer; it is a so-called organic building, a strange dream-castle, consisting of a mass of brick with not a perpendicular external wall in view. Its leaning buttresses are filled with offices, offering a suggestion of swallows' nests and clouds.

My destination with the Konings on our evening outing is the nearby village of Giethoorn where almost all the houses stand on little individual islands along a small central canal. The farmers here still use wide, flat-bottomed punts to move their hay. The houses are all reed-thatched – thanks to subsidy from a conservation-conscious government. Giethoorn is calm and pretty, with ducklings on the water and plenty of other families out for a saunter. There is every suggestion that in summer it may be a hell on earth, or water, rather, with thousands of little motor boats for rental chugging up and down the canals and the nearby lake. When the Koning children were small and times were quieter, the family kept a caravan here for summer holidays. For Sieni as a child it was a world of untold happiness, of secret waterways and boats and bathing. Next, the family had a sailing boat, and now they have a motor boat with comfortable sleeping quarters. Sieni holidays on her own while for three weeks every summer her parents explore their country by water. Every town and village in the neighbourhood seems to have its own inland harbour, full of pleasure-craft. It is a world of democratic boating, open to all.

Next morning, in biting wind although it is late May, I make my way as previously arranged to a handsome old house where one of Wolvega's two veterinary practices has its headquarters. Berend Brummelman, specialist in the larger animals, has agreed to take me on his round of the farms. The four vets, all men, are sitting round a table with their female administrator. They already know what visits they have to make and they are discussing individual programmes, who should take which farm and in what order so as to make economical use of the day. Diaries are out, coffee is on the table – a huge vacuum flask of it on a silvered tray with cream and cups and sugar. There is a computer primed with relevant information as a back-up, an animal pharmacy, immaculate underground in the old wine cellar, an X-ray unit and an operating theatre for smaller animals. You would have thought, amongst this sleek modernity and under ornamental plaster ceilings, that things would be pretty serious. Certainly the business gets done. But there are continuous ripples of laughter round the table and several jokes that stop them in their tracks. Jelle Kramer, the oldest and most senior of the vets, seemingly some seven feet tall and generally with a quiet manner, more than once rolls his head right back on his shoulders to roar with laughter like a sea-lion. The morning conference is an engaging spectacle.

Berend Brummelman's long grey car is loaded to the gunwales with vaccines and medicines for cows and horses and all the impedimenta of his trade. There is a slightly heady smell of disinfectant. Brummelman himself is serious and concentrated, gives questions full consideration. He pilots us across a landscape quickening with green, new crops showing through black plough. But mostly it is pasture for here we are in the Netherlands' main dairy region. In the south and east of the country there are plenty of pig and poultry farms, immensely intensive. Round Wolvega it is black and white cattle. There is also the unexpected extra of trotting horses, Wolvega having a trotting course coiled in the best civic fashion round a running track and sports ground behind the former mayoral offices.

Our first call is at an entirely typical farm – huge old barn behind a quite modest house, its name inscribed in large letters high on the façade, a scatter of modern buildings near the barn, one of them housing the modern dairy parlour. All cows have four stomachs, Brummelman assures me, stirring dim memories of school biology. In the case of our patient here at Cornelia-Sate – the name of the farm – one of the stomachs has shifted. We join the farmer in a dim shed, straw underfoot, and after a certain amount of heavy breathing on all sides and stethoscope work by Berend Brummelman, the decision is taken. We will roll the cow and try to shake her innards until the stomach slips back into place. Quickly the cow is trussed in a rope and spun on to her back, feet in the air like a dog wanting its belly scratched. We juggle the cow from side to side. I am in charge of one of the ropes and succeed, so it seems to me, in having my big toe totally crushed under one of the cow's vertebrae. I stifle my cry of alarm, afraid that Brummelman will write me off too early in the day as an hysterical assistant.

The stomach yields to this informal treatment and we all go into the Cornelia-Sate kitchen for coffee and home-made ginger biscuits the size of dishes. The couple, in their late fifties, have three children but none of them is working on the land. A new motorway is being constructed along the edge of his territory, and the farmer claims he doesn't care a button. 'It won't make any difference to me,' he says. 'I only wish it had come straight through the house so I could have taken early retirement on the proceeds.' There's a corner cupboard with a mass of blue and white Delft pottery, blue and white dishes with oriental patterns on the walls, and masses and masses of flowering plants in pots.

On our next call we see something now a little unusual – one of the big barns still being used in the original way. The farmhouse is a former holiday home, now the retirement home, of a one-time school manager and he has left things so far as possible in their original state. This means he has his haystack right in the middle of his barn. The barn is the size of a church, its soaring thatch held up on what seem mighty forest trees. The cattle would have spent the winters in stalls ranged round the central haystack. It's an impressive sight, and one typical of how the region used to be. Many Dutch barns are quite magnificent and there are different kinds in different parts of the country, their intimate details the subject of weighty tomes. In some, particularly in the east, the family hearth was open to the cow-stalls, with only the bedrooms and parlour divided off by a partition. Most varieties can be seen at the Open Air Museum at

Arnhem but it is a thrill to encounter a good one in, as it were, the wild.

Next, on to a bachelor living alone with his aged mother. Brummelman has been called in for the rather menial task of hoof-trimming but he does it uncomplainingly while the farmer chats on about football, Friesland and the past. He is an Ajax supporter, used frequently to make the trip to Amsterdam to watch his team in action. He and several other farmers whom we visit still speak Fries, the language of their former independence. You do not hear it at all in Wolvega. He coaches me in a little Frisian rhyme involving tricky pronunciations: 'Butter, rye bread, green cheese – if you can't say them you're not Fries.' He tries me out on German, his leading foreign language. All children had to learn German at school during the war, he says, and he recalls a British Lancaster bomber coming down near his village, its crew unharmed but swiftly seized by the Germans. Before we leave we are pressed into a ramshackle shed to admire a trotting horse with foal which the farmer is looking after for a neighbour.

Some farms are small, some bigger, though none really substantial in this area – the definition of size is by the number of cows in milk and it ranges from 20 at the previous farm to 180 on the next. Here I find myself engaged in a serious discussion. There is trouble in Holland, given the intensity of farming, with the quantity of nitrates and phosphates seeping into the water table. Slurry is a problem too, and dairy farms have been forbidden to spread it during the winter months when it cannot be taken up by plant growth and mostly goes into the water. There's an argument over just which months the slurry-spreading should be banned. Farmers have been told to fill in special forms giving details of their own slurry-spreading and 900 have simply torn up the forms in protest. The farmers I am talking with half approve the action, half deplore the reputation they feel the Dutch have gained for instant protest and unsociable behaviour. It is clear they are thinking of Amsterdam and drugs and squatters.

The most surprising aspect of the day is our visit to a duck decoy, a place with a little artificial lake and a complex set of devices to trap wild duck. Brummelman has never been here before during seven years in Wolvega. Nor, as it turns out later, has Jelle Kramer, the senior vet, during his whole career. 'No,' says Kramer, 'it is a secret place.'

It is astonishing how well the decoy is hidden, a trick you might think impossible in flat and open country. From across the fields all we can see at first is a little mound of dike and the tops of small trees. Approaching, we realize that the dikes form a rectangle. Inside, it is all tender young trees, soft grass and virulent nettles, the whole enclosure ringing with birdsong, and the lake screened off by a high palisade of reeds. There is a technical term for every aspect of this business. (The English word 'decoy' is itself formed rather oddly from the Dutch, using the plural portion of the word for ducks – *eende* – and the word for cage – *kooi*: *eende kooi*, in full, cut down to the English 'decoy'.) The duck-catcher is a neighbouring farmer. He goes to a shed and dons an old grey raincoat. He has a peaked cap and a whistle round his neck and he slings a satchel of grain around his middle like a van Gogh sower. Instantly, we are in the nineteenth century.

Next he leads us to the tall reed palisade and we peer through a hole like a letter box at the tranquil little lake where ducks are gaily bobbing. Most of these, says the duck – catcher, are domesticated birds used for leading on wild duck. August is the best month for trapping. We enter a complex system of blinds, little walls of reed with spaces between them giving on to the water, and here the duck-catcher, invisible to his quarry, throws out grain as bait. The tame ducks do obligingly come cruising into the narrowing channel, one of four traps in a system as elaborate as the defences of a castle. If there were wild duck behind the tame ones, the duck master would contrive to hurry them on from behind with a mild scare and so deeper and deeper into the trap. He explains that dogs were originally used as well. Waterfowl, it seems, are naturally curious about dogs and a specially trained dog would enter the palisade through a little pipe, run up towards the trap, then out again by a pipe higher up, round and round in circles until the duck were moving up towards him. Then the dog would make a round a little further up again through another set of pipes – round and round and round, further and further up, until, by a combination of bait and dog, the ducks were finally lured into the cages at the end of the reed palisades. Sad for ducks, no doubt, but for Brummelman and myself, on a cold May afternoon, a place that had allowed us to glimpse a past that was fragile, deeply appealing in its vulnerability.

That evening, back in Wolvega, I dine with my hosts the Konings. Hands folded, eyes closed, we pause for a moment in lieu of grace and then it is '*Eet smakelijk*', 'enjoy your meal', the ritual words for the start of any meal. First there is soup. Then there are several dishes of vegetables, all meticulously prepared and lightly cooked – salad, stuffed tomatoes with cheese, or it might be cauliflower with cheese, or chicory wrapped in a thin slice of ham. With these there are gravy and potatoes and a small slice of meat. The average serving of meat in Holland is about 100 grammes, far less than in most European countries or in America. Ask Mrs Koning what is for supper and she will not say 'grilled steak' but will instead reply with the names of the vegetables she is preparing. Puddings are mostly based on milk, originally a way of using up surplus milk in a dairying nation.

It is true that in Holland today there is a mass of fast food, hamburgers and so forth, sold on the streets and consumed on the streets. You see people munch sausages in supermarkets, a kind of eating public as a royal levee. *Frites* or chip potatoes, eaten with mayonnaise, are also ubiquitous in public places. Town centres smell of them. And, as you might expect in the land of multinationals, there is plenty of processed food, with frozen meals and TV dinners. This may in part reflect the fact that few Dutch homes had ovens until the present generation, there being no ready supply of cheap coal as in Belgium or Britain. Quality bakers filled the gap and still do a brisk trade.

All the fast and processed foods appear to belong to another way of eating from that practised at the Konings. It is as if there are two separate food cultures. One is dedicated to fairly repulsive foodstuffs; the other, though not a *haute cuisine* in the French sense, is dedicated to first-class produce, freshly and interestingly cooked and with the emphasis on vegetables. The longer I spend in Holland the more I like it.

Most families have a cooked meal in the evening and would consider it odd to have a hot lunch too. Lunch, in fact, is much like breakfast, with thinly sliced cold meats and cheese on open slices of bread – rye bread, often enough in Friesland. Dutch cheese is far more varied, and far more delicious, than the bland, waxy substance sold to Holland's unsuspecting neighbours. Given the Dutch propensity for endless cups of coffee with evaporated milk called *koffie-melk*, you might well think the fat intake from lunch and breakfast would be high. But watching Wolvega families in action soon leads to the conclusion that people in fact eat carefully and with an eye to health. A trip round the food shops of Wolvega also reveals considerable differences from other cultures. Butchers, bakers, greengrocers and fishmongers still exist as separate shops. They are spotlessly clean and sell goods which are already half-way prepared for cooking. Fillets of fish are skinned; vegetables are cleaned and may be sold ready cut for salad or soup-making; the butcher sells meat ready for the pan or oven – veal with paprika or neatly wrapped roulades of beef. It is not fast food exactly; it is more a matter of care taken and value carefully added.

Alcoholic drinks in Holland are surprisingly cheap. Dutch beer is mostly lager, not perhaps so interesting as in Belgium or Germany. Dutch gin, or 'genever', drunk on its own, ice-cold, from thimble-sized glasses, is perhaps an acquired taste – but a taste well worth acquiring. There is little public drunkenness in Holland, no need to prove oneself one of the boys by boisterous beer-swilling.

Later that evening in Wolvega, on the day of the duck decoy, I go back for a second visit with Berend Brummelman to one of the farms we have seen earlier. Brummelman, as I have discovered while roping cows with him, is thin as wire and hard as gun-metal. He cycles seriously and competitively, plays tennis on summer evenings and in the winter he skates. Our visit now is about skating.

This takes a little explaining. Wolvega, of course, is not a beauty spot in any sense. But many of the towns of Friesland definitely are – pretty little Sneek (pronounced as 'snake'), for instance, Franeker with its ancient but long-defunct university, Leeuwarden the capital, Hindeloopen with its painted interiors. Eleven of these old Frisian towns are bound together in a single chain by a 210-kilometre skating race held only when it is cold enough for every inch of the waterways that link them to be rock solid ice. In the rare years when this 'Eleven Town Race', the Elfstedentocht, is held, the whole country simply abandons whatever else it is supposed to be doing on the day of the race.

The decision to hold the race is taken just two or three days before the event, but all over the country, every winter, serious skaters train in earnest against the possibility of a big freeze. Farmers are the best of all, followed, apparently, by school-teachers. Only some 400 will qualify as competitors in the Elfstedentocht. Hundreds of other skaters, who must also be extremely tough and extremely proficient to be allowed to start, follow behind the competitors as touring skaters, racing only against the clock and to complete the course. The race itself begins soon after 5 a.m. in the blackness of the winter morning; it will take the winner about seven punishing hours.

There was an Elfstedentocht in 1963. The weather was too cold. Only some 150 skaters finished and many of these had frostbite. Every Dutch citizen old enough remembers the anguish and drama. For twenty-two years after that, there was never a hard enough frost for long enough to allow the race to be held. Then in 1985 the lakes and canals iced hard. An Elfstedentocht was proclaimed and duly raced – and won by a young farmer from just near Wolvega, his name Evert van Benthem and his position as a national hero immediately assured. To universal joy it froze again in 1986. Again, van Benthem won. And on this occasion Berend Brummelman was one of the touring skaters who came behind. Being himself a part of the event he naturally missed it on television. But one of the dairy farms on his rounds has a video of the whole proceedings and little by little, over a period of many months, Brummelman has been popping in to see a little more of the video. He himself took twelve hours to complete the course and was pleased he was fit enough to be back at work next day. There are awesome tales of Frisian farmers doing the milking at 3 a.m., popping out to win the Elfstedentocht, then straight back home at night for the evening milking.

On the way out to the farm I confess to Brummelman my fears that I may be bored by the video. We sit in the farm parlour comfortably resting our arms on a table covered by a carpet – in an unbroken tradition from the carpeted tables of seventeenth-century painting. There are big Delft ornaments, polychrome, not blue and white, on top of a heavy dresser. There is an endless supply of strong coffee and farmhouse cake. We watch the race in snatches, then fast forward, then watch some more again. We are trying to sample the whole of the panorama. Little by little it takes an irresistible grip on me.

First, in the darkness, the competitors have to run two kilometres to the start, skates round their necks – sufficient ordeal, one might have thought, for a single day. The skating, when it begins, is often fierce, not graceful, arms flung up and wide behind, then pumped hard down to gain momentum. Within an hour or two the blackness gives way to a feathery, frozen grey. The skaters pump and pump, thunder into checkpoints, thrash their way out again. Sometimes they ease up and skate with their arms behind their backs. Even so, they are going so fast that they lean forward at what appears a perilous angle.

Now the sun is rising. A tinge of pink. Hour after hour, as we whizz through the video, the skaters work their way across the frosty polders, whizzing on black canals past moored boats fast

209

in ice and through town centres where spectators dance and clap. Now there is gold in the sky and gold among the frozen grasses. Evert van Benthem, at one point several minutes behind the front skaters, has worked his way forwards but is instantly challenged. The race is fierce. Van Benthem falls behind, his assailant begins to go away from him. Van Benthem counter-attacks, passes his opponent. Then suddenly we see the opponent rise for a moment to an upright position, coasting a few metres to ease the pain. And in that moment van Benthem goes away, uncatchable over the black ice. Now he is skating alone down a narrow lane between spectators who threaten to trip him as they try to take his photograph, then out on to a wide fairway and home at last across the finishing line, both arms above his head but fast, still fast, triumph and exhaustion mingled in his face under the freezing sky.

Robert Blauw is the Reformed Church dominie of Wolvega, affable in check trousers, open-necked shirt and jersey with a partridge embroidered on the left breast. He was born in Nijmegen in the last year of the war. The allies had taken up positions here after being stopped at Arnhem and Blauw spent most of the first year of his life either in blackout or underground in a cellar.

Like an increasing number of clergymen he seems quite pleased to be out of the hurly-burly of the Randstad. He has spent five years of his career in Zeeland in the south and another five on the northern island of Texel; and he is happy now, he says, to be in Wolvega, a fine place for small children and a town where people have plenty of time for one another. While some of the north is still stiff and stratified, with a layer of large farmers and big shop-owners, Wolvega was impoverished until fifty or sixty years ago. Its people lived off reeds they cut for thatch. This lack of an upper crust, Blauw argues, gives the town a specially democratic feeling, an openness which allows for the friendly greetings I have heard each morning in the street. Nor is it particularly denominational in atmosphere, he says, enumerating ways in which the pillars of *verzuiling* are either crumbling away or never amounted to so very much.

Catholics, though outnumbered by all the Protestant sects combined, are the largest single religious group in Holland. Wolvega is a little more Catholic than the population at large. About half of those who go to church here are Catholic and the remainder Calvinist Protestant, divided between Reformed (Hervormde) and strictly Reformed (Gereformeerde). Each of these three groups used to have its own schools, alongside the schools provided by the state. But now the Protestant schools have amalgamated. There is a single Christian sports club which brings all the communities together. And where, before the war, Catholics were forbidden to have Bibles in their homes, there are now joint Catholic and Protestant Bible studies five nights a week, with the Catholics, apparently, rather more inclined to literal interpretations than the Protestants.

Dutch Catholics, as is common knowledge, have had a hard time with the Vatican. Ordinary Dutch communicants, and a great many priests as well, have wanted to form their own individual compact with God through Bible reading just as the Protestants traditionally do. They are in favour of contraception. They are not averse to women priests, they take a strong line on social issues. Meanwhile the Vatican has tried to hold them back, working through a sometimes reluctant hierarchy of bishops and archbishops. Little by little, the hierarchy is being forced to reduce the room for manoeuvre which it has tried to allow to priests and communicants. The result could be a slow falling away of Catholic church members.

For the Protestants, too, there have been great issues. One of the small Dutch churches is ready to marry homosexuals and give them its blessing. Others will tolerate homosexual couples but will not bless their union. There was also a huge rumpus over South Africa: should the churches be ready to give money, even if theoretically to finance medical supplies, to externally based opposition groups involved in the armed struggle? Some said yea and some said nay and a limited amount of money was passed on.

What happened over all, according to Robert Blauw, was that some of the churches went out ahead of public opinion on some issues – issues, he implies, where a conservative community like Wolvega might find it hard to follow. Now it is a matter of everybody learning to live with the diverse opinions aroused in what he calls 'the democratic explosions of the 1960s and 70s'.

But never forget, warns Blauw, the moral passion of the Dutch, their conviction of righteousness when acting in accord with what they hold to be the word of God. It is not so long ago, he says – and the facts can be checked out at the excellent St Catherine Convent Museum in Utrecht – that seven out of ten of all the Christian missionaries in all the world, both Protestant and Catholic, were Dutch. It is not entirely clear whether he thinks this was a good thing.

During my stay in Wolvega I also visit a lower level secondary school. Here I have the opportunity of watching a dedicated teacher who has succeeded over the year in imparting a remarkable amount of English to a class of thirteen-year-olds. Though the majority are willing, there is a surprisingly difficult group of boys, not aggressive but unmotivated and entirely disobliging. The teacher refuses to be ruffled, goes on trying to teach the rest. The methods are relatively old-fashioned, based on a text-book, with reading round the classroom and then a series of questions on the text. But it is clear that most of these children will soon be among the large number of young Dutch people who can speak English clearly and purposefully. It is a reminder that the Dutch are among the great linguists of Europe.

I visit the house of Jelle Kramer, the senior vet of the practice which had welcomed me. If Mr Kramer appeared seven feet tall, his two sons, both back at home for a few days from university, must have been nine feet tall at least. One evening, because I asked them, not because they volunteered, the elder Kramers fell to war stories. Mr Kramer had been a young boy on a farm at the start of the war and things were mostly not so bad. He remembered that it was brilliant weather when the Germans came. 'Yes,' said Mrs Kramer, 'you would have thought it would be thunder and lightning.' Come 1944, there was no hunger on the farms to compare with the sufferings of the Randstad, but yes, each village had its informers and collaborators and the rest of the people were frightened of them. And yes, after the war the collaborators melted away with great rapidity. Each farm kept a continual lookout against the Germans and for himself the worst moments had been when he had to hide to escape forced labour. He remembers the windows trembling at night as Allied bombers rumbled across the sky towards Germany. Because his family had a – forbidden – radio none of them lost confidence that the Germans would finally be beaten.

Mrs Kramer had been a small child in The Hague in 1940. One morning she was in the bathroom watching her father shave when behind him through the window she saw distant parachutists falling earthwards. This, of course, was the arrival of the Germans and she has always remembered the date, partly because it is living history but also because it was just before her birthday. Peeping through the curtains, believing herself invisible, she saw horse carts taking patients away from the hospital after it was bombed. In the winter of 1944, from the same windows, she saw people collapsing on the streets from hunger. Her family set off in search of food with a pram containing everything they could possibly barter. She darts upstairs to find a letter written to her grandmother earlier in the war – 'Mother can always find everything,' says one of the immense young Kramer boys.

'If there wasn't a war I'd like to spend a few days with you,' the letter starts. It ends, before the appropriate multitude of kisses, 'Mother is at her wits' end because there's nothing to mend stockings with.'

Later, I spend almost the whole of a day with Dr Jan de Haan, one of Wolvega's five GPs. This is a revelation in several ways.

The first, though the least surprising, is the very high standard of cleanliness and material provision, with everything that might be needed plentifully and pleasantly supplied. The gleaming instruments, even the practice's computer, seem part of caring rather than an attempt to terrify. Dr de Haan appears to be in sympathy with his patients, treating them as equals. Like the dominie, he is wearing an open neck shirt.

The next point of interest is that an experiment is under way in the practice and, as I begin to grasp the details, I realize that in a profound sense this typifies the aspirations that lie behind social behaviour and organization in Holland.

All doctors have assistants. These are quite highly trained and manage a large part of the doctor's routine business, doing the administration, giving injections and so forth. But Dr de Haan has required his assistant, Hanneke Zonderland, to act as a preliminary screen or filter, listening to patients' symptoms on the telephone and advising them whether or not they need to see the doctor. She is to treat some minor ailments herself without recourse to Dr de Haan. If all this can be done successfully, it will obviously relieve the doctor of a great deal of peripheral business. But how can it be managed so that important early warning signs are not missed and the doctor remains properly responsible? And how do the patients themselves react? Jan de Haan and Hanneke Zonderland have been working together on these questions for eight years. At one time they saw 1,000 patients separately, one after the other, compared results and found them promising. They have set up ground rules such as the number of hours a child with earache may be dealt with by Hanneke alone before she must refer the case to the doctor. They have determined the limits of patients' willingness to expose their problems to Hanneke and they make it easy for patients to communicate solely and directly with the doctor. Under these conditions, the scheme is up and running.

What they are doing, it seems, is using a methodical approach to improve individual lives. They are doing it seriously and conscientiously, almost, it appears, as a matter of conscience.

The undertaking is impressive and enlightening. It comes as no surprise to learn that Dr de Haan has been invited to lecture a day a week at Groningen University and that he is in demand as far south as Tilburg on the strength of his ideas.

The ideas flow over other issues, too. De Haan and Hanneke take their mid-morning break in the family kitchen with Mrs de Haan. We talk about the position of women. Both Allie de Haan and Hanneke Zonderland accept that women were indeed bound to their homes till just a generation ago by the large size of their families. But they do not believe this will break down now that families are smaller. Both are emphatic that women stay at home not for negative reasons but because of the deep value they attach to home, the immediate family and the wider domestic circle.

Then there is the question of *nivellering*, the equalizing of society. According to Dr de Haan, the costs of medical practice are rising faster than the rewards. He has a smaller car than he used, his wife's car is changed less often. This is one small aspect of *nivellering*. Later in the day we see houses the size of hotels in which doctors of an earlier generation have lived and worked. Even though their own house is extremely agreeable and a source of daily renewed pleasure for the de Haans – split-level, open-plan and, like the Konings', with a sense of space – it is clear exactly what he means.

As the child of what he calls 'working-class parents', de Haan is willing to speculate freely about social class, sees it as definitely existing but diminishing in importance. There was no opportunity for his father, a highly intelligent man, to go to university. For him there was – and he took it. His brother-in-law is a factory worker and, though they live in different parts of the country, they see each other every birthday. There is no question of a newly created class barrier intervening between them. He obliquely makes the point that of all family occasions in Holland birthdays are the most important. Dutch people are traditionally 'at home' on their birthdays, and if they don't want to be, have to tell everybody that they are not 'celebrating' it.

Pursuing our inquiry into the extent of class division, Jan de Haan takes me along with him on a series of house visits. Everywhere we go, thanks to his easy relationship with patients, I get a warm welcome. We see beyond contradiction that people of differing degrees of wealth do subscribe to common standards, at least so far as houses are concerned. In most countries these values and standards would clearly be described as middle class. Every house we enter is impeccable, reflecting, to outward appearances, a life under conscious control. The tables and cupboards are wooden and solid, sofas and chairs are deep and comfortable. Every house has its own indoor garden: pot plants and cut flowers. Almost all have blue and white china pots and ornaments, most often ranged along the top of cupboards.

What does vary immensely is the size of house. We encounter one old lady living in the tiniest of dwellings, her bedroom reached by stairs like a ladder on a boat and, when you get there, the bedroom itself like a boat's cabin. De Haan clearly believes this a matter of comparative poverty, not choice. I quite forget to ask him a question that has preoccupied me for years. Stairs in Holland, especially in the tall canal houses of Amsterdam, often seem almost vertical. What happens to old people with rheumatism or bad legs? (The answer, I discovered later, is that the elderly have priority for ground-floor accommodation). We visit two old people's homes. One is new and has plenty of space. Another is miniature again. Dr de Haan is affronted. 'This', he says, 'is the kind of place working-class people used to have to die in.' Ringing behind the phrase is justification and welcome for *nivellering*. As we go out we glimpse the old people having lunch together in a small hall. Many of the men are wearing suit and tie.

Finally we visit an old lady living in a 'granny house' beside the main house of a farm. She is eighty-six years old and in the last three years has filled six weighty manuscript books with her recollections, stories and copied verses. All are written in a strong, diagonal, old-fashioned hand. Entering the house, we find her composing a poem in honour of her own long-dead mother. An ancient photograph hangs on the wall, showing the mother's serious face under its tight Frisian hat with side-wings, almost like a helmet. The mother's look in the photograph is serious, even a little stern and the daughter, now in her own old age, is in the act of praising her for all the work she did in her lifetime – invisibly, not making a fuss about it. Caring for the family and home is real work, proper work, the poem says, even though at times there is no honour in it. Dr de Haan is visibly proud of his patient, visibly moved by the poem.

I think what I have discovered in Wolvega is a capacity to feel and to express feeling not generally found in some other countries, my own among them. This goes along with a careful and methodical approach to life – and perhaps this is the central paradox of Holland.

Finally though, it is time to leave the little town of Wolvega and to return, as often, to the Randstad. For just one moment, as I re-enter it, urban Holland seems crushed and crushing. But even in untypical Wolvega, I felt I had been privileged to see something of the true nature of the country – workaday, perhaps, domestic certainly, but full of a sense of justice too and, because of the honesty and practicality, the modesty and the mixture of conservative and radical, both solid and delightful under those Dutch immensities of sky.

Bibliography

The bibliography has been compiled to give a general impression of the wide range of works available in English. Some titles have been included because they are typical of their period or genre, others because they are indispensable to a deeper understanding of matters discussed in the text. Editions quoted are generally those I have used myself, though in some cases extra bibliographical information has been included.

GENERAL WORKS

Baena, Duke of, *The Dutch Puzzle*, Boucher, The Hague, 1966. Intriguing work by an admirer of Holland.

Feltham, Owen, *A Brief Character of the Lowlands*, London, 1652. Engaging curiosity.

Huggett, Frank E., *The Dutch Connection*, Government Publishing Office, The Hague, 1982. Brief, helpful and readable.

Huggett, Frank E., *The Modern Netherlands*, Praeger, New York, London, 1971.

Jungman, Beatrix, *Holland (Peeps at Many Lands)*, Adam and Charles Black, London, 1908. A children's book showing stereotypes in the making, charming illustrations.

Lucas, E. V., *A Wanderer in Holland*, Methuen and Co., London, 1905. Excellent book, strong on English literary references.

Newton, Gerald, *The Netherlands: an Historical and Cultural Survey*, Benn/Westview, London/Boulder, 1978. Hard-going but exceedingly useful, particularly on modern developments.

Schuchert, Max, *The Netherlands*, Thames and Hudson, London, 1972.

Sitwell, Sacheverell, *The Netherlands: A Study of some aspects of Art, Costume and Social Life*, Batsford, London, 1974. Good on the less fashionable late seventeenth and eighteenth centuries.

Temple, Richard Carnac ed., *The Travels of Peter Mundy in Europe and Asia: 1608–1667, IV: Travels in Europe, 1639–1647*. Hakluyt Society, London, 1925. An entertained and entertaining writer.

Temple, Sir William, *Observations upon the United Provinces of the Netherlands*, London, 1673. Shrewd and durable.

Temple, Sir William, *Memoirs*, London, 1700.

Veraart, J. A., *Holland*, Macdonald, London, undated (World War II). Wartime attempt to explain an ally to an ally.

HISTORY

Baxter, Stephen, *William III*, Longman, London, 1966.

Burnet, (Bishop) Gilbert, *History of His own Time*, William Smith, London, 1838 (single vol. edn.). One of the great works, endlessly fascinating on William and Mary and their period both in Holland and in England.

Carasso, Dedalo, trs. Michael Hoyle, *A Short History of Amsterdam*. Amsterdam Historical Museum, 1985. Useful, scholarly.

Chapman, Hester, *Mary II: Queen of England*, Jonathan Cape, London, 1953.

Dresden, Sam, *Humanism in the Renaissance*, Weidenfeld and Nicolson, London, 1968.

Geyl, Pieter, *The Revolt of the Netherlands*, Benn, London, 1958 (first pub. 1932). See text, chapter three, for discussion. Helped correct Motley version of struggle against Spain. Still good but now superseded.

Hamilton, Elizabeth, *William's Mary*, Hamish Hamilton, London, 1972.

Huizinga, J., *The Waning of the Middle Ages*, Penguin, London,

1953 (first pub. 1924). Dated but a leading work of its period, more fine sweep than substantiated argument.

Israel, Jonathan I., *The Dutch Republic and the Hispanic World*, Clarendon, Oxford, 1982. Admired by historians, ranges out beyond Holland.

Kenyon, J. P., *Stuart England*, Penguin, London, 1985 ed.

Kossmann, E. H., *The Low Countries, 1780–1940*, Oxford, 1978. An indispensable work, offering outstanding interpretative insights.

Lambert, Audrey, M., *The Making of the Dutch Landscape*, Seminar Press, London and New York, 1971. Another indispensable work, may soon need updating.

Motley, John Lothrop, *The Rise of the Dutch Republic*, (first pub. 1856), 1904 ed. Bell and Sons, London. Contains account of Motley's life. Marvellous misleading work, discussed in text, chapter three.

Murray, John M., *Amsterdam in the Age of Rembrandt*, David and Charles, Newton Abbott, 1972. Interesting work by American scholar.

Parker, Geoffrey, *The Dutch Revolt*, (first pub. 1977), Penguin, London, 1985. The indispensable, up-to-date work setting the record straight on the sixteenth and early seventeenth centuries. See text, chapter three.

Robb, Nesca A., *William of Orange*, Heinemann, London. 2 vols, 1962 and 1966. A good read on William III.

van Veen, Dr Johan, *Dredge Drain Reclaim*, Martinus Nijhof, The Hague, 1955. A passionate work full of surprising information.

Wedgwood, C. V., *William the Silent*, Jonathan Cape, London, 1946. From the heroic school of historiography.

Wilson, Charles, *Holland and Britain*, Collins, London, 1947. Early version of work now reprinted as *The Dutch Republic*. Full of fascinating facts and *aperçus*. Original ed., outstanding illustrations.

van der Zee, Henri and Barbara, *William and Mary*, Macmillan, London, 1973. A popular biography. Well worth attention.

SECOND WORLD WAR

Frank, Anne, *The Diary of Anne Frank*, Pan Books, 1954. (First published in Dutch, 1947.) Extremely moving and remains a central document. See text, chapter eight.

Frost, Maj.-Gen. John, *A Drop too Many*, Buchan and Enright, London, 1982. Lively and combative.

Giskes, H. J., *London Calling Northpole*, William Kimber, London, 1953. An extraordinary tale. See text, chapter eight.

Golden, Lewis, *Echoes from Arnhem*, William Kimber, London, 1984. Useful introduction by General Sir John Hackett.

Hackett, General Sir John, *I Was a Stranger*, Chatto and Windus, London, 1977. Outstanding both as a war book and an account of Dutch domestic life.

Hazelhoff, Eric, *Soldier of Orange*, Hodder and Stoughton, London, 1972. Bravura account of soldiering. Filmed.

Hermans, Willem Frederik, *The Dark Room of Damocles*, Heinemann, London, 1962. A subtle and mordant novel. See text, chapter eight.

Hillesum, Etty, *Etty: a diary*, Jonathan Cape, 1973. This extraordinary account of persecution offers insights to balance against those of the younger Anne Frank. See text, chapter eight.

Maas, Walter B., *The Netherlands at War 1940–45*, Abelard Schuman, New York, 1970. Useful, readable.

Mulisch, Harry, *The Assault*, Penguin, London 1983. Another powerful and subtle novel, recently filmed.

Powell, Geoffrey, *The Devil's Birthday: the Bridges to Arnhem*, Macmillan, London, 1984.

Ryan, Cornelius, *A Bridge too Far*, Hamish Hamilton, London, 1974. This powerful popular work on Arnhem did much to open up debate. Filmed.

Simoni, Anna, E. C., *Publish and be Free*, a catalogue of clandestine books printed in the Netherlands 1940–45 in the British Library. The Hague, 1973. See introduction.

Urquhart, Maj.-Gen. R. E., *Arnhem*, Cassell, London, 1958.

Warmbrunn, Werner, *The Dutch under German Occupation, 1940–45*, Stamford University Press, Stamford, 1963. Scholarly work.

ART AND ARTEFACTS

Alpers, Svetlana, *The Art of Describing: Dutch Art in the Seventeenth Century*, John Murray, London, 1983. Adventurous and controversial polemic, highly readable but will it damage your outlook? Discussed in text, chapter five.

Brown, Christopher, *Scenes of Everyday Life: Dutch Genre Painting of the Seventeenth Century*, Faber and Faber, London, 1984. Good book by a British authority, ample illustration.

Cabanne, Pierre, *Van Gogh*, Thames and Hudson, 1963. Still very much in evidence but tends to the romantic interpretation.

Fourest, Henry-Pierre, *Delftware*, Thames and Hudson, 1980. Clear and helpful, extremely pleasurable.

Friedländer, Max, *From van Eyck to Bruegel*, Phaidon, 1956. Reissued, black and white, in 'Landmarks in Art History' series, Phaidon, 1981. (Originally published in German, 1916.) This book and the author's sixteen-volume work on the same subject are truly among the landmarks of art history. Though often concerned with establishing the *œuvre* of individual painters, they offer brilliant and memorable characterizations of the work.

Fuchs, R. H., *Dutch Painting*, Thames and Hudson, 1978. An individual interpretation from one of the most interesting Dutch museum directors of the day, sometimes uneven.

van Gogh, Vincent, *The Complete Letters*, Greenwich, Conn. and London, 3 vols., 1978. Still an astonishing and illuminating collection.

Gibson, Walter, S., *Bruegel*, Thames and Hudson, London, 1977. Robust and useful.

Gombrich, E. H., *The Story of Art*, Phaidon, 1953. Gombrich's chapter on Northern Realism still has much to offer.

Gowing, L., *Vermeer*, Faber and Faber, London, 1952.

Hammacher, A. M. and Renilde, *Van Gogh: a documentary biography*, Thames and Hudson, London, 1982.

Hauser, Arnold, *The Social History of Art*, Routledge and Kegan Paul, 4 vols, London, 1962. (For Dutch art see esp. vol. 2: Renaissance, Mannerism, Baroque.)

Hulsker, Jan, *The Complete van Gogh*, Phaidon, Oxford, 1980. The central work on van Gogh, large and humane but never hysterical. Thorough discussion of life, drawings and paintings.

Jaffé, Hans L. C., *Mondrian*, Thames and Hudson, 1970. Large work, full of insight, method may seem dated.

Kitson, Michael, *Rembrandt*, Phaidon, Oxford, 1982. Useful introduction to the paintings.

Roberts, Keith, *Bruegel*, Phaidon, Oxford, 1982. Another useful introduction.

Rosenberg, Jakob et al., *Dutch Art and Architecture 1600–1800*, Pelican History of Art, Penguin, London, 1977. Offers a useful and sympathetic map of its large period and a comprehensive bibliography.

Snyder, James, *Bosch in Perspective*, Prentice-Hall, New Jersey, 1973. Contains interesting excerpts of critical writing over the centuries.

Stechow, Wolfgang, *Dutch Landscape Painting of the Seventeenth Century*, Phaidon, Oxford, 1966.

White, Christopher, *Rembrandt*, Thames and Hudson, 1984. A biography, with critical insights. Good starting point for Rembrandt. Good on Rembrandt in Amsterdam.

SOME USEFUL EXHIBITION CATALOGUES

'Piet Mondrian 1872–1944 ... Centennial Exhibition', The Solomon R. Guggenheim foundation, New York, 1971.

'Dutch Landscape: The Early Years, Haarlem and Amsterdam 1590–1650', National Gallery, London, 1986. ed. Christopher Brown. Excellent, particularly on origins.

'The Hague School: Dutch Masters of the 19th century', Royal Academy, London . . . ed. Ronald de Leeuw. Weidenfeld and Nicolson, London, 1983. Outstanding, the essential introduction. Good essays by Ronald de Leeuw, John Sillevis, Charles Moffett, Herbert Henkels.

'De Stijl: 1971–1931: Visions of Utopia', Walker Art Centre. ed. Mildred Friedman, Phaidon, Oxford, 1982 (paperback 1986). Useful essays, good illustrations.

MUSEUM CATALOGUES AND OTHER PUBLICATIONS

The following have all proved helpful. Some are considerable pieces of critical writing in their own right:

Kröller-Müller Museum, Dutch Museums (I), Staff of the museum, Haarlem, 1985.

Fries Museum (Leeuwarden), Dutch Museums (II), Staff, Haarlem, 1978.

Van Abbe Museum Eindhoven, Dutch Museums (IV), Staff, Haarlem, 1982.

Het Catharijneconvent, Dutch Museums (VII), Staff, Haarlem, 1983.

OTHER USEFUL MUSEUM PUBLICATIONS IN THE NETHERLANDS

'Guide: The Netherlands Open Air Museum' (Nederlands Openluchtmuseum), Arnhem, 1985.

'Mauritshuis, The Hague: Paintings', by Magdi Toth-Ubbens, Knorr, Hanover, 1982.

'Treasures from the Rijksmuseum, Amsterdam', by Emile Meijer, Scala/Philip Wilson, London, 1985. Better than its title.

'Piet Mondriaan in het Haags Gemeentemuseum (Piet Mondrian in the Haags Gemeentemuseum)', The Hague, 1985.

MUSEUM PUBLICATIONS FROM OTHER COUNTRIES

'Groeningemuseum, Bruges: the Complete Collection', by Dirk de Vos, Die Keure, Bruges, 1983.

'Dutch Paintings (National Gallery Schools of Painting)', by Christopher Brown, National Gallery, London, in association with William Collins, 1983.

GUIDE BOOKS

I have used mainly Fodor's *Holland*; *The Rough Guide to Amsterdam and Holland*; *Roaming Round Holland*; and *Holland: a Phaidon Cultural Guide*. None is adequate on its own. Fodor is middlebrow and chatty. *The Rough Guide* is good for travelling cheaply and also strong on art. *Roaming* is undoubtedly the book for family travel and useful facts of a domestic nature, clearly the one for those planning to settle in the Netherlands. The *Phaidon Cultural Guide* has a good number of entries which often disappoint because of their brevity.

Index